HAWK

BOOKS BY STEVEN BRUST

The Dragaeran Novels

Brokedown Palace

THE KHAAVREN ROMANCES

The Phoenix Guards
Five Hundred Years After
The Viscount of Adrilankha,
which comprises
The Paths of the Dead,
The Lord of Castle Black,
and
Sethra Lavode

THE VLAD TALTOS NOVELS

Jhereg	*Phoenix*	*Dzur*
Yendi	*Athyra*	*Jhegaala*
Teckla	*Orca*	*Iorich*
Taltos	*Dragon*	*Tiassa*
	Issola	

Other Novels

To Reign in Hell
The Sun, the Moon, and the Stars
Agyar
Cowboy Feng's Space Bar and Grille
The Gypsy (with Megan Lindholm)
Freedom and Necessity (with Emma Bull)
The Incrementalists (with Skyler White)

STEVEN BRUST

HAWK

TOR

A TOM DOHERTY ASSOCIATES BOOK

NEW YORK

HAWK

Copyright © 2014 by Steven Brust

Edited by Teresa Nielsen Hayden

A Tor Book
Published by Tom Doherty Associates, LLC
175 Fifth Avenue
New York, NY 10010

www.tor-forge.com

Tor® is a registered trademark of Tom Doherty Associates, LLC.

The Library of Congress Cataloging-in-Publication Data is available upon request.

ISBN 978-0-7653-2444-3 (hardcover)
ISBN 978-1-4299-4482-3 (e-book)

Tor books may be purchased for educational, business, or promotional use. For information on bulk purchases, please contact Macmillan Corporate and Premium Sales Department at 1-800-221-7945, extension 5442, or write specialmarkets@macmillan.com.

First Edition: October 2014

Printed in the United States of America

0 9 8 7 6 5 4 3 2 1

This book is dedicated to the memory of
Enos Harold Hunley (1944–2010),
who kept his eyes open when he was needed.

ACKNOWLEDGMENTS

Thanks to Corwin for constant technical support, and to Jennifer for the handling of life details. Speaking of life: Thanks, Martin. I was given outstanding criticism on this one by Emma Bull, Pamela Dean, Will Shetterly, Adam Stemple, and Skyler White. Alexx Kay (http://www.panix.com/~alexx /dragtime.html) did some very useful continuity checking for me. Also thanks to everyone who contributes to The Lyorn Records (http://dragaera.wikia.com/wiki/Main_Page). A special thanks to Jim Macdonald for the throat-cutting and Teresa Nielsen Hayden for the wonderful line edit, and to Terry McGarry for the copyedit. Finally, a warm thank-you to The Flying Karamazov Brothers, who, albeit unknowingly, inspired this one.

Additional proofreading and continuity checking by sQuirrelco Textbenders, Inc.

THE CYCLE

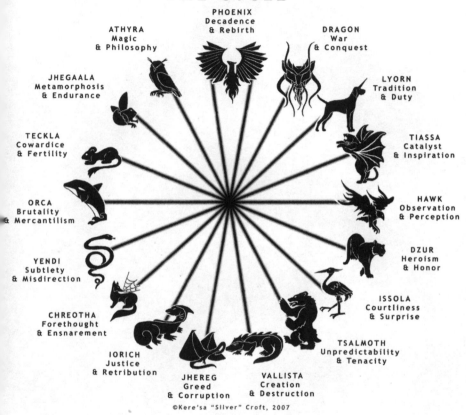

PHOENIX
Decadence
& Rebirth

DRAGON
War
& Conquest

ATHYRA
Magic
& Philosophy

LYORN
Tradition
& Duty

JHEGAALA
Metamorphosis
& Endurance

TIASSA
Catalyst
& Inspiration

TECKLA
Cowardice
& Fertility

HAWK
Observation
& Perception

ORCA
Brutality
& Mercantilism

DZUR
Heroism
& Honor

YENDI
Subtlety
& Misdirection

ISSOLA
Courtliness
& Surprise

CHREOTHA
Forethought
& Ensnarement

TSALMOTH
Unpredictability
& Tenacity

IORICH
Justice
& Retribution

JHEREG
Greed
& Corruption

VALLISTA
Creation
& Destruction

©Kere'sa "Silver" Croft, 2007

Prologue

My name is Vlad Taltos. I used to be an assassin, until—

The criminal organization that operates as part of the House of the Jhereg has rules. One is that you do not threaten the contact between the Organization and the Empire, because they need that guy to keep the Empire happy. I kind of broke that rule a little.

There's also a rule that you do not testify against the Organization to the Empire. I kind of broke that rule a lot.

I had reasons, having to do with an estranged wife, a rebellion, and some guys really pissing me off. The Jhereg is not that interested in my reasons. So, yeah, now I'm an ex-assassin, and now the Jhereg wants to kill me, and they're happy to use any sort of personal connections, blackmail, magic, or influence to do it. This is not a comfortable position.

When you have a price on your head you've got nothing: no contacts, no access to your operating capital, no chance to see your estranged wife and eight-year-old son. You move around to anywhere you think will keep you ahead of the hired killers. You do whatever work comes your way. You rely on anyone who's still talking to you: a notorious thief whose name makes everyone around you check his pockets; an undead Enchantress famous for destroying anyone who comes near her; a sorcerer known to have sacrificed entire villages to his goddess; his even more hot-tempered cousin; and a flying lizard of a familiar with a nasty sense of humor.

Bottom line: As long as you're wanted, you're not staying anywhere.

Part One

Eyes of the Hawk

1

MAKING A STAND
OR
MAKING TRACKS

Several years ago, I was getting drunk with four or five of the most powerful sorcerers in the Empire—like you do—when Daymar told a story. We were in the library of Castle Black, having just finished doing something dangerous and preposterous, and our host, Morrolan, pulled out a case of a really good white wine from Descin. Sethra Lavode, the Enchantress of Dzur Mountain, was there, as was Morrolan's cousin Aliera, and I think the Necromancer, and of course Daymar.

The more we talked, the more we drank; and the more we drank, the less I can recall of what we said. But I remember that at some point in there they started telling stories of the various rites of passage among the different Houses. You know, some tests or things you go through before you're considered fully part of the House, or maybe an adult, or officially a bloodthirsty asshole, or whatever it is your House values.

All the Great Houses except the Teckla and the Jhereg have them, and they're all different. The Dragonlords—Morrolan and Aliera—told of having to make tough command decisions during a combat exercise. Sethra recounted different tests among the Dzur, the Tiassa, and the Iorich across much of history, which she could do, having lived through all of history and a little more besides. I talked about a couple of traditions among Eastern witches; including the one that had got me the jhereg that was, at that moment, sitting on my shoulder telepathically making smart-ass remarks.

Daymar turned out to be a surprisingly entertaining storyteller for a guy who never seemed sure where his imagination stopped and reality started. I don't remember a lot about what he said, but I remember enjoying it. And there is one piece that must have stuck with me. I know this because years later I abruptly remembered it, setting off, well, I guess everything that I'm about to tell you.

Here's the bit of what he said that I suddenly remembered: "I had to hide from the Orb while I did it." I must have been pretty drunk not to react at the time, but—jumping forward to now, to a time when I was on the run from the Jhereg and concentrating all of my energy on living through each day—I woke up from a light sleep and said aloud, "Verra's tits and toenails!"

I sat there in a dank, windowless, cell-like room, with my back against the stone wall, and let things play out in my head. Then I stood up and started pacing. There wasn't enough space in the room, so I went out and started pacing up and down the hall.

"Okay," I said into Loiosh's mind after a while. "I might have something."

"Think soup and bed rest will cure it, Boss?"

"Something that might get me out of trouble with the Jhereg."

Silence in my mind. Then, "Really?"

"Maybe."

"What—"

"*Find Daymar. Have him meet me across the street,*" I said.

Loiosh didn't reply; I opened the door at the far end of the hallway and he flew out, followed by his mate, Rocza. A moment later she returned and hissed at me. That was another time when I was glad she and I couldn't speak with each other, although, really, she was communicating just fine.

I don't know. If I hadn't been on my way to see my kid, I might not have decided it was time to risk everything. I wonder. I mean, it probably wouldn't have changed things, but that's the sort of thing you wonder about later.

So, yeah. A couple of days before I suddenly woke up with that memory of Daymar, I was on my way to visit my kid at the home of my estranged wife in South Adrilankha when someone tried to kill me. Loiosh warned me. "*Boss,*" he said. "*There are two people up ahead, hiding. They're Dragaerans. I think there's a Morganti weapon.*" He didn't actually say, "They're waiting to kill you," but he also didn't tell me that water is wet and rocks are hard (nor that water is hard, but never mind that for now).

I stopped. This part of South Adrilankha was full of cottages set at varying distances back from a narrow road dotted with large deciduous trees. I figured the trees were planted there so their leaves would catch the stench of the slaughterhouses and keep it close to you. That way, even on days like this when the breeze wasn't from the south, you had a little reminder of why you hated this part of the city. I stepped behind one of the trees and spoke to Loiosh.

"*Goodness,*" I said. "*Whatever could they want?*"

"*Imperial representatives, wanting to present you with an is-land kingdom?*"

"*That's just what I was thinking they were.*"

"*As you would say: Heh.*"

"*How far ahead?*"

"*Fifty yards or so.*"

"*In other words, right in front of Cawti's house?*"

"*Yeah. Also—*"

"*What?*"

"*Another guy, leaning against the house itself.*"

"*That doesn't make any—*"

"*Colors of the House of the Dragon, Boss, and a gold half-cloak.*"

"*That makes perfect sense.*"

It was a dilemma. The assassins—I had no doubt they were assassins because I'm not an idiot—were in front of the house my kid lived in. I could come around behind them and hunt the hunters, but that would bring the whole mess to my front door, in a fairly literal way. Yeah, Cawti was there, and she could certainly handle herself. But murder tends to get noticed, sometimes even in South Adrilankha. And there was a Dragonlord, an Imperial Guardsman, on duty. That would mean the Jhereg couldn't get me, here and now; but I couldn't get them, either. Put it another way: Much as I wanted to take them down, it seemed like the best thing would be to just walk away.

But if they were watching my house (dammit, *not* my house; my ex-wife's house), it meant it would never be safe to visit there.

"*Boss, it never has been safe to visit there.*"

"*Yeah, I know.*"

"*And why the guardsman?*"

"Norathar. I mean, the Dragon Heir, not the boy. I'll bet you six dead teckla she arranged for that gold-cloak to be there, to keep Cawti and the boy safe."

I chuckled a bit to myself as I imagined just what Cawti must have said about being protected. I'd have loved to have eavesdropped on that conversation. Probably psychic, though. Too bad you can't listen in on someone else's psychic conversations.

For now, I kept myself hidden, I studied, and considered. I discovered that my right hand had gone to the hilt of Lady Teldra, about whom more later. I relaxed and let the hand fall to my side while I thought.

Yeah, sometimes I think. It isn't what I do best, but occasionally I just give it a shot anyway.

If I were the assassins, and there was an Imperial Guardsman right in front of where I thought the target would be, what would I do? That was easy—find a different place to "take my shot," in the idiom of my homeland. Where? Well, ideally, a place where there weren't any Imperial Guardsmen? But okay, if I wanted the guy really, really bad, and I couldn't find anywhere else? Maybe—*maybe*—I'd try to arrange for the guard to be distracted long enough for me to make the attempt anyway. It would be complicated, tricky, expensive, and risky; but maybe.

Well, no, to be more precise, *I* wouldn't do that, but it was possible these guys would. After all, there were two of them doing a job that usually only one did—assassins usually work alone. Having two of them waiting for me was, to be sure, an honor of sorts. But like the guy on the Executioner's Star said: Except for the honor, I'd have preferred to skip the ceremony.

"*What do you think, Loiosh?*"

"You know what I think, Boss. You should walk away right now."

"Yeah. Talk me into it."

"If I had to talk you into it, you wouldn't be asking me to. Let's go already."

There was nothing to say to that. Loiosh landed on my right shoulder, Rocza on my left, and I turned and walked back the way I'd come. After a few hundred feet, I stepped off into an alley, and took back streets all the way to the Stone Bridge, which leads back to the City. Instead of taking the bridge, however, I cut north on a street whose name I never learned. In a few minutes, I saw a dilapidated building off to my right that had the vertical parallel lines—drawn or painted above the door—that indicate, in the Easterners' district, a place that lets out rooms for the night.

"The street would have fewer vermin than that place," said Loiosh. *"And probably be safer."*

I didn't answer him.

I paid for a room from the fat, grizzled woman in the chair next to the door. She grunted a number at me.

"Are there actually numbers on the rooms?" I asked her.

She squinted at me, and opened her mouth. She didn't have many teeth.

"Up the stairs, second door on the right. If you have a bag, carry it yourself," she added, which wasn't necessary because she could see I didn't have one, and because I wouldn't have trusted her with it if I had. It was the kind of place the lower order of prostitutes avoid as too disgusting.

She glowered at me, I think just on principle; but when I started moving, my cloak shifted, and she could see the hilt of

my rapier, and she stopped glowering, and I knew if we had
any more conversation she would be very polite.

The room was about what you'd expect. I tested the bed.
I'd slept in worse. Of course, that was on the ground, but still.
There was an empty water pitcher, which indicated a pump
room nearby, so it could have been much worse. There was a
window big enough for Loiosh and Rocza to fit through, but
no way to close it, or even to block any light that came
through unless I drove a nail into the wall above it and hung
my cloak there. I considered going out to find a blacksmith.
There was a chair and a small table with a washbasin on it.
The chair looked safe, so I sat in it, and relaxed for half an
hour or so while I considered nails and other matters.

"Boss, there really is a lot of insect life in here."

I grunted and stood up.

You could say that I was unable to perform any witchcraft
because of the amulet I wore that made me invisible to magical detection, but it wouldn't be strictly true. I took a selection
of herbs from my pouch, put them in the tin water basin, and
lit them. Just because I couldn't invoke any power didn't mean
I couldn't use what I knew, and what I knew was how to drive
at least most of the insect life out of the room. After that, it
was just a matter of leaving the room for a couple of hours
while the herbs did—

"Boss! There's someone in the hall."

I froze, my hand on the doorknob.

There'd been occasional people walking up and down the
hallway all along, but Loiosh wouldn't have mentioned this
one without reason.

"Check the window."

He flapped over there, stuck his head out. *"No good, Boss; two of them out there."*

"Two? Two outside, and one inside? Three of them? What is this organization coming to?"

"There might be more than one outside the door, Boss. I can't tell for sure."

I looked around for a place to hide. I mean, there wasn't one, and I knew there wasn't one, but I looked anyway, because you do. I could jump out the window where I knew there were two of them, and, with any luck, Loiosh and Rocza could distract them while I recovered from the jump enough to, you know, not die. But aside from any other problems, I wasn't sure I could fit through the window. I could wait and deal with the unknown or unknowns who, I presumed, were getting ready to smash my door down, and—well, same problem. If it were me on the other side of the door, I'd blow the damned thing up and rush in before the dust settled. Crap. If I were in a farce, I'd hide under the bed. In a play full of exciting fake violence I'd . . .

Hmmmm.

The room didn't have a real ceiling, just bare rafters with the roof a few feet above them.

"Boss, seriously? That's what you're going with?"

"Got a better idea?"

I stood on the bed frame and jumped, catching hold of one of the rafters. I pulled myself up, which wasn't as easy as it should have been. Either I'd gained weight since coming back to Adrilankha, or else the extra hardware I'd picked up recently was weighing me down. But I got there, stood on the beam, and put my other hand on the slanting roof for balance.

Loiosh and Rocza flew up next to me and door blew in, almost knocking me off the beam in spite of my grip.

From above, all I could tell was that there were two of them, one of them holding a dagger and the other a Morganti broadsword. I mean, you don't exactly *see* that it's Morganti, unless you're in light bright enough to notice that there's no reflection from the metal, but it doesn't matter. You know it's a Morganti weapon. Even wearing a Phoenix Stone amulet, which pretty much makes you deaf to both sorcery and psychic phenomena, if you're that close to a Morganti weapon, you know.

They charged into the room ready to kill, stopped, looked around. I took a deep breath and a grip on the rafter. After a moment, they went over to the window and looked out on the street. The one with the dagger shrugged his shoulders. The other one turned around, looked up, saw me, opened his mouth, and got both of my boots in his teeth. He didn't go out the window, which is what I'd been hoping for, but I could hear the crack when his head hit the sill; I didn't think I'd have to worry about him for a bit.

The other one turned to me. I'd fallen to the ground after my heroic leap, so I rolled back out of range while Loiosh and Rocza got in the assassin's face in a very literal, biting, fill-him-with-jhereg-venom kind of way. I got to my feet and recovered my balance, then I threw the basin of burning herbs in his face, then drew a dagger and stabbed him in the throat, angled up to get the base of his brain. In a move that had become almost automatic, I stepped to the side to avoid the stuff that would require laundry services if it got on my clothes. The other guy seemed to be unconscious. I stabbed him in the throat too, just to be sure. I left the knife there.

Then I stood in front of the window and looked down at the other two, spreading my hands in a "now what?" gesture.

They turned and walked away.

What I really wanted to do next, just for effect, was to go back downstairs and demand a new room of the landlady on the basis that mine was full of vermin, the washbasin was dented, and the door was broken. But I didn't. I went back down the stairs and, ignoring her, walked out the door. If she had any presence of mind and a few connections, she'd sell that Morganti broadsword on the gray market for enough to retire on.

I took a sharp left, taking me off in a different direction than the two button-men had gone.

I wondered how they'd found me.

After a couple of blocks I stopped, rested against a building, and let myself shake for a while. I don't know, maybe two minutes, maybe five.

Evening was coming on.

I'd been in Adrilankha for several months; too long to be in one place with assassins after you. Loiosh was no longer bothering to tell me how stupid it was for me to hang around. I couldn't argue with him, even before the Jhereg stationed outside Cawti's place confirmed it. The price on my head was high enough to be tempting to anyone.

I had to get out of the city, but I didn't want to. My son was here, and I'd only managed to see him a few times. My friends were here, and I'd hardly seen them at all. My life—no, my life was no longer here; my death was here. Sorry if that sounds a bit over-the-top, but as far as I could tell, it was simply true.

"*Quit whining, Boss.*"

"*I'm not whining, I'm reflecting.*"

"*Then quit reflecting with that tone of mind.*"

"Maybe we should go to Szurke and see my grandfather."

"Good idea."

"Or I could spend some more time back East."

"That'd be good."

"Or maybe the Kanefthali Mountains."

"I've always wanted to see those."

"Or—"

"Oh, stop it, Boss. If we're just going to wait here until you're killed, at least don't pretend—"

"Damn, Loiosh. Getting a little bitchy in our old age, are we? Ouch. Cut it out. I'm not saying we're going to stay here—"

"No, you just don't plan to leave."

I didn't answer him, a policy I should have adopted several minutes before. Or maybe years.

"Ha," he said.

Rocza, who'd been flying around for the last minute or so, landed on my shoulder again, shifting from foot to foot, which was her way of saying she was hungry. We found a bakery, where I paid too much for a couple of buns stuffed with too little kethna that was too sweet. The baker's assistant tried very hard to keep his eyes off the weapon at my side. I didn't speak to him. I picked up a can of weak beer from a street vendor nearby and walked, looking around.

Eventually I found what passes for a park in South Adrilankha—a place where some grass and weeds had grown up in a large vacant lot with a few low bushes and couple of scrawny trees. I sat down and leaned against one, and ate the buns and fed some to Loiosh and Rocza. It was a good place, because no one could sneak up on me without my familiar seeing him. Although here, in the middle of the Easterners' district, I should be safe enough.

When we were done eating I relaxed for a while. There was a nice breeze coming in from the City, so for once South Adrilankha didn't smell like the slaughterhouses to the southeast. My mind kept coming back to the conversation with Loiosh, and I kept shoving it aside. What I needed to be thinking about was how I'd been found in that flophouse. There were very few possibilities, and all of them were bad. Or it was something I hadn't even considered possible, and that was worse.

Okay, relax. Let's look at all the possibilities, one at a time, and figure out—

"Boss," said Loiosh. "You're being watched."

"Yeah?" I said, looking around. "Where? Who?"

"Other end of the park. Sight-spell. Dragaeran. Jhereg colors."

I felt my breath catch, and my heart gave a couple of test thuds to make sure it was ready. I was in South Adrilankha. I was in the Easterners' quarter. I had walked away from the flophouse and gotten lost among back streets and unmarked alleys. There's no way the Jhereg could have found me here. No way.

Except that they had.

I didn't reach for a weapon; I didn't even move. Not yet.

"I need to see," I said. "And send Rocza on a sweep of the area in case there's more than one."

"Already doing it, Boss."

"Good. Here I come."

Colors swam; some of them disappeared, new ones occurred. My vision wavered, steadied, and I could see the man he'd spoken of. We moved closer. He was staring into something in his palm, then glancing in the direction where my body waited.

And, for just a second, his eyes flicked up toward me. It wasn't much, he didn't hold it for long, but it was enough. I returned to my body.

"Loiosh! You and Rocza, out of there now!"

"Boss, what—?"

"Get height and distance. Move!"

And I could feel Loiosh's response—the jolt of fear—and could only assume Rocza had been given the message as well.

I had, it seemed, gotten to my feet, and drawn Lady Teldra. I was walking toward the Jhereg. I was aware that there was probably another assassin around, maybe more. I hoped so. I was suddenly in a mood to kill as many of them as presented themselves. I had just enough presence of mind to have Lady Teldra stay alert for the minuscule wavering around objects that tells you that someone is using an invisibility spell. It's always the little things that bite you in the ass.

The Jhereg turned and ran. It was very undignified. I was never going to catch him, and I had no intention of throwing Lady Teldra. I looked around for someone else to kill, but I saw no other Jhereg in the area. In fact, I saw no one at all.

Yeah, well, pull a weapon like Lady Teldra out, and that's what's going to happen. The least sensitive lout will get the feeling that there's something bad out there. Anyone with any psychic ability will feel like all the denizens of the Nightmare Abyss have come climbing out singing "Dirge of the Red House." So, no, there was no one around.

"Boss? What's going on?"

"Where are you?"

"Half a mile up on an updraft, and almost over the ocean-sea. What's—"

"Stay there for a bit."

"Boss—"

"Just for a bit."

I looked around the area again, carefully. I moved around just enough to make sure the spindly trees and weeds weren't concealing anyone.

"What's going on, Boss?"

"A fluffy kitten tea party."

"Boss—"

"Just wait."

It felt like all of my nerve endings were right on top of my skin—like all of my senses were strained to the limit. There's a kind of exhilaration that comes with this feeling, but I don't recommend it. There was movement in a tree off to my left. I spun that way, raising Lady Teldra, who had taken the form of a shortsword for the occasion. It was just a fucking squirrel. I looked around some more. There was still someone. Somewhere nearby.

Lady Teldra was naked in my hand, and there was still someone around the edge of the park, moving from tree to bush, trying to stay out of my sight. I had to give him credit for balls, if not sense. Just one? Too soon to say.

There was almost a hundred feet between me and anything that could be used for cover. There is no way they'd come at me in the open like this, and I'd be fine with it if they tried. And no invisibility spell or illusion ever cast would fool Lady Teldra if she was alert and looking. She may not be the best at casting spells, but she can detect and disrupt them like nothing you've ever seen. So I waited.

I don't know how long I waited, because when you're standing like that, no idea what will happen, trying to be ready for anything, it's hard to keep track of how much time is passing. But after what felt like an hour but was almost certainly closer to five minutes, I smelled smoke. Then I saw it rolling toward me; thick smoke, thick enough to let someone get right up to me before I could see him. He needn't cast a spell on me; he just needed to cast a spell on himself to permit him to breathe and see through the smoke. He? I hoped he, not they. If there were more than one, I could be in trouble. Jhereg assassins usually work alone; but, like I said before, sometimes there are teams of two. And I'd just proven that sometimes there are four. Four, for the love of all things broken.

"Boss?"

"*Stay where you are, Loiosh. I got this.*"

There are times when—no, I won't explain. I turned and ran just as fast as I could away from the smoke. And, yes, I knew there was a pretty good chance that either I was doing just what they expected, or they had contingencies for me running like that. Barlen's scaly arse. Sophisticated trick they'd pulled on me. Flint, steel, a pile of leaves, and a wind spell. To get me, the button-man probably had a big stick.

I'm not all that fast a runner, and Dragaerans have longer legs than we poor, short humans; but there was always the hope no one was chasing me. There was a puddle of water in the middle of the park from yesterday's rain—a big enough puddle to slow me down. I swung right to avoid it, and in front of me was a long, low shrub; perfect for someone to be hiding behind. Just in case, I swerved at the last minute, dove over it, and rolled to my feet. And, sure enough, there he was—just where he should have been. If I'd had time, I'd have been astonished—how often do you find an assassin where you're expecting one?

But I didn't have time.

He was very fast, that one. He drew a Morganti longsword and had a dagger in the other hand, and he was showing every sign of knowing how to use them. The sword came down in a fast arc from my left, toward my head. I took a step back and parried with Lady Teldra, while drawing a fighting knife from behind my back, but he was awfully quick, and very good, and there was what at first felt like a dull, weak thud in my right arm just at the elbow, but then there was a whole lot of pain, then there was numbness and Lady Teldra dropped to the ground; then there was panic. Well, almost.

He came at me with both blades then; I stepped back, tried to draw my rapier, but my right arm wasn't working. He missed me, and then came in again, both weapons from the same angle, this time coming down from my right. I didn't have a clear idea of what was behind me. I couldn't look. Loiosh and Rocza were a long, long way away. My primary hand was disabled, and he had a Morganti sword and a long fighting knife coming at me. More important, Lady Teldra was on the ground and I kept getting farther away from her. And this guy may not have been the best assassin I'd ever met, but he was an awfully good fighter.

I was becoming concerned.

I took a step back and to my left as he struck again, this time the blades coming from completely different angles; I only just barely avoided the knife. I felt wetness on my right hand, which meant there was some feeling there, and it was bleeding. I threw my knife at him, aiming at his chest. It hit him point-first, which wasn't bad for a left-hand shot, but there wasn't enough strength for it to stick. It checked his progress for a moment. The good news was, a whole lot of the stuff I keep around to throw was set up to be drawn with my left hand, figuring I'd have a more convincing argument in my right. I drew out three shuriken and sent them at him, and one went into his cheek, making him pause again. I tested my right hand to see if I could do anything with it yet. I couldn't. I continued circling to my left, hoping to make my way to Lady Teldra; if I could pick her up, I knew she could heal me.

He apparently figured out what I was doing—which was disturbing on several levels—and moved to interpose himself. For the first time, I got a look at him: a narrow face, dead gray eyes, broad shoulders, hair cut short enough to be bristles. Neither of us said a word.

I carelessly threw a handful of darts in his direction—he couldn't know that I hadn't gotten around to dabbing poison on them—and pulled a knife from my boot. Then, with the same motion, I stepped in to him, committing everything I had to a shot at his right arm, hoping for a combination of surprise and an unexpected angle of attack from inside the arc of that big fucking sword.

I got it; the knife sank in, and something connected with my right side, feeling like I'd been punched there, but I had gotten a good, satisfying thrust at his sword arm. The Morganti sword fell slowly, like I could watch it spinning on the way down. And with the same slowness, I drew the blade from his arm at the same time as he pulled his from my side.

Insofar as you do anything that can be called *thinking* in situations like that, what I thought was that he'd either stoop to pick up his Morganti weapon, or, more likely, stab me again with the knife in his left hand. I didn't figure him to punch me in the throat.

I drove my knife up under his chin at the same time as he brought his right fist into my throat. He hit my throat in the right place—I mean, for him—and really, really hard.

I'd gotten him. Yay.

Now all I had to do was figure out a way to breathe.

His knees went, and he started to go down; it seemed to me that it was only then that the Morganti sword hit the ground. I don't know. Most of my attention was on my throat; my brain was screaming that it really wanted some air, please. Right now.

When your windpipe is crushed, you can go maybe a minute or two at the best of times—and already panting from the exertion of surviving a fight is hardly the best of times. How much time did I have before I blacked out, then died? Twenty seconds? Twenty-five? I think Loiosh said something into my mind, but I didn't have the attention to spare.

My first thought was Lady Teldra, but I was too disoriented; I had no idea which way to move, and whatever odd arcane sense might have told me where she was, was too busy screaming about getting air.

And my right arm still wasn't working.

Seriously. This was starting to become a problem.

I had a knife in my hand. A fighting knife—mostly blade. It was good for cutting and slashing bellies and faces; it was never made for stabbing, or, if you will, puncturing. But it did have a point—ask the guy who'd just tasted it.

If there's no other way, you can always cut your own throat.

I really, really, really do not recommend this as a way to pass an evening. Listening to someone with a monotonous voice recite an epic poem in a language you don't speak while you're hungry and need to find a privy is better than cutting your own throat. Well, okay, maybe as bad. Fortunately, I didn't have time to think about it; if I had, I probably wouldn't have done it.

I was, somehow, on my knees, and black splotches were forming in front of my eyes. I found the spot with the fingers of my left hand. My left hand was still holding the knife, so I gave myself a shallow cut on the right side of my neck, just so I'd be able to feel stupid later when I realized it. My fingers searched my neck. Take your time. *Breathe!* There's the throat-knob, now down—*Need need need to breathe!*

I slid the point in. It hurt. Harder than sliding the knife in, though, was not sliding it in too far; you don't have much leeway in there before going all the way through the wind-pipe, or even nailing an artery, and if I did that I'd see a red spray through the black splotches, and then nothing, ever. Worse (though I didn't give it any thought at the time) was that, while I had made a very careful and thorough study of Dragaeran anatomy, I hadn't ever bothered to find out the differences between Dragaeran and human. But, like I said, I didn't think about that as I was doing it; this was just not the moment to consider that, and, as the man said, there was no time to learn it now.

But here I am talking to you, so I must have managed it.

I held the knife where it was, sticking out of my throat, then I twisted it a little to open a gap for air. That *really* hurt. I leaned forward so the blood would flow out that way instead of going down my throat and making me cough.

And I inhaled.

Let me summarize: It was absolutely no fun at all.

And yet, I'll tell you, that first rush of air felt so good, I wondered why I had never thought of doing this before.

Then I almost fell on my face, but with the knife still

stuck in my throat holding my windpipe open, that would have been a tactical error. I reminded myself that, if I didn't do something fast, I'd just bleed to death, and having gone through all the work of cutting my own throat only to have it prove useless would be more annoyance than I could stand. Of course, if the other assassin was still lurking nearby, and he managed to find me, the whole thing was moot. And I couldn't see how he wouldn't.

But you deal with one problem at a time.

"*Boss!*"

I couldn't concentrate enough to make a coherent reply. My right arm wasn't working, and my left was weak, and getting weaker. I knew I'd been badly stabbed in the side; I couldn't tell exactly where, which was almost certainly a bad sign. But I became aware, then, of Lady Teldra; maybe six feet away. I went toward her, trying to move the knife as little as possible while walking on my knees, until, just short of where I needed to be, my knees refused to work any more and the world started spinning. I became aware that I was on my side and I made sure I hunched over so the blood wouldn't go down my throat and pushed myself with my feet and rolled over on my back on top of her and then blood *did* go down my throat and coughing was maybe the worst thing ever, except I don't remember much of it. I knew, as the world collapsed into a contracting tunnel of light, that she could heal me. I knew because she'd done so before; but then I'd been holding her in my hand. I wondered if she could do that while I was just sort of lying on top of her.

Interesting question, I decided.

The tunnel collapsed.

2

MAKING TRACKS
OR
MAKING A HOLE

There's a long time in there where I don't know what happened, but I figured that either the other assassin didn't manage to find me, or, more likely, didn't know how helpless I was and decided he didn't want to take on me and Lady Teldra by himself.

The other possibility, that he was going for help, didn't cross my mind.

I know I dropped the knife I was holding, but Lady Teldra must have healed me fast enough to keep me breathing. At some point, I realized I was staring up at an empty sky, and I became aware that Loiosh and Rocza were next to me. I felt a little ill, and I knew that if I tried to stand I'd get sick, so I lay there. This stuff is hard to reconstruct after the fact.

"*Boss?*"

"*I think we're—*" I had a moment of panic thinking of Lady Teldra, but then I connected her with the profoundly uncomfortable lump digging into my back. I rolled over. My right arm was working, so I took her into my hand. She felt warm, and almost seemed to be vibrating, though none of my senses were very reliable at that moment.

"*I think we're okay,*" I said, and closed my eyes.

A little later I became aware that I was shivering.

"*Am I bleeding?*"

"*I don't think so.*"

My left hand was working, so I reached up and felt my throat. It hurt, but my fingers came away dry. I wondered if I could do something strenuous like, I don't know, sit up. I tried. The world spun but settled down after a while.

From time to time, Loiosh or Rocza would take off, fly around for a bit, then land again; the other would stay near me like I was a nest full of eggs.

"*I think we can conclude they're gone,*" I said.

"*Good call, Boss. What happened?*"

I tried to get to my feet, made it as far as my knees. I sheathed Lady Teldra, then used both hands to stand up. A few feet away was the body of someone who had almost been good enough. Almost will kill you. I put him out of my mind as I tried to walk. I wobbled for a bit, and the world spun; but after a minute it seemed like I might be able to move. I tried a step. It worked. I tried another.

"*Boss?*"

"*Just let me concentrate on walking for a bit.*"

In a few more steps, I was doing all right—if I'd been seventy years old and had let myself go. But I moved. I worked my way back to the place in the park where I'd started, where I had a good view in all directions. It was dark, but lights from the City worked with the enclouding to provide a bit of illumination.

I stopped there, breathing heavily, and tried to figure out my next move.

I said, "*I don't know how they found me, but—*"

"*Boss, are you all right?*"

"*I'm fine. A bit dicey there for a minute, but it's the first attempt I'm worried about.*"

"*The first attempt? How many were there?*"

"*Just two, I think. But—*"

"*You think?*"

"*I'm pretty sure. But—*"

"*Pretty sure? You're pretty sure how many times—*"

"*Loiosh, be quiet for a minute. I'm trying to tell you something. It's the first attack I'm worried about. I mean the second. The first one here, in the park.*"

"*Oh, well that's good. I'm glad you weren't worried about the one where you had to cut your own throat. No reason that should worry—*"

"*You were the target, not me.*"

There was a significant pause, then, "*Oh,*" he said.

"*I should have been expecting this. It's the obvious way to weaken me. And with the second attempt, the guy went for my sword arm. His whole plan was to make me drop Lady Teldra. They know enough about me to be very dangerous.*"

"*We'll have to be more careful,*" he said.

"*I need to find a place to hide, to hole up for a few days while I recover.*"

"*But if they can find you—*"

"*Yeah. Need to figure out how they did that.*"

"*Maybe figure it out before we go into a confined space without much visibility?*"

"Right. Good plan."

"So—"

"Shut up. I'm thinking."

"It's good to see you're open to new experiences," he said.

I ignored him and, standing in the park on a chilly night, weak, trembling, and distracted, I tried to work things out.

Sethra Lavode had once found me in the wilderness by tracking Loiosh, but she was Sethra Lavode; could anyone else do that? I could ask her, but that would entail its own risks. I went through the list: Sorcery required a link to the Orb, and the amulet I wore, a combination of gold and black Phoenix Stone, ought to prevent that. There was necromancy, but that was just a specialized use of sorcery. Elder sorcery? I was no expert, but I'd never heard of anyone doing anything as subtle as a location spell with it. Psychic skills? Witchcraft? The other part of my amulet should prevent those from working.

So, perhaps it had been Loiosh someone found a way to locate. But in that case—

"Loiosh?"

"Maybe, Boss, if it happened while I was sleeping. But I'm pretty sure I'd notice someone casting a spell on me or Rocza."

"Sethra managed without you knowing."

"She's Sethra."

"I'm going to have to ask her, aren't I?"

I didn't like it that they'd taken a shot at Loiosh. I didn't like that at all.

There was a mild breeze, a bit chilly, and carrying the scent of pine needles. I had sheathed Lady Teldra, but I still had the park and the nearby streets to myself. It was sort of eerie, being alone in a place that was usually crowded. For a while, it was like time stopped, held its breath waiting for something to break. Loiosh and Rocza perched on my shoulders; they, too, were unmoving. The place had cleared because I'd drawn Lady Teldra—I held something so terrifying that it could clear a park and the surrounding streets.

So why was I so bloody scared?

I suppose it might have something to do with the fact that they'd come so close to killing me that I'd had to cut my own throat as the only alternative to dying.

There was a bronze plaque on the ground not far from me, naming the place as Kodai Park; who Kodai was I have no idea. Be nice to have a park named after you. I hope whatever he did was worth it. I hadn't realized that it really was a park— I thought it was just a place no one had built on. Nice that there are parks, don't you think? I heard sounds from some distance away—cries, maybe; violence perhaps. But they weren't coming any closer so I ignored them.

I don't know how long I stood there—maybe a quarter of an hour, maybe more—but eventually foot traffic started up again, and a few people walked through the park. Soon someone would find the body, and either scream or ignore it; and maybe inform the Phoenix Guards, who might or might not bother to look at it.

"Boss?"

"Yeah, we should move."

"And soon."

"The question is, where to?"

"Well, Boss. Out of the park might be a good start."

"I need some sort of destination."

"Just pick—wait. Something . . ."

"Loiosh?"

"Something's coming toward us."

"*Some* thing, *Loiosh?*" Well, I decided. This can't be good. I put my hand on Lady Teldra's hilt, wondering if the effort to draw her would make me fall over.

Loiosh said, "*It's . . . oh.*"

I saw it. A dog—the big, loping kind, coming up to me, tail wagging. I'd seen that dog before, fairly recently, so I waited. It sniffed at my feet, then my hand, then wagged its tail some more.

"Hello, Awtlá," I said aloud. It came out in a whisper, and ragged, like there was something wrong with my throat. I almost cleared my throat, but realized in time that doing so was probably not my best move. I tried speaking again. "If I knew how you found me, would I know how the Jhereg found me?" It didn't hurt to talk, I just sounded bad.

Awtlá seemed very happy to see me. My feelings were more mixed. It was a very, very bad sign that I could be found. But Awtlá was one of the familiars of a warlock—of *the* Warlock—who as far as I knew was friendly. More significantly, I was in absolutely no condition to either defend myself or run away. So I decided to wait for further developments. Loiosh flapped his wings and hissed at Awtlá, who jumped up on his back legs to either eat him or lick him; I backed away because having a dog on my chest would make me fall over.

The next thing that ought to happen was the appearance of a cat. I looked around.

"*There, Boss. By that hedge.*"

Yeah, I could just see it. It wasn't approaching me; it seemed to be giving itself a careful bath.

Then he himself appeared. I couldn't see him all that well in the gloom, but well enough to recognize him. He looked me over. I nodded to him.

"Hello, Lord Taltos," he said.

"How did you find me?"

"You really need to stop wasting so much time with small talk," he said.

I waited.

He shrugged. "You were found by the will of the Empress."

I licked my lips. "You aren't making that up, are you?"

"No. She used the Orb."

"And, what, it was just coincidence that the Jhereg found me on the same day?"

"No. She became aware that you'd been attacked."

"She was right about that."

"She wasn't certain you'd survive."

"Yeah, me neither."

"The Jhereg found you?"

"Kinda," I said.

"There were more looking for you," he told me.

"Were?"

He said, "Have you noticed we look alike?"

"Human, dark hair, mustache, yeah I've noticed."

"That would explain it."

"You met some Jhereg?"

"Three. Not far from here. They met Awtlá and Sireng. One had a Morganti weapon."

If you've been paying attention, that was where I realized that the guy had gone off to get friends. "Yeah, Morganti," I said. "A lot of those around lately. They should be illegal."

"They *are* illegal."

"Oh, right. Nothing personal, but I'm glad they found you instead of me. I'm not in any shape to—"

"I can see that."

I nodded. "But wouldn't they have been embarrassed to find out they'd destroyed the wrong soul?"

The Warlock nodded. "Yeah, that would have been bad. Glad I was able to save them from that."

"So you don't know how they found me?"

"No. You have a lot of blood on you."

"Your powers of observation—"

"How much of it is yours?"

"A lot of it."

"I see. How are you?"

"Glad to still be on my feet, what with one thing and another. But, overall, I'd say pretty poor."

He was silent for a moment, then his two familiars began to move. They started walking in large circles around the park. I watched them for a few moments, and, yeah, there was a wolf and a dzur where a dog and a cat had been. I really wished I knew how they did that.

He said, "You know I can't heal you while you wear that amulet."

"Yeah."

"I could give you some basic emergency care."

"Lady Teldra has handled that already, thanks."

"Lady—? Oh. Yes, of course. You know about the limitations on that, right?"

"Pretend I don't for a minute and tell me."

"A device like that can—"

"Device like this?"

He shrugged. "Any energy-magic conversion device."

"Ener . . . Um. Okay."

"It can only do so much until it receives more energy."

"Receives more energy," I repeated. "By which you mean—kills someone, destroying his soul?"

"Yes," he said.

"That doesn't make sense. When I carried Spellbreaker—"

"Were you wearing that amulet then?"

"Um."

"If she can draw energy from the Orb, she doesn't need to feed."

"So, if I can find a safe place to take the amulet off, she'll be all right again?"

"Maybe. It depends on how awake she is, how much awareness she has to pull in energy to use later. That isn't something I'd know."

"You know a lot about this sort of thing for an Easterner."

"I try to be useful to Her Majesty."

I bit back an observation that would have been vulgar and said, "I suppose. So, how did the Jhereg find me?"

"Sorry, no idea."

"Just when I was sure you knew everything."

"Not everything. Not even most things. Just a lot of things."

"I was thinking they put some sort of spell on my familiars."

He looked at Loiosh. Rocza flapped her wings and hissed; Loiosh hissed at her and she settled down.

After a moment, he said, "No."

I very much wanted to say, "Are you sure?" But I resisted; it would just have annoyed him. I muttered.

"What?" he said.

"It would be very, very convenient to figure out how the Jhereg found me. That way, I could maybe, you know, keep them from doing it again. I'd prefer to avoid another attack, even if I manage to recover from this last one."

He shrugged. "My guess is they followed you."

"Yeah, not likely."

"Why not?"

"Because we've been watching for it."

"This is outside my area of expertise, but, you can't follow someone who's watching for it?"

"It's pretty damned hard without a whole lot of people."

"And does the Jhereg have a whole lot of people?"

"I . . ."

"Yes?"

"You really think it's that simple?"

"I don't know. Have you been somewhere they could have expected you to be? Somewhere they could pick you up?"

"Yes, but—"

"Hmmm?"

"Gods of the Paths! They'd have needed five, six different people with the way we were watching for it, all of them with illusions so they looked human. And they'd have to pay each of them for several days to make sure they caught me when I finally showed up, plus paying the sorcerer. Do you have any idea how much that would cost?"

"Well, no," he said.

"A lot."

"And do they want you badly enough to spend a lot?"

I didn't answer. They did, of course. Was it really that simple? They'd picked me up at Cawti's, followed me, set up an attack at the flophouse, and, when that didn't work, followed me until they could set up another?

Someone was spending a lot of gold. I mean, a lot.

"Loiosh? What do you think?"

"I can believe it, Boss. You did really annoy them. But you know them better than I do."

Yeah, I really did annoy them.

"You'll thank Her Majesty for me?"

"She said to tell you no thanks are necessary. You hold an Imperial title. That makes it her duty to render aid when needed, and if she notices."

"Uh-huh. You'll thank her for me?"

"I will."

"And, ah, thank you as well."

"I serve Her Majesty."

"Yeah. About that. Think Her Majesty might manage to forbid the Jhereg from trying to, you know, kill me and stuff?"

He shook his head. "She'd like to. She is not, of course, unaware of your situation. But that's an internal House matter, and she can't interfere."

"But she can send a rescue party?"

"That's different. They tried to kill you. That's illegal."

"But—"

"If they'd just be kind enough to admit they were trying to kill you, she could tell them not to."

I shook my head, which I ought not to have done. "Yeah, I get it."

His cat and his dog—just a cat and a dog now—came back. The dog curled up by his feet, the cat rubbed his leg then sat down and started licking itself. Loiosh hissed at the cat, I guess just on general principle; the cat pretended Loiosh didn't exist.

"You should get somewhere safe," he said.

I nodded. "That's next on my list. Right after I figure out where."

"I could escort you to the Palace."

I shook my head. "That's the last place I want to be."

"Then maybe you should see how far from Adrilankha you can get how fast?"

"No, I'm sticking around. And that means—"

"Why?"

"Why? Why am I sticking around?"

"Yes."

"He asks good questions, Boss."

"Shut up."

Aloud I said, "They've threatened my son."

"We're watching out for him, and for your ex-wife."

"And I'm tired of running from them. I want this settled."

He started to speak, then just nodded.

I said, "I need to stay in South Adrilankha, at least until I'm feeling better. Dragaerans stand out here a bit more, Jhereg in particular. It's easier for me to vanish, and harder for the Jhereg to be sneaky."

"How'd that work out today?"

I shrugged.

"All right," he said. He didn't sound convinced. "If you know of a place where you'll be safe."

"I'm still thinking about—oh."

"Not bad, Boss. Sort of safe at least."

"Thanks for the reassurance."

"You've thought of a place."

"I think so."

"Need an escort?"

"There are no Jhereg around now, are there?"

"No."

"Then no, thanks. I'd as soon keep this private. No offense intended to you or Her Majesty."

"None taken. Best of luck to you, Lord Taltos. That is, Count Szurke."

He turned away, his familiars following. I really hoped he was right about there being no Jhereg around, or I was going to feel very foolish for a short time.

I started walking east, then turned north. I was still slow, but getting better. Above all, I was hungry: very, very hungry. The more I thought about it, the more convinced I was that the Warlock was right—that it was nothing more than a bunch of Jhereg following me around, and taking whatever shots at me they could. It didn't have to be any one of the big bosses committing that much money. A group that big? Sure. The amount being offered for me was so high that a group of eight or nine could conceivably get together and agree to help each other and split the bounty afterward. It was hard to imagine a group that size trusting each other to the point where they could see each other starred—the main reasons assassins work alone is because no matter how much pressure the Imperial Justicers apply, no one can testify to something he doesn't know about.

But, yeah. Sometimes you need to take a leap and accept that the improbable has happened. Sometimes you even need to accept that the impossible is more possible than you'd thought. I considered this and all its implications as I made my slow, painful way through South Adrilankha.

After taking an hour to make a ten-minute walk, we reached an area that for reasons I'd love to discover someday is called the Noose. I took Calf Lane to stay off the main thoroughfares.

The houses here were wooden, old, rickety, three-story, and held eight or nine families each, and they all smelled bad. There were piles of refuse and rats to scurry around them, and here and there well-controlled fires in the middle of streets where someone was risking a conflagration in order to reduce his trash for a while. Some of the buildings had once been shops but now held families; a few of the houses now sported signs indicating a smith, a cobbler, a physicker, a tailor. I passed the place my grandfather had once lived, but I didn't stop; I didn't want to see what it had become.

A little past it was a tiny cottage with a tent attached to the front, looking both out of place among the larger build-ings and absurd just by itself. The entrance to the tent was covered with a quilt that had floral patterns in red and blue. Often the home of a witch is indicated by any of several sym-bols that depend on which culture the witch came from; but a witch who is well known in the neighborhood needs no sign.

I pushed the quilt aside and entered.

She looked up at me from an odd legless chair—like a cushion with a back—where she sat with her knees drawn up, reading. She was around fifty years old but looked older: her face weathered, her hair stringy and mostly gray. Her eyes—a deep, penetrating brown—fell first on Loiosh and Rocza, then on the sword at my side, then on my face.

"You're the young Taltos boy, aren't you?"

"Yes, Auntie," I said. My voice was still pretty raspy. I again almost cleared my throat, and again remembered in time to not do that.

"Tea?"

"Please."

I sat silently while she puttered. She served us a strong

herb tea with hints of cinnamon and orange. I waited while
she tasted hers, looking me over with narrow, evaluating eyes.
A few wisps of hair fell over her forehead. I was pleased that I
could swallow the tea without discomfort. Thank you, Lady
Teldra.

"Well," said the old woman said after a moment.

"Thank you for the tea, Auntie."

"What do you bring me?"

"Gold," I said.

She sniffed. "Gold gold, or copper?"

I drew an imperial from my pouch and passed it over. She
studied it, and I could see her trying not to show how impressed she was. Eventually she gave up the struggle, and let
herself smile. She still had many of her teeth, though they were
yellow.

"Are you hungry?"

I managed a dignified nod that understated my hunger by
a great deal. She disappeared, then came back with large bowl
and a small one.

"Oh my," I said. "Are those what I think they are?"

"Probably."

"Who grows red mushrooms around here?"

"I do," she said and offered me the bowl. I took one, dipped
it into the garlic butter, and took a bite. The burn spread over
my tongue and mouth and I grinned. The last person I knew
who grew red mushrooms had been my father, years and years
ago. He had served them lightly steamed, coated in garlic butter, and with a scallion wrapped around each. These were just
steamed and dipped in garlic butter, which is all you need. In
a pinch, you can skip the garlic butter. I felt my face flush, I
started sweating, and I ate another one.

I think it was just about there that I remembered that my clothes were covered in blood.

"Auntie," I rasped. "About my appearance—"

"Eat first," she snapped, as if annoyed that she had to explain something so obvious. I didn't argue.

The burn from red mushrooms (which, fortunately, affects the front of the mouth and not the throat) hits immediately, but it also accumulates, so by the fifth one my mouth was seriously concerned that I was trying to get information from it, and it would have told me anything I wanted to hear if it had only known what to say. She brought out some langosh, however, and that helped.

"Thanks," I said.

She sniffed. "I'm not a laundry service. You'll have to find your own way to clean up."

"I know, Auntie."

"You need rest."

I nodded.

"But that isn't why you came to me. Nor was it for red mushrooms." She sniffed again, as if red mushrooms were the only reason any right-thinking person would visit her.

I shook my head.

"Well?"

"I need a safe place to stay," I said. "Just for a day or two, while I recover."

She studied me, her eyes unblinking. "How is your grandfather?"

"Well. He's in an Eastern province, just this side of the mountains. Lots of wildlife, lots of privacy. He likes it."

"You'll give him my regards?"

"I will."

She considered a little longer, and I waited for her to decide.

Let me explain: Stabbing someone to death isn't easy. I know how often you see it in the theater, but on the street, it doesn't work like it does on the stage. You can't simply put steel into someone and expect him to become dead. People just naturally don't want to die, and have bodies that are designed to keep on living. If you have a thrusting sword like a rapier, or even better, a shortsword, and you can nail the heart, you're going to be all right; but it needs to be perfect, and it's hard to use anything as big as that without giving the target enough warning that it could turn into a fight—and you don't want it to turn into a fight, because then it won't be perfect, which means something might go wrong. That's why most "work" is done with knives, and killing someone with a knife requires knowing what you're doing.

There is a significant difference between a fight and an assassination. Usually, when I'm fighting, I try for wounds that will slow my enemy, or throw him off, or make it more difficult for him to fight me. That's why I cut so much—cutting someone's face, or arm, or belly, or leg, will interfere with his plans even if it won't kill him. The times you can actually get in a perfect killing strike are rare in a fight. The whole point of assassination, in fact, is to get the target into a position where you can take one perfect shot for a vital spot, and hit it. Even then, a great deal of the time, the victim won't die instantly; he'll just lie there, in shock, until he bleeds to death or his organs shut down. I mean, it often isn't even clear exactly when death occurs. But most of the time, it doesn't matter. Nail a guy's brain, and he's dead, even if he's still breathing for a bit. Generally speaking, that's good enough.

But I didn't have a pattern of movements, and I certainly wouldn't agree to a meeting, which made it very hard for anyone to set me up with a perfect shot; it didn't give them a lot to work with. In a situation like that, if I'd even agreed to take the job, I'd have just exercised patience and waited for the target (me, if you're paying attention) to make a mistake. But the Jhereg wanted me really badly, and I was skilled enough to make it hard for them—so someone had just put out the word that anyone who managed to stick a Morganti blade in me would make a lot of money. They were spending a lot of money on having people watch for me, and they'd made some arrangement to get out word when I was spotted.

I mean, the death thing—if it's a Morganti blade they've stuck into you, that's different. Doesn't much matter where you're hit, you're dead. Really dead. All the way dead. Depending on how strong the blade is, probably pretty fast, too.

The result was that a lot of incompetent people were taking shots at me. And that meant two things: one, that there were going to be a lot of attempts that were less than expert; and, two, sooner or later they were going to get me unless I got out of town really fast. It also meant that all of the places I usually went would be watched: Kragar's office, Cawti's house—for all I knew they were even watching Castle Black and Dzur Mountain.

I'm explaining this to you; it isn't what I was thinking about then. I sort of knew it, and I was sort of too messed up to care. Yeah, sometimes things are complicated.

What I did know was that I needed to be somewhere safe for a few days; to rest, to build up my strength. Just for a while. Someplace they couldn't find me, at least until I was in shape to maybe survive another attempt.

Just because you figure that one of them is going to get you eventually is no reason to make it easy for them.

Well, is it?

She raised a hand, studied me, then let it fall.

"You cannot remove that amulet even long enough to be healed?"

"No, Auntie. If I do, I'll be found."

She sniffed. "You need longer than a few days. You're already falling apart. You've been foolish, and are being more foolish every hour, and you need rest."

"Yeah," I said.

She considered. "Your grandfather would want me to help you."

"You knew him well?"

"I knew him well enough to know he would want me to help you."

"I'm pleased to hear you say so."

She nodded. "Very well, young Taltos. I will keep you hidden for two days. After that, we'll see."

"Auntie, do you know from whom you're hiding me?"

"No," she said. "Now, come along."

3

Making a Hole
or
Making Plans

She led the way out of the tent. In a few steps, we were in front of a dilapidated wooden ironware store. We went in. Auntie had a key, which brought up some questions I never found the answers to, but meant we didn't have to wake up a clerk. She led me through the place and out the back into an alley that was so narrow I rubbed against the walls on both sides. It was only a few paces, however, and then we went through a door and down several steps. After a moment, I smelled kerosene and there was light. She was holding a lantern, and I was in a narrow hallway of rough stone. It went thirty or forty paces before we came to a wooden door on the left. She opened it, and hung the lantern next to the door.

"Here," she said. "I'll bring you food and water, and a bucket so you needn't leave."

"All right."

"And blankets."

"You are kind."

She scowled. "Take off your clothes, I'll see they're cleaned."

"You are very kind."

She sniffed. "Do not do anything foolish, young Taltos. Or rather, anything else foolish."

"I'll try not to, Auntie. And I can pretty much promise that I won't at least until I have my clothes back."

She looked at Loiosh, sitting calmly on my right shoulder, and nodded. They were communicating. Not psychically, just—you know—communicating. I suspect if I'd had a better idea of what they were telling each other, I wouldn't have liked it, so I didn't ask. I stripped down and handed her my blood-covered clothes; fortunately, the cloak hadn't been in the way of the blood, so I didn't have to show her most of my weaponry. She saw the harness, and determinedly ignored it while I removed it.

Yeah, yeah. I was wearing the harness you gave me, with the fancy strange sticky stuff you can pull off and put on again, and I had a few weapons attached to it. There. Are you happy?

She left. I sat down, mostly naked, with my back against the wall, and closed my eyes. Presently, she came back with a pile of bedding and a bucket, then left without a word.

"Boss?"

"Yeah?"

"Can you really hide down here, doing nothing, for two days?"

"It'll make me crazy, but a different kind of crazy. I figure, right now, that's an improvement."

"Didn't think you had it in you, Boss."

"Never underestimate my sense of self-preservation."

"Boss, I've been with you all along, remember? You just barely have a sense of self-preservation."

"Shut up."

I threw the blankets onto the hard floor, stretched out,

and shook for a little while. When I was done with that, I closed my eyes. Sleep didn't come, but I didn't mind so much; it was good just to lie there. I did nothing for, I don't know, maybe a couple of hours, and I think I dozed off for a bit in there.

I sat up, my back to the wall, legs stretched out.

"Boss?"

"Yeah?"

"I'm bored. Rocza is bored."

"Get used to it. Remember when I was in jail?"

"Which time?"

"The first time. It was a lot like this."

"Tedious?"

"Exactly."

"How much longer?"

"Loiosh, don't start counting the hours. It'll make it worse."

"What then?"

"I'll get the door. You two head out. Fly around. Eat dead things. I'm going to stay here."

"Just leave you here?"

"Loiosh, all I want to do for a while is nothing. There isn't any good reason for you two to do nothing. The whole idea is for nothing to happen."

"I know that's the idea, Boss."

"Go."

I walked down the hall, opened the door, and let them out.

"And be careful," I said.

"You telling me that is pretty funny," he said.

I went back to the room, stretched out on the blankets, closed my eyes, and did nothing for a while.

Oh, relax. I'm not going to make you listen to how I did nothing for two days. It was hard enough to make myself go through it once; I have no interest in living it again. I did the things you do when your life involves sitting around and waiting. That my prison term was self-imposed helped a little; I always knew I could walk out if I wanted to.

The next day she came back with my clothing. I felt less helpless wearing clothes, although I know how stupid that is. While I dressed, I said, "Why can I still speak with my familiar, when I can't send or receive psychic messages, or perform witchcraft?"

"You think I'm an expert on Phoenix Stone?"

"Yes," I said.

"Well, I'm not."

"So it was just a wild guess when you identified it so quickly."

She glowered for a moment. Then she said, "You are bonded with your familiar."

"Yes."

Her face twitched, and I realized she was trying to find words to describe something that words weren't good for. "If you removed the amulet, I could show you," she said.

"I think I'll pass."

She nodded. She frowned, then said, "When you communicate with your familiar, it is more like speaking with your own arm than it is like psychic communication."

"I don't use words when I speak with my arm."

"I'm surprised you can use words at all."

Okay, I asked for that.

She said, "Psychic messages for the elfs can come through their device—the Orb—to make it easier for them. Or directly, mind-to-mind the way we do. Either way, it is a question of attuning your mind to resonate with the mind of the other."

I was right, she knew something about this stuff. It would be amusing—on several levels—to hear a conversation between her and Daymar. Alas, I was denied that pleasure.

"I think I'm with you," I said.

"The Phoenix Stone interferes with and changes how your mind emits the vibrations on the psychic levels, so none can hear you, and, at the same time, you cannot reach out."

"And when I communicate with Loiosh?"

"He does not receive the vibrations of psychic energy. He is part of what emits them."

I spent some time trying to make sense of that. Then I said, "All right, so knowing someone well enough to reach him psychically means knowing how his mind works well enough to permit your mind to be in sync with it, whereas you're bound to your familiar in such a way that he is almost thinking your thoughts with you."

"Yes."

"That's why he can help with spells."

"Yes. For a witch, the training is the opposite."

"I don't—"

"Hush. When communicating with another, you must learn to alter your brain's emissions enough to adjust to another. When communicating with your familiar, you must learn to separate your thought from his enough to hear and send words."

"I understand," I said. "Well, I don't, but I understand more than I did. Thank you."

She sniffed, nodded, and went back upstairs.

She came back a few more times and we had a few more

conversations. Some of them were interesting, but that is the only one that had any effect on the matters we're discussing today, so I'm afraid you must go the rest of your life without learning what they are. If that bothers you, feel free to write a letter. Fill it with threats and obscenity and send it to Sethra Lavode, Dzur Mountain. Let me know how that works out for you.

I sat, rested, recovered. I let things play out in my mind, things like how they'd found me, and what I might have to do to keep them from finding me again. I started to go through the list of enemies I'd made, but it was too long and just made me feel hopeless. And a stupid part of me—the part that had never grown older than six, I suppose—cried out that it wasn't fair.

Fairness matters to me. I've heard Eastern rebels speak of equality; I've heard Iorich advocates speak of justice. I'm not sure if I understand either of those concepts; they seem, I don't know, too far from my experience to grasp, or else I just don't have the sort of mind that can work with them. But I've always been concerned with fair. In a sense, that's why I could do what I did for so long—it might not be justice to kill some poor son-of-a-bitch who was skimming from his boss; and it certainly made him and the boss unequal. But it always seemed fair to me. He knew the rules, he knew the risks.

And, yeah, I'd broken the rules: I'd threatened the Imperial representative of the Jhereg and I'd testified to the Empire. But the fact is, I'd had no choice. Cawti was threatened. And I was scared and I was furious. I don't know, it looks different from the perspective of years, but I still don't see what else I could have done.

So, yeah, there was that voice inside loudly howling that

it wasn't fair. Usually, I was too busy—or maybe I tried to keep myself too busy—to pay attention to it. But there, in that basement, staring at walls, it rolled over me from time to time.

Oh, skip it; you don't need to hear about it. I do apologize; my intention isn't to make you listen to me complain. I know how wearying that is. But I'm also trying to tell you what happened, the whole thing, the why as well as the how; and that's a piece of it, all right?

I also considered the information I'd gotten about Lady Teldra. I mean, was I starving her by not letting her destroy souls? Should I, I don't know, just go out and do that? I didn't think I could. I didn't think she'd want me to. It certainly explained why I wasn't feeling better, though; I mean, why she'd only partly healed me. I'd drained her. I got the image in my head of one of those water-pulleys you see in the North: once the water has emptied out of them, they can't lift any more until you fill them. I had never imagined Lady Teldra like that, but maybe she was.

Which meant that I might need her to do something sometime, and she'd be unable to do it. That was not a comforting thought.

I fell asleep and dreamed I was operating a water-pulley, then that I was in one. Dreams are stupid.

My hostess brought bread and cheese from time to time, and once some tough peppery sausages, and more red mushrooms, which made me very happy (although my mouth raised some objections). Most of the time I did nothing, and tried very hard not to think. Loiosh spent a lot of the time just flying around the city; he was happier than he wanted to admit to know that, at least for a little while, I was pretty safe.

I know I liked that part of it. No friends, no enemies, no gods; just four blank walls and the sound of my own breathing.

Did it help? Yeah, I guess some. It seems like sometimes, if your body is wasted, ruined, falling apart, your mind is a bit more willing to accept doing nothing without going crazy. At least, sometimes. I think that's what made it tolerable.

What I wanted to do was take Lady Teldra, find as many high-up Jhereg as I could, and kill as many of them as possible before they got me. I wanted to do that very, very much. And there were certainly advantages to the idea: it was unlikely, if I made things that bloody, that they'd actually be able to nail me with a Morganti weapon; and just dying might be considered a win.

Is it sad when dying is a win?

The problem was Cawti and the boy; if I did that, then I had no doubt the Jhereg would go after them—before they got me, as a threat, or afterward, as revenge.

I couldn't do it.

I sat in the room, relaxed, tense, angry, calm.

So, what is it that sparked the idea? Was it frustration? Boredom? Anger? Dreams of water-pulleys? Half-conscious musing on fairness?

I don't know. Doesn't much matter, I suppose. I'd like to say I dreamed it because there would be a certain charm in that, but I didn't. I was doing a lot of sleeping, a lot of resting, a lot of nothing. I wasn't even thinking that much about my predicament; or, rather, it would be more accurate to say I was doing everything I could not to think about it, just for a while. I'd been there two days, and it was getting close to time to be on my way, which meant making a decision I wasn't any closer to making. The knowledge that I was going to leave the place was stirring up a combination of anticipation and fear. Yeah, it would be good to be out, but. You know.

In any case, that's when it hit me. That's when everything changed. Because if you are at the point where things are intolerable, and then suddenly you see a way to fix them, there isn't a lot of question about trying it, no matter how crazy it seems.

I was lying on my back, fingers clasped behind my head, staring at the rough texture of the ceiling, and then I drifted off, and then I remembered what Daymar had said on that long-ago evening. It wasn't like I dreamed it, it was more like the memory woke me up. Does that make sense?

Suddenly it was there, and then I paced the halls and pieces of a plan started falling into place. When enough of them were in place, I told Loiosh to find Daymar.

This was going to be difficult, tricky, probably futile, and certainly unpleasant. But all in all, not bad if you use cutting your own throat as the standard of comparison.

I was pretty sure I could do the part that ought to be impossible.

I was pretty sure I could sell the part I had to sell.

But the issue, as it always seemed to be, was: repercussions. How could I protect myself and expose myself at the same time, when I didn't know who exactly I'd be protecting myself from? And, if that turned out to be impossible, how could I find out who I needed to protect myself from?

My grandfather, in teaching me the human style of swordsmanship, had said over and over that there was no way to control what your opponent did—that you had to be prepared for the guy to make any decision available to him, and be ready to respond. He was trying to make me understand the importance of being adaptable to changing circumstances. But the point is, he would repeat that there is no way to control your opponent's actions. And then one time he added, "Except one."

"What's that?"

"Give him a perfect shot at your heart."

"But then I'll be dead, Noish-pa."

"Yes, Vladimir. That's why we don't do it."

Well, okay, then. If you can't control where the attack comes from, limit where the attack goes, right? Create your own opening, so that you've made your preparations for whoever charges into it. That might be feasible, if I were careful.

It would take bringing some high-powered Jhereg together, and then running a game on them. There would certainly be sorcery. How to work around it? The amulet? No. Lady Teldra? Not the greatest sorcerer of all the weapons I've heard of, but still able to hold her own when needed.

Only, yeah. I had to assume she wouldn't be available. Was there any way to—yeah. It is much more difficult to enchant a living thing than a dead object—that's why objects were teleported before they figured out how to do people, right? So that meant I could maybe find a way to do *that*.

Or, wait. Hold it. Whole different idea. Castle Black? There would be a certain elegance in, just at the right moment, getting to Castle Black where the Jhereg wouldn't dare touch me, or else put someone else in exactly the position I'd been in so many years before. Elegant and amusing, but no; there was another piece to it: Morrolan. I couldn't put him in that position. At least, not if there was another way that had a reasonable chance of working.

And there was a way. And it did have a chance of working. Maybe even a reasonable chance. If I could just figure out . . .

Resources. I was going to need a lot of resources. Both the kind you hold in your hand, and the kind that walk and talk. The latter are always trickier. Who to call on? Cawti? No, I couldn't drag her into this without also dragging in the boy, and that wasn't going to happen.

Kiera or Kragar, or both. Two old friends; two people still willing to help me in spite of the Jhereg, and with contacts deep enough that maybe—maybe one or the other of them could get what I needed.

The idea, you see, fell into two distinct pieces: Part one, convince the Jhereg they didn't want to kill me. Part two, stay alive while completing part one. Tricky, because, even if this worked, word would get out—word had to get out—what I was doing. And a lot of Jhereg were very, very unhappy with me. All of which meant that there was bound to be someone—someone or someones—who was just flat-out not going to let me get away with it, no matter what. I'd made too many Jhereg too mad.

So, while I was pretty sure I had the first part figured out, the second part was going to be harder. After pacing for a while, I became convinced that I just couldn't figure out the second until I'd spoken with Kragar or Kiera.

So, then.

I went back to the room I'd been sleeping in to make sure I hadn't left anything there; I wouldn't be coming back. I checked the dagger in my boot and the throwing knife up my sleeve, and the things on the harness. I strapped the rapier to my side with Lady Teldra just in front of it, and the various things in and under my cloak. I looked around the room again, and gave it a silent thank-you. Then, Rocza riding discontentedly on my right shoulder, I went down the hall and out, leaving the clammy mildewy stench of the basement for the stink of South Adrilankha.

I stopped to thank Auntie and tell her good-bye. She sniffed, nodded, and asked if there was anything else I needed.

"Do you know any place nearby I can get cleaned up a bit?"

"Nine doors down that way and across the street. It doesn't look like it, but they let rooms, and they'll have a pump and a basin. Give them a coin, and if they give you any trouble tell them I sent you."

"All right. Good. Thanks. Also, do you have some koelsch leaves? I'm out."

"They aren't good for you."

"I know. But neither is dying."

She grunted, went into her house, and emerged with a small leather pouch. "Six coppers," she said.

I handed her a silver coin. "Keep it," I said.

She nodded. "Good luck," she told me.

"Thanks."

I followed her directions and found myself in the sort of flophouse I'd been staying in lately. I entered, flipped the landlady a coin without saying a word, and went up the stairs to use the pump room and get myself a little more prepared to face the world. Or Daymar, at least. The water was cold. They had a small mirror there, and I took some time to study myself; yeah, I still looked like me, except I now had a small white scar on my throat.

When I'd told Loiosh to have Daymar meet me "across the street," I meant a place I'd discovered some weeks earlier, while wandering about South Adrilankha. They were called Len and Nieces, and they made klava and sold pastries. The pastries weren't all that good, but the klava was excellent, and the baking and the roasting coffee overpowered the smells from outside. I walked down three steps and into the place with its seven identical round tables, and paused to take a deep breath before seating myself. There were two other tables occupied, both of them by old men and women—human, of course. That is, what the Dragaerans called Easterners, like me. Dragaerans refer to themselves as human, and I'm usually too polite to correct them.

The people at the tables were either the same ones I'd seen before, or the same type. One look at them, and you knew they spent all of their time here. I had mixed feelings about that: maybe it's a useless waste to spend every minute of your life doing nothing more than sitting around gabbing; but maybe it's not a bad thing at all. I don't know.

Claudia—one of the nieces—brought me klava and a cream-filled sweet roll, as always without a word. She wasn't used to people openly carrying weapons, and didn't know what to make of me. The first time I'd come in, Len had asked me to remove my sword while I was there; I'd looked at him until he went back to his counter. Since then, it had become obvious that I made them uncomfortable, but it wasn't like there was anything they could do about it. And I didn't care that much. Does that make me a bad person? I don't care that much about that, either.

The klava was even better than usual that day; the sweet roll was all right, but my brain was working too fast to give either of them the concentration they deserved. I kept checking the door for Daymar, which was pointless: it would be hours at best before Loiosh would be able to find him, assuming he was in the City.

I had to hide from the Orb while I did it, Daymar had said.

Every citizen of the Empire is linked to the Orb. It permits sorcery and is how you can tell time, and, if you have information vital to the Empire or are really stupid, you can reach the Empress instantly and directly. The amulet I wore was powerful enough so that I couldn't even detect the Orb if I was too far from it, but the Orb could still find me.

I knew two ways to hide from the Orb. You could give up your citizenship, and then the Orb couldn't find you, but you wouldn't be able to use sorcery. The other is a short-term solution: You concentrate on blanking out your mind, thinking of nothing, imagining a big, black, empty well. I'd done that once for a little while, just to see if I could, but I didn't think I'd be able to pull it off if I were in danger. In any case, neither of those methods would help in this case. But neither of them would have done Daymar any good either, so there might be a third way. If there was, it might have something to do with what Auntie had just told me about attuning one's mind, which seemed reasonable, based on my experience with sorcery and my knowledge of witchcraft. And, if so, it might be just what I needed to set things in motion.

That's a lot of maybes. And if it went wrong, I'd be dead. But if I did nothing, I'd be dead anyway—the last few days had convinced me of that, if nothing else.

I gestured to Claudia. She brought me more klava, still not looking at me. I guess something strange happens in the heads of Easterners when they're around someone like me—they feel like I'm one of them, but not. Come to think of it, I feel the same way. The last time I went back East, I found out—no, skip it. I did a lot of reminiscing while I was waiting for Daymar, and I told myself the story of how I'd gotten into this mess, but you don't need to hear about it.

I had just finished my second sweet roll—this one tartberry—and was drinking my fourth cup of klava when there was a pop of displaced air, and Daymar was sitting in front of me, floating cross-legged a few feet off the ground. Loiosh flapped over to me.

Daymar looked around. "Why are you holding a weapon?"

I got up off the floor and made the dagger vanish. "It would take too long to explain," I explained.

I picked my chair up while Daymar seated himself in a more traditional way. By this time, there was only one table of old men—they were studiously not looking at the commotion. Len and Claudia were, in fact, staring at Daymar, but when I looked at them they got busy doing other things.

I turned to Daymar and smiled.

Part Two

WINGS OF THE HAWK

4

MAKING PLANS
OR
MAKING CONVERSATION

"Aren't they used to having humans in here?" he asked.

I didn't take the trouble to correct him about who the humans were because, like I said, I'm too polite. I said, "Not humans who suddenly appear in the middle of their place, no."

"Oh," he said. "Why not?"

"It's not done," I said. "In the East."

"Oh."

Loiosh settled on my left shoulder, Rocza on my right. I called over for a klava for Daymar; when it was delivered, he said, "It's good to see you, Vlad."

"You too," I lied.

"When I saw Loiosh, I concluded that you wanted to see me."

"Good thinking."

"He let me get the location from his mind, so I teleported."

"Yes," I said.

"So I was right?"

I nodded.

He sat back, tilted his head, and waited.

"I wanted to ask you about something," I said.

He nodded. "All right, I'm listening."

"You wish me to ask you, then?" I said, keeping my face straight.

He shrugged. "I don't know. It's up to you. I wasn't doing anything important. And I'm not in a hurry. So, take as much time as you want."

Explaining the joke to Daymar seemed like a poor use of my time, so I said, "It goes back to a remark you made some years ago. We were sitting around Castle Black, and you mentioned a Hawk rite of passage you'd undergone."

"I don't remember that," he said. "I mean, I remember the rite, but I don't remember talking about it."

"We were all a little drunk."

He nodded, waiting, his big eyes fixed on me. He has a way of looking at you that simultaneously indicates total concentration, and a distant abstraction. I'm not sure how he does it. But then, I'm not sure how he does most of what he does.

"You said something about a time you'd hidden from the Orb. Could you expand on that?"

I hadn't thought about predicting what he'd say, but if I had, I would have been right. "Why would you want to know about that?" he said.

"Just curious," I told him.

I don't believe there is anyone else in the world who would have accepted that as a reasonable answer under the circumstances, but Daymar just nodded and said, "All right. What exactly do you want to know?"

"How did you do it?"

He tilted his head as if I'd asked him the sum of two and two.

"The link to the Orb comes in on a particular set of psychic channels. You just route those around you for as long as you need to hide."

"That's all?"

"Yes."

"I hadn't realized it was that simple."

He nodded. "That's all it is."

"Well, good then."

"Is there anything else?"

"Yes. How do you reroute a psychic channel?"

He blinked a couple of times, tilted his head again, and frowned. "Vlad," he said, "are you jesting?"

"Remember," I said, "I'm an Easterner."

"Oh, yes, of course. Sorry. What is this?"

"Klava," I said. "You've had it before."

"Have I? Oh. Did I like it?"

"I think so."

He nodded and drank some more.

"So," I said. "Rerouting the channels will make you invisible to the Orb. Is that something I could do?"

"Well, first you have to identify the right channels. Then it's just a matter of—hmm." He looked at me and his brow furrowed. I'm pretty sure he was trying to get inside my head to test my psychic abilities, or power, or something. After a moment of being unable to do so, he looked puzzled and said, "Phoenix Stone?"

I nodded.

"I can't get past it to tell. Could you remove it?"

"Uh, that would be a bad idea. There are people looking for me."

"Looking for you? I don't—"

"To kill me. Were I to remove the Phoenix Stone, they'd find me, and then they'd kill me, and I would be sad."

"Oh." He considered. "Why do they want to kill you?"

"We've discussed this before, Daymar. It's the Jhereg. I offended them."

"Oh, yes. I'd forgotten. Can you apologize?"

"Sure. The trick is getting them to accept the apology."

"Oh. They're not very forgiving, are they. I remember that."

"Right. But I'm beginning to think there may be a way to."

"Oh?"

"Maybe."

"How?"

"That's why I'm asking about hiding from the Orb."

He did the head-tilt again. "Hiding from the Orb will help convince the Jhereg to accept the apology?"

"Not hiding from the Orb, exactly. But the Orb is how most Drag—humans communicate psychically. I know, you don't. But most of them do. That means that if it's possible to hide from the Orb, then it might also be possible to tap into those channels of the Orb."

"Tap in?"

"Identify the channels psychically, manipulate them with sorcery to direct them to, say, me."

"But then you'd—oh!" His eyes widened. Then he frowned. "Wouldn't that be illegal?"

"I imagine it would. So, if you'd be so kind, explain."

He gave a sort of shrug. "All right. It's pretty simple; after you've identified the channels, you just externalize your thought-stream so you can shape it, and—"

"Wait. Slow down."

"Vlad, how much do you know about the basics of psychic manipulation?"

"Not that much."

"How about how sorcery works?"

"Not that much either. I just use it."

"All right. Do you understand the Sea of Amorphia?"

"I know what it is. I mean, I know it's amorphia."

"And you know what amorphia is?"

"Ah, sort of."

"It is simultaneously matter and energy, and—"

"Wait. What does that mean?"

"It means—" He stopped, frowned, and it was like I could see him back up to take another run at it. He said, "Amorphia is chaos: material randomness."

"Um—"

"The Orb is a device for imposing dimensionality on its formlessness, thus permitting sorcerous access to amorphia, through the Orb."

"Daymar, does 'imposing dimensionality' actually mean anything?"

"I think so."

"All right. Please explain how this relates to hiding from the Orb. Or, more specifically, to identifying the channels through which someone is reaching the Orb."

He did, and we'd each had another cup of klava by the time I realized that I was never going to be able to manipulate the channels myself—whether I had the psychic power I didn't know, but I most certainly didn't have the skill. I also had a deeper understanding of the relationship between physics and sorcery, and between sorcery and amorphia. And the beginnings of a headache.

But I also understood manipulating the channels well enough to know my plan might work. I didn't need to be able to do it, you see. Well, I sort of did, but only once, so I was perfectly willing to cheat on that part. The point is, it had to be possible to do it. If it were possible, I could make it happen. Because I know people. Like Daymar.

When he'd finished the explanation, I said, "Thanks, Daymar. I appreciate you taking the time. Now let me tell you what I'm going to try, and you tell me if it'll work."

"All right."

He listened, and his eyes widened. "Why didn't I ever think of that?" were his first words.

I bit back the obvious reply and said, "Because you aren't both a witch and a sorcerer. There aren't many of us who are. Morrolan might have thought of it, but it would never cross his mind to do that. Will it work?"

"I could do it."

"Yes, but can I? Using the equipment I talked about?"

"I can't think of why not," he said.

I nodded. "Good then. And thank you once more."

"You're welcome," he said. "Is there anything else I can do for you?"

"Yes," I said. "I think a great deal. But not just now."

"Oh? What, then?"

"I'll get back to you."

"All right. I'll open up for a few minutes on the hour."

"Thanks," I said. "But—"

"Oh, right. You won't be able to reach me."

"*So, I'll be spending yet more time flying around Pamlar University?*"

"*Unless you have another idea.*"

"I'm not the idea guy."

"No, you're the one who flies off to find Daymar."

He called me something impolite.

Daymar vanished with a pop of displaced air. It got me more glances from those in Len's. Then he popped back in.

"Oh," he said. "Was that rude? Should I not have done that?"

Sometimes I just have no idea what to say. Daymar went through the door this time.

I left a few coins on the table at Len and Nieces and headed out to deal with urgent matters that had been building up since my third klava. Then I walked about half a mile away and found a flophouse. Loiosh and Rocza took a flight around the place to make sure it was safe.

"So, Boss, about this plan."

"Yeah. Give me some time to think about it."

"All right."

Then, "Boss?"

"More time, Loiosh."

"All right."

Then he said, "Just tell me one thing: Will the spell work?"

"Daymar just said it would."

"I know. Will the spell work?"

"Trying to build up my confidence, are you?"

"That's my job."

I gave the landlord some money, started the room fumigating, and walked back outside. I strolled a bit, but it made me nervous, so I went back to the flophouse, hanging out near the desk where the landlord determinedly didn't look at me. After a while, I went back to the room, smothered the burning herbs, and let the place get started on airing out. I'd have opened the window except that it couldn't close, so there was no need.

I sat on the bed, I stood up, I paced, I sat down, I leaned against the wall, I struck my palm with my fist, and I said, "Yeah, Loiosh, I think we can maybe do this."

"Boss, do you know what you're saying?"

"Yeah. There's a chance I can get my life back. Or get killed, of course."

"You've almost gotten killed in worse causes."

"Yeah."

"What do we need?"

"A way to make a Jhereg think like an Orca."

"That seems possible."

"Yeah, if we can make him see things like a Hawk."

"That sounds harder."

"There may be a way. We'll need some things. Lots of things. The first steps will be to get a good supply of cash, and to find Kiera."

"Which one first?"

"It doesn't matter. All right. Let's go steal the Jhereg Council."

"And we're off!"

Loiosh sounded positively excited. I couldn't remember the last time he'd sounded excited about something that wasn't on the order of telling me that if I didn't duck I was going to be dead.

I was feeling somewhat the same. It wasn't just the last few days, of course; I hope I've gotten at least that much across. The Jhereg had been after me for years—wanting me not just dead, but *dead* dead. Soul dead. Killed with a Morganti weapon. I'd been looking over my shoulder all that time, running around, too scared to settle anywhere even for a while. I'd learned that my ex-wife had given birth while I was gone, and

I now had a son. I'd fought personal demons and impersonal gods and wandered through buildings that couldn't exist to do impossible things. I had discovered that I had a destiny, and blown that destiny right off the table. I'd run, fought, hid, and schemed. I was tired of the whole thing. And now, maybe, maybe. After all of this, a "maybe" was more precious than platinum, more delicious than Piarran Mist. In all of these years, this was the first maybe I'd had. I gripped it, held it, studied it from every side. I was pretty close to giving it a name and a food dish.

A beautiful, beautiful maybe.

Now to make it real.

I threw my cloak back on and headed out to get things started.

The first step was easy enough, just tedious. I had to pass through pretty much all of South Adrilankha and then cross the river. I've been told that before teleportation became commonplace, the city used to be full of carriages, but now you can only find them near the Palace where they charge too much to take too long to get to too few places. There are cabriolets, but I just didn't like the idea of having my face exposed while not being under my own power. That left renting a horse, or walking, and I'd ridden on horseback before, so that was out.

I'd gotten used to doing a lot of walking in the last few years, so it wasn't too bad—it just took a long time. Adrilankha, in case you've never been there, is not a small city. It was afternoon when I finally reached the part of Adrilankha where I used to be important—which was also the part where I was most likely to be spotted by those who wanted to do harmful things to my person. Loiosh and Rocza flew above me in slow circles, alert to anything.

I felt a quickening of my heartbeat, and tried to relax. There was a lot to do, and a lot that could go wrong; this wasn't the time to let my emotions drive the team.

There were four different places where, in the past, I'd left messages that I wanted to see Kiera. The message I left this time was the same at all four: "Please tell Kiera that the little guy is hungry for apples."

And something happened in there that's worth relating, because it turned out to be important, though I didn't realize it at the time.

The Hook is a tiny area on the western side of the city, just touching Lower Kieron. There are no Jhereg operations there. I was leaving a message at a place called the Fruit Basket, and I saw a kid being hauled off by a couple of Phoenix Guards. He wore the colors of the Orca, and if there's any House I hate, that's the one. But he was young. He was Dragaeran, not human, so the ages don't line up, but he looked like the same age as my son. I guess that's what did it.

Anyway, I couldn't help it. I approached them.

"Move along, whiskers," said one of them, not even stopping, and I got annoyed. I dug into my pouch, pulled out my signet and showed it to them. I got all the reaction I could have asked for: wide eyes, open mouths, and I think they even turned a little pale.

The woman said, "My lord, apologies. I didn't know—"

"That any Easterners had Imperial titles. Yeah. I'm Count of Szurke by the grace of Her Majesty. What is the boy accused of?"

"Cutpurse, m'lord."

One look at him said he was guilty.

"May we proceed?" said the man.

I considered. "Not yet." I turned to him. "What's your name, boy?"

"Asyavn, my lord." The name wasn't unlike that of a Teckla boy I liked. I frowned and turned toward the Phoenix Guards. I started to say, "Let him go," then reconsidered. I was going to need to collect a lot of things. "Get his imprint, and suspend the arrest."

"Until?"

"A year and a day. If he's done nothing in that time, it never happened."

"As you say, m'lord."

When they'd taken a psychic impression of him, they left. I turned to him, and he seemed a little frightened. He said, "You could have just freed me."

"Yeah," I said. "But I prefer being able to find you to collect the favor you owe me."

He looked even more frightened, and seemed very close to bolting. "What do you want me to do?"

I said, "Nothing just now. I may need some help in the future though. What do you do besides cutting purses?"

"I dive and salvage some," he said.

I smiled. "Do you indeed? Well. If I need some diving and salvaging, or a purse cut, how do I find you?"

He told me a few places he could usually be found, and I told him that a Jhereg might come looking for him, then sent him on his way. It was a minor stroke of good luck, as such things go, but it turned out to help.

I went back to arranging to make contact with my old friend Kiera the Thief.

It was long, slow, and painful to get into each of the places I wanted to leave a message without taking more chances than

necessary; but not all that interesting to relate, so let's just say
I did it, and by the time I was done I was seriously hungry—for
apples or anything else. I stayed on major streets and hung with
big crowds as much as I could while heading past Malak Circle to
Windchime Market, and from there north to a tiny place called,
appropriately, Tiny's, where they made a decent if not outstanding peppered breaded kethna. The real attraction, though, was
across the street where there was a smaller place selling baked
cinnamon apples filled with sweetened flavored iced cream;
fresh apples when in season, dried when not. Kiera had heard me
talking about it often, and I was pretty sure she'd take the hint.

Good news: She had. Bad news: She'd gotten the message
sooner than I'd calculated on, so I didn't have time for the
kethna.

She smiled and kissed my cheek. Somehow, she never made
it seem like she had to bend over to kiss me, even though she
did. "Hello, Vlad."

"Kiera. You look wonderful. You haven't changed at all."

That was a sort of joke, by the way; Dragaerans live for a
couple of thousand years if someone like me doesn't kill them
first. Kiera either missed the joke or ignored it. She said, "Are
you safe here?"

"Not terribly. But I needed to see you."

She looked around. "Maybe another place?"

"Loiosh and Rocza are watching; this is about as safe as it
gets. The Jhereg would have real problems setting something
up here, even if I were spotted. Although—eh, never mind."

"Although what, Vlad?"

"They've taken a couple of tries without any set-up. Just
random attacks, hoping for the best. As you can see, I lived."

"You look pale. Were you wounded?"

"A bit."

"Vlad, you need to be careful."

"Yeah, well."

"All right. You know best."

"You haven't been speaking to Loiosh."

She chuckled politely. "What's been going on?"

"Someone's been trying to kill me."

"Yes. The whole organization."

"That isn't what I mean. I know they want me, but someone wants me even more."

"I'm listening."

"They took some random shots at me."

"So you said."

"Sloppy stuff—just finding me and taking a whack. That isn't how it's done."

She nodded; even though she wasn't an assassin herself, she knew how this sort of thing was generally handled. "Go on."

"Unless I'm completely missing what's going on—which is possible, but not likely—they used at least eight guys. And they were Jhereg, not hired Orca. I mean, they were getting paid."

"Eight?"

"Eight. Following me, taking shots two at a time, following me to the next place. Yeah."

"Eight?"

"At least."

"That's . . ."

"I know."

"Think it's something personal?"

"Could be. Someone is behind it, and it's costing that guy a lot. A whole lot. It's a bad investment. A bad gamble."

She nodded. "Who do you think it is?"

"No idea, no good way to find out."

"I could ask around."

"And?"

"Yeah, you're right. Probably nothing."

I said, "Anyway, that brings us to this meeting."

"What do you need? If I can do it, Vlad, you know I will. What is it?"

"A couple of things. First, I need the Jhereg shaken up."

"What do you mean?"

"I need them talking about something that isn't me. There'll be rumors flying around about me—I know, because I'm going to start them—and at the same time, there has to be something else going on that takes their attention. Something big. I need them wondering about me, and looking away at the same time."

"Well, you could always kill someone high up in the Organization. That generally does it."

I winced. "Maybe," I said. "I'm not terribly partial to, you know, just killing someone for effect."

"I could steal the Jhereg treasury."

I chuckled. "That didn't work out so well the last time someone did it."

She spread her hands.

"Yeah, okay," I said. "I'll think about it."

"What else do you need?" she said.

I took a deep breath and let it out slowly. "A long time ago—by my standards—"

"So, a few years?"

"Yeah. About eight years, nine years. And the incident in question must have been a hundred or so before that."

"Wait. What?"

"Sorry. Eight or so years ago you made a reference to an incident that had happened a hundred years or so before that."

"I keep forgetting what a good memory you have."

"I have a terrible memory, Kiera."

"You have a good memory for the oddest things. All right. What incident?"

"You mentioned a phoenix made of gold jade."

"I did?"

"Yeah."

"Was I drunk?"

"A little."

"All right. What about it?"

"You were talking about the lock on the display case."

"I remember that lock."

"And you mentioned using an enchanted lockpick."

"I must have been *really* drunk," said Kiera.

I was going to need Kiera's enchanted lockpick.

I need to explain.

I got this story from Kiera, and most of the names are probably wrong because she was drunk and most likely lying about them. But that's fine because you don't need to know the names anyway; I just want you to understand a bit of the background, all right? If all the names and stuff confuse you, forget it; that isn't the point.

It was never about stealing the jade. Not that gold jade isn't beautiful, and three-quarters of a pound of it was worth a fortune even before Nescaffi had put his genius to it. But stealing the jade was only a means to an end. There was a man named Scaanil who coveted anything and everything by

Nescaffi. It was all about Scaanil, and that made it about the jade.

Which made it about the lock on the display case.

Nedev, who owned the jade phoenix, had good taste in art, and a lot of money; the case had been designed by Tudin of Threehills, which meant Kiera was far and away the best choice to steal it, if she could be persuaded to take the job. She could.

The enchantment that secured the lock was by Heffesca of Longlake, which sent Kiera to Litra.

Litra wasn't the name she was born with; she took it five hundred years ago when she moved to Adrilankha. No one knew where she came from or who she was before. She had the dark complexion and sharp features of the House of the Hawk, though of course she was now a Jhereg. She took the name Litra, which was the Dragaeran form of a Serioli word that means "to scrounge."

Litra lived in the Captain's Corner district, surrounded by the ramshackle dwellings of petty merchants. Her own home blended in, but in fact it continued down more than fifty feet below street level, and it was in the subbasements that Litra did her work. Since the Interregnum, she was known as one of the best at what she did.

So, Kiera gave her details of the position and composition of the pins, the position of the stepper, the weight of the hammer, and the complex interleaving of spells that would preserve the integrity of the lock, verifying the identity of anyone attempting to open it, and sounding an alert if it was opened.

Litra listened carefully, then said, "I've always wanted to go against Heffesca."

"I've always wanted to go against Tudin," said Kiera.

"Three days," said Litra.

"I'll be back then."

And she was, and she got the jade, and she put it into the hand of the man who'd hired her, and a week later Scaanil's severed head turned up on the street outside the Undauntra's Arms, where the sorceress who'd hired Mario for the job ran her business.

And that's what a very drunk Kiera had told me that evening. Some conversations you remember.

"Well, yeah, you were kind of drunk."

"All right. What about my lockpick?"

"Mind if I borrow it?"

She looked at me. "I'm not sure what to ask first."

"You want to ask why."

"Yes. You're right. Why?"

"I don't want to tell you."

"Why didn't I see that coming?"

I smiled.

"All right. How long will you need it?"

"Not long. A week at the most."

"What are the chances that I'll get it back?"

"Fair. If you're willing to find my dead, soulless corpse and loot it, they go up to excellent."

"It's like that, is it?"

"Isn't it always?"

"Pretty much."

She studied me through slitted eyes. "Give me a hint."

"I might be able to get myself out of trouble with the Jhereg," I told her, because she deserved to know, and because I knew I'd enjoy watching her face when I said it.

"Really!"

The expression on her face was all I could have wanted. I was beginning to enjoy this.

"Maybe," I told her. "I'm not sure yet, but, yeah, I just might manage to pull this off. It'll be tricky, and I'm going to need help, but yeah."

She nodded and her eyes seemed to light up. "How?"

"By offering them something they want as much as my head."

"I can't imagine what that might be."

"I have a good imagination," I said.

She glanced around the area again, then turned her attention back to me. "Money, of course. But it would have to be a lot of it. Are you planning to knock over the Dragon treasury?"

"Nothing so direct, or impossible."

She studied me for a minute or two, then said, "It has to be either a scam, or a new business."

"A scam would be temporary."

"That was going to be my next sentence. What's the business?"

"Remember when I said I don't want to tell you?"

She looked like she was about to argue, then she said, "All right."

"So I can use the lockpick?"

"You're sure it wouldn't be better to just have me open the lock?"

"I'm sure. I may not even need it. In fact, if things go as I hope, I won't need it. But if I do, you wouldn't be—never mind. I'm sure."

"All right. What's the best way to get it to you?"

"Do you have any favorite drops?"

"Several. Do you know Filsin's tannery?"

"I've seen it."

"Go around to the back, face the door, turn and take three paces to your left, and at knee level is a loose stone. The pick will be there by this time tomorrow."

"Thank you, Kiera."

"Good luck," she said. She kissed my cheek again, then she was gone.

I knew what I wanted to do next. I couldn't think of any way to do it, and it wasn't at all necessary to my plan, but I wanted to go visit my estranged wife and my son, because if this was going to kill me I really ought to say good-bye. But the Jhereg would be watching her and watching the house.

So much for what I wanted.

I only learned of my son when he was about four. That kind of thing happens when you're on the run, and is one of the reasons I was tired of running. One of the big reasons. Do you have kids? It's kind of a big deal. You don't know how much kids matter until you have one. He was eight now, and I'd only seen him a few times. The last time I'd shown up to see him, he'd smiled and run toward me with his arms out.

Loiosh was silent while I tried and failed to figure out a safe way to see Cawti and Vlad Norathar. Eventually I sighed and said, *"All right. On to the next step."*

5

MAKING CONVERSATION
OR
MAKING DEALS

The bar was still mostly deserted, and no one was paying attention to me.

"What's the next step, Boss?"

"My old friend Tippy."

"The money guy?"

"Right. Then a jewelry store."

"Boss, seeing Tippy is dangerous."

"What do you suggest instead, Loiosh?"

"You could just rob the jewelry store."

"What I want, I can't steal. Besides, that requires a set of skills I don't have. And what I want in the jewelry store isn't in the jewelry store. And the money isn't for that—it's for, um, incidentals."

"You're enjoying this too much, Boss."

"Indulge me."

"I still think it would be easier to rob some place than see the money guy."

"No," I said.

He didn't say anything; I got the feeling he was sulking.

"Oh," I said.

"What?"

"I just figured it out. All those years on the road, when we were robbing the road agents. You liked that, didn't you?"

"So?"

"You just enjoy robbery."

"Well, if someone has something, and you want it—"

"I understand. But that isn't what we're doing now, Loiosh. This all has to be done right. It's complicated, and liable to get messy. I can't risk improvising."

"All right," he said.

"Glad I have your permission."

"Heh," he said.

Loiosh and Rocza flew out and let me know it was safe. I walked fast but not too fast, heading north toward the harbor, then skirting up Overlook, hooking around and back down Pressman's Hill to enter the Little Deathgate area by the back door, sort of.

Little Deathgate has a reputation for being one of the roughest areas in the City. It's not entirely undeserved, but it is exaggerated. As I understand it, it goes back about two hundred years to when there was an especially nasty turf war over control of the area. It was long and bloody and, for the Jhereg, very expensive in both money and Imperial notice. When it finally ended, there were almost no Jhereg operations in the area, and therefore no reason to keep the streets safe. There is, yes, a lot of street crime; but if you're openly armed and you look like you can handle yourself, you can walk around the area day or night with no real worries, except for any Jhereg assassins who might be looking for you.

I'd been to Tippy's a couple of times, but it took a bit of looking to find the way amid the tiny, twisting streets, most of which had no names. Eventually, as dark was falling, I recognized the ugly off-white house with two stories and three doors.

"*Anything, Loiosh?*"

"*Seems okay, Boss.*"

I stood outside the middle door and clapped three times, then twice more, then twice more. I waited for half a minute, then walked away. I strolled the neighborhood for twenty minutes, then worked my way around to the right-hand back door of the house. I waited for a couple of minutes, then it opened and I stepped inside. I was in a small, square, dimly lit room with two comfortable chairs and one table. Tippy sat in one of the chairs, I took the other. The first time I'd been there, I'd noticed that my chair was more comfortable than his. And would take considerably longer to get out of. That's the kind of thing you notice. It proved that Tippy was no fool, even if he looked like—

Um. How to describe him?

Imagine, for a moment, that you're walking through a forest and you come across a woodsman's hut. You clap, you enter, and there, in this one rustic room, you see someone wearing the full Phoenix regalia: gold garments with tall collar, flared hem, courtier sleeves, and ruff-top boots. Well, a visit with Tippy always seemed a bit like that. He wore the gray and black of the Jhereg, but everything was either silk or velvet, and there were bits of lace at his throat and wrists and his boots gleamed in the light of a pair of wall lamps. He had rings on every finger, pendants, and he had poked holes in his ears and other parts of his face to hang more jewelry from, which is a custom that, I'm told, was lost with the Interregnum.

Other than that, he was young, a bit short, with an angular face, a strong chin, and a sharp nose. And very white teeth that he displayed whenever possible. I have a theory that the delay he always insisted on as part of the meeting protocol had nothing to do with security, but was all about giving him time to dress. I don't know.

"Hello, Vlad. Can I offer you anything?"

"No thanks," I said.

"I assume you need money that clinks?"

I nodded.

"How much?"

"Two hundred."

"How soon?"

"Thirty hours, if necessary. Now would be best if you can do it."

"Thirty hours will be two-twenty for two. Now is two-fifty for two."

"All right. Now."

He pulled out an inkpot, quill, sand, and a blank draft. I filled it out and passed it to him.

"Anything else?" he said.

"One thing."

"Yes?"

"You're good with money."

"Thank you."

"I mean, you know how money works, in and out of the Jhereg. You understand finance."

"Up to a point. Mostly I know how to move money around so it can end up somewhere without appearing to come from where it came from."

"Yes, yes. But you have an idea of Jhereg business, and what it earns?"

"All of it? No."

"No, not all of it, but—"

"Vlad, what are you getting at?"

"Suppose I had an idea for a new business venture."

"For the Jhereg?"

"Yes."

"Big enough that they might, ah, that it might change your situation?"

"Exactly."

He whistled. "That would have to be . . ."

"Yeah."

"All right. What about it?"

"Who in the Council would have the authority to make that decision?"

"A majority vote. The others would have to go along with it. Though it'd be smart to arrange for all of them to get a slice, if you can manage it."

I nodded. "The real question, though, is who is the big one. Who do I need on my side?"

"I have no idea. That isn't at all my area."

"All right. Just checking. I'll see you next time I need money that clinks."

"Watch your ass, Vlad."

"I will."

I left him with that thought and headed back out into the Adrilankha night.

"Boss? You knew he wouldn't know that."

"Yeah. I just need a rumor to get started in a few places."

"Aren't you just the clever one. All right. Jewelry store next, then?"

"I'm going to hold off on that for a little. There's something I

*need to do first, because if it doesn't work, I can just stop before I
waste all my time."*

"So, what then?"

"A visit to an old friend."

"Which old friend?"

"An old friend who wants to kill me."

"That doesn't limit it all that much, Boss."

I kept to the poorest-lit areas, because it made me feel safer.
It was a long way to the south and a little east, and took me
through parts of the City I didn't know; that made me feel less
safe.

It eats at you all the time, when you're being hunted.
When you're moving, you see them everywhere; when you're
holed up, you imagine them figuring out where you are. After
a long enough time, it wears you down, you start seeing—

"Quit whining, Boss. Where are we going?"

"Somewhere safe."

"Was that sarcasm?"

"Yeah."

"Just checking."

The homes hereabouts were bigger, more luxurious, and
many of them had fences and grounds. There were fewer
Jhereg, but more patrols of Phoenix Guards. Suspicious Phoenix Guards: I had to show my Imperial signet twice.

I stopped just short of a particularly big house, surrounded
by a high fence, with a pair of alert-looking fellows in the colors of House Jhereg. They wore cloaks, and no weapons were
visible; but either they were guarding the house or a pair of
random strangers just happened to be standing by the gate
looking very alert for no reason.

"Boss, this is—"

"Yeah."

"We need to—?"

"Yeah."

"Okay. Brash, or sneaky?"

"Yeah, that's the question, isn't it. What do you think?"

"If brash doesn't work, they'll be alerted to sneaky, if sneaky doesn't work, you can't pull off brash."

"Well done, Loiosh. You've managed to state the problem."

"Flip a coin?"

"Take a fly around the perimeter for me; let's see if sneaky is even possible."

"Am I reporting, or are you coming along?"

"I'll come along."

Across the narrow street and down a short distance was a place between two of the smaller houses where, by pulling my cloak around me, I could effectively be invisible. I crossed and waited there with Rocza, who kept shifting from foot to foot on my shoulder while Loiosh took wing. I relaxed, and fell into a sort of half-awake state, letting the images from Loiosh enter: guards in pairs, looking annoyingly alert; little knobs every fifteen feet on the fences, almost invisible sparkles around the doors, a vision distortion around the windows. Also, really thick-looking bars. One vision of the lock on the back door. Kiera could have handled the lock. I could handle the spells with Lady Teldra, only not without alerting every one of those guards, which in turn would make things bloody, as opposed to sneaky.

I returned to my own body. Loiosh returned.

"Brash, then?" he said.

"Brash it is."

"Then let's go."

"A moment. It takes me a little while to build up to brash."

"Since when, Boss?"

There was no answer to that, so I went back across the street, right up to the pair of Jhereg flanking the gate.

They were good. One took a step forward, no weapon drawn; the other immediately began scanning the rest of the area and, I had no doubt, alerting someone. Bad guards either under- or over-react, and either can be exploited by sneaky types. Yeah, brash was the right choice this time.

I walked up until the short one—he was still a head taller than I was—was right in front of me, somewhere between sword range and dagger range. If you do enough fighting, you'll start to automatically notice distances. The point here wasn't that I did, it was that he obviously knew what he was doing. He had the dead eyes of someone who's done "work." He didn't show fear, or curiosity, or, well, anything. His boss had been able to afford good help, and had gotten it.

"I want to see your boss," I said. "Let him know Vlad Taltos is here and wants a meeting."

He couldn't keep his eyes from widening a bit. Yes, he'd heard of me. And that meant he knew he could become rich right here and now. I watched the wheels spin in his head as he weighed the pros and cons; it wasn't what he was being paid to do. And I might not that be that easy to take down.

But it was a *lot* of money.

I slowly eased my cloak aside, set my hand on the hilt of Lady Teldra, and raised her about a quarter of an inch, then slid her back in. He got enough of a taste of Lady Teldra to help him make up his mind. A fraction of a smile quirked his lip for a fraction of a second, then he said, "Your message is delivered," and about the time he had finished speaking, there were four more of them there.

I acted like it was no big deal, and I waited.

It was natural that they'd get the forces out, whether their boss agreed to see me or not. It was just a question of protecting him while he decided if he wanted to see me.

"Boss? This is making me uncomfortable."

"Me too. But I need to see this guy. They're just making sure. They're afraid of me."

"I know, but—"

"But you're right. Scout the area."

Loiosh stayed where he was, but Rocza launched herself into the air. The guys around me let their eyes flick to her, then come back to me. Still, none of them had drawn a weapon.

"Three more coming toward us, Boss. No, make that five. From the back side of the house."

"Shit," I suggested.

"Half a minute," he added.

Aloud, I said, "Tell the ones who are approaching to stop, or I'll get nervous. Your boss will either see me, or not. You don't need any more protection."

He looked at me.

"Boss, they're still coming."

"Last chance," I told the guy.

The guy in front of me reached for a dagger.

"Morganti!" Loiosh screamed into my mind, but he needn't have bothered; that's a feeling you can't miss. Then things happened fast.

My first thought was, *Dammit, this isn't how I wanted it to go down;* my second thought was, *Just how many of those things are there in this town?* After that I was too busy to think.

Loiosh was in someone's face, and I threw a knife in the general direction of another, and, I remember clearly, there was a horrible fraction of a second when I reached into my cloak for a shuriken that wasn't there.

In the back of my mind, I realized I wasn't in shape for this, either physically or mentally. I had no time to indulge the feeling, so ignoring it was easy.

I know I was rolling on the ground, and then I was on my feet, and since my cloak wasn't good for anything else I undid the clasp with one hand and threw it into a face. I turned quickly and one of them was coming at me with a sword, so I moved in on him to throw off his distance and he cut my left arm below the elbow but I put my dagger into his throat, then Loiosh yelled for me to duck to the side, and I did and something missed me. I drew my rapier, and took a step backward toward the street.

Three of them were still up. One of them was bleeding badly from two different wounds on the same arm, and the other two were swinging wildly at Loiosh and Rocza, who were darting just into range then back out again. It's hard to fight flying things; I like to have them on my side.

I drew Lady Teldra with my left hand. The presence of a Morganti weapon that powerful instantly spread out and assaulted the mind of anyone in the area who had one. A mind, I mean. She took the form of a wide-bladed, leaf-shaped fighting knife, and she felt very good in my hand.

"Facedown on the ground," I said, "or I start using this."

Loiosh and Rocza backed off to give them time to decide. I tried very hard to hide how much my hands were shaking. And my knees. My side, which I'd thought Lady Teldra had completely healed, was aching in a bad way.

"Now," I explained. I sincerely hoped they understood the explanation, because if they didn't it would be bad for them, and very likely worse for me.

They dropped their weapons and dropped to the ground as the reinforcements arrived. The Morganti dagger was lying on the ground; I kicked it away. Loiosh and Rocza landed on my shoulder and I said, "I just want to talk to your boss. If he doesn't want to see me, I'll go away," I added. "And let him know that if lets me in, he'll have a lot of chances to ambush me inside the house."

They looked at me.

"Please?" I said. And gave them my warmest smile. I've learned that it doesn't show weakness to be polite when you are holding a Great Weapon.

One of the new arrivals—a pale man with almost no neck—seemed to be in charge. After a long enough pause for messages to go back and forth between a couple of minds, he said, "All right, you can come in."

I hesitated. Did I dare trust him? The reinforcements were still standing and there were a lot of them. As if on cue, a bunch of them turned and walked away. All right, then. I sheathed Lady Teldra and my rapier, and retrieved my cloak. "Thanks," I said.

Two of them led the way for me, and the rest went back to their positions. The ones who'd been on the ground got up, and, without even wasting a dirty look on me, started to help the ones who were injured. The one I'd gotten in the throat looked like he might not make it.

The door opened and I was met by an enforcer dressed as a butler. He acted like a butler, too. I'd have believed that's all he was if it weren't for his eyes.

It was a very impressive home. I'd been there before, and I'd been impressed then, too. I was escorted up a long, white, curving stairway to what I'd think of as a study—a few books, a desk, a pair of chairs, some small sculptures and expensive paintings and psiprints—except that it was closer to the size of a ballroom than a study. Okay, I'm exaggerating. The chairs looked comfortable enough. I picked the one that didn't go with the desk and stood next to it, waiting. The butler left, the two-man escort remained; not exactly watching me, but not exactly not watching me.

All together, like old friends, we stood there and waited for the guy generally known as the Demon. My left arm dripped blood on his floor, and it served him right as far as I was concerned. I studied his desk. It was pretty clean. There were a few papers on it, a quill pen, and what looked like a pile of handkerchiefs. Maybe he perspired a lot? There were a couple off to the side that seemed to have been used. I wondered if I could steal one without either of the guards noticing. I leaned over the desk.

"Back away, please," said one.

I stuffed the handkerchief in my sleeve as I backed away.

At a meeting like this, the time you're kept waiting is a good indicator of where you stand. In this case, it was less than two minutes. He came in briskly, as if he had not the least worry that I might be there to kill him. He sat down in the chair next to the desk, not behind it, and nodded toward another. I sat in it, and he made a gesture to the two enforcers; they stepped back until they were out of earshot, but close enough to watch me. Which is probably why he had such a big study.

"Lord Taltos," he said.

"Demon."

"Can I get you anything?"

"No, thanks."

"How did I get to be the guy you always come to?"

"Because I knew you wouldn't try to have me killed."

"Is that it?"

I smiled.

He shrugged. "Seemed worth the shot. Did you kill any of them?"

"Not sure. Maybe one."

He swore softly and without much conviction.

"I was trying not to, but I was also kind of busy staying alive. That seemed the higher priority."

"People do underestimate you, Taltos."

"I know."

"All right. I have tickets for a concert tonight, so let's get to it."

"I want to propose a business venture."

"Uh-huh."

"For you, and for the Jhereg."

"Very kind."

"Very lucrative. So lucrative, in fact, that in gratitude, you'll cancel all the ill-feelings directed toward me."

He studied me. After most of a minute, he said, "That would have to be *extremely* lucrative."

"It is."

"Tell me."

"What if you could listen in on psychic communication?"

His eyebrows went up. "That would be useful."

I continued. "What if you could sell that service?"

"Well, yes. That would be lucrative."

"What if you could also sell the service of preventing it?"

"Well, all right. You have my attention. You can do that?"

"I think so, yes."

"You think so?"

I shrugged. "If it turns out that I can't, you haven't lost anything."

He said, "There would need to be proofs. A lot of proofs. Enough so that I'm not only convinced it works, but that it wouldn't be possible to fake it; and then I'd need some independent verification on that. From a sorcerer I trust."

"That's more or less how I figured it."

"How long will it take to set up your proof?"

"A few days."

"I can't guarantee your safety in that time."

"You mean you won't."

"That is correct."

I nodded. "I don't expect any reward until I've delivered the technique, and proof that it works. If someone manages to nail me before I've done that, tough luck for both of us. I just want your word that, if I deliver, you'll take the price off my head."

"Is there a catch?"

"You mean, like, it's so hard to do it's impractical? Or it would alert the Empire, or, I don't know, some reason why you'd regret the deal after you made it?"

"Yeah."

"Then no catch. That's part of the deal. You judge if you're happy with it."

"You'd trust me with that?"

"That's the other reason I came to you."

He nodded. "You have my word."

"Good, then."

"A few days, you say?"

"If I'm not killed setting it up, a few days should do it."

"What will you need for the test?"

I shrugged. "Someone not in the room to communicate with someone who is in the room. Someone he—you—can communicate with, which means you'll have to know him, I suppose. I shouldn't know who that is, or who you'll be talking to. Any of you. We'll want two or three tests so you can be convinced. Sorcerers present, so they can see what I'm doing well enough to duplicate it. Probably better in an area that isn't too crowded. And we'll—"

"Why?"

"My lord?"

"Why somewhere deserted?"

"Not deserted. It doesn't have to be deserted. But the fewer people speaking psychically, the cleaner the test will be."

"And the easier?"

"I'm not sure. Maybe."

"So then, somewhere just a bit out of town?"

"Yeah. And that way it isn't in someone's territory, which might be a good idea politically. For me, an ideal location would be comfortable, out of town to cut down on unknowns, but not too far out of town because I have to walk. West or north would be better than east because it's easier to get to. But none of those things are required. You pick the place."

"What about protection?"

"For me? None. Your word is good."

"All right. What else?"

"Nothing. What do you need?"

"As you say, at least three tests, with three different people."

"All right."

"In addition to those tests, I'd like one where I'm sending the message instead of receiving it. Is there a problem with that?"

"No, should work just as well."

"Good."

"What else?"

He frowned. "Let me consider."

"Take your time," I said. "This is the first safe place I've been in in some time."

He chuckled. Then he said, "All right. I'll find a place. And if it works, you'll be clear—no, I'll go further. It'll be strictly hands-off of you, family, and friends, as long as you don't do anything else unseemly."

"More than reasonable," I said, because it was.

He nodded. "I can't do more than that; you're on your own getting there."

"Yeah, so you said."

He tilted his head and studied me. "I like you, Taltos. If I could give you a few days of safety, I would. But, this may shock you, there are some who are not only greedy, but don't like you."

"And yet, I'm such a pleasant fellow."

"I have to do a balancing act. If this comes through, it won't be a problem to have your name taken off the shine-on-sight list. But I'll need at least two other Council members to witness the demonstration. If I know them, they'll want to be there in person. I would."

"Sure."

"And that means they'll need to feel safe."

"I understand that."

"Would you consent to a hostage?"

There were only two possible hostages. "No," I said.

"I didn't think so." He considered some more. "All right. First of all, your, ah, winged friends can wait in the street, or above the street. In any case, outside of the room until we're finished."

"Boss! Don't you—"

"Done," I said.

He gestured toward Lady Teldra at my side. "And you will leave that outside."

"No," I said.

"Deal-breaker," he said.

"You know enough about weapons like this to know that just isn't going to happen."

"I trust you," he said. "Probably exactly as much as you trust me. And that means not enough to put you in a room full of people you hate and let you keep a Great Weapon."

"So, you don't mind sending us out of the room, but—"

"I don't mind putting you exactly where I need you to be, no. Now shut up."

"What about this," I said. "You're going to need sorcerers in the room anyway."

He nodded, listening.

"Think one of them could find a bonding spell strong enough to keep her in her sheath? We'd just need an hour or so."

He frowned. "A spell strong enough to keep it sheathed if, um, if it doesn't want to stay that way? If the sorcerer is good enough, and takes enough time, yes, it should be manageable."

"Good," I said. "Ask your people. You must have some who know what they're dealing with and can give you a straight answer."

"And you'd go along with that?"

"Yes."

He nodded. "I think we can manage that."

"Good, then. Is there anything else you want?"

He considered, then shook his head.

"You'll get back to me when you've settled on the place?"

"I will. Presumably a message delivered to your friend Kragar will find you."

I nodded.

"And you know how to reach me when we're ready. I'll need thirty hours' notice, no more."

"Good, then." I stood up.

He smiled. "Vlad, it will be good to have you back in the Organization."

"I can hardly wait myself," I said. "Now, if you'll excuse me."

"By all means," he said.

I stood, bowed, and headed out the door.

6

MAKING DEALS
OR
MAKING SMALL TALK

My back itched all the way to the street, but Loiosh and Rocza were keeping watch. As I passed through the gate, I caught the eye of the short guy who'd been there before. I thought about asking how his friend was, but there was no way to do so without making it seem like I was sneering, so I just kept walking.

"Boss?"

"Yeah?"

"Can you really do that? What you told the Demon?"

"Daymar says I can."

"But can you?"

"I guess we'll see, won't we?"

"Boss—"

"Yeah, I think so. With enough help and enough gear."

"And you think the Demon will keep to his deal?"

"What do you think?"

"What's next?"

"A decent night's sleep while I figure that out."

"And a meal?"

"*Yeah. Almost dying used to scare me; now it just makes me hungry. I wonder what that means.*"

"*It means we should find something to eat.*"

"*Yeah.*"

I hadn't left anything in the flophouse in South Adrilankha, so I took us back toward Little Deathgate where there was a good collection of inns, as well as plenty of street food. I like street food. On this occasion I got flatbread with lamb, onions, carrots, peppers, and whole garlic cloves, and I picked up a bottle of cheap wine to wash it down. I rented a room in an almost invisible hostelry off a street with no name. We went up to the room. None of us, I suppose, were as alert as we should have been, between having survived the attack and eating, but nothing happened. Sometimes you catch a break when you don't deserve it.

I got undressed and lay down on top of the blanket with my cloak over me—not trusting the bed itself to be free of wildlife—and closed my eyes. And that's when I started shaking and sweating. The attack had happened hours ago, and I'd gotten through the meeting with the Demon, and a walk through a scary part of town, and *now* it was hitting me? *Now* I couldn't shut my eyes without feeling that Morganti blade, and seeing images of steel flashing toward me? That made no sense.

It took me a long time to fall asleep.

I woke up fully alert and a bit scared, my hand reaching for a weapon.

"*It's all right, Boss. Nothing going on.*"

I nodded and got up, got clean, and got dressed.

Just across the street was a coffee vendor. I bought his cheapest mug and filled it, figuring it would keep me going until I found klava. Then it was a long walk, Loiosh and Rocza flying overhead, all the way back to Malak Circle, where there was a shop I'd patronized for years.

I stopped in the doorway of a leathergoods store across the street, and watched it. This was my old area, and this store was a place I had been known to patronize. In other words, this wasn't safe at all. Loiosh didn't say anything, but I could feel his nervousness, a reflection of my own. After ten minutes, I said, "Okay, I think we're good."

"Okay, Boss."

I didn't recognize the man behind the counter. "Who are you?" I said by way of introduction.

He was young and a Jhegaala and he didn't know quite how to respond to an Easterner who carried a sword and wasn't obsequious. While he was working it out, I snapped, "Well?"

"Nyier," he said. "I'm helping out."

"All right, Nyier. Then you can help me out."

I spent a lot of money there, but I came away with two fighting knives, three more throwing knives, six shuriken, two more daggers, and four darts that would be useless if I couldn't get what I needed to mix up a batch of nerve toxin. It wasn't as much as I used to carry, but it was considerably more than I'd had on me for the last few years.

I left the place carefully and took myself all the way back to Little Deathgate and the inn I'd stayed at. It was still early, so I shouldn't have to pay anything for the room.

It took three full hours to arrange my new toys in places where I could get at them easily but they wouldn't clank as I walked. Apparently, that was a skill that required constant practice. Who knew?

When I was finally done, I had a brief interaction with

the host, who wanted extra money for the room. He fumed
and ranted. I gave him the cold look. The cold look won the
argument. Lucky for him: if it hadn't, I'd have glared. Then I
set off once more for Malak Circle, aware of how stupid it was
for me to be there. But a lot of what I needed to do was nearby,
so it seemed a reasonable place to start what I figured was
liable to be a fruitless search.

"*I need a base of operations, Loiosh. Somewhere I can have a
reasonable chance the Jhereg won't find me, and that's close enough
to the action that I don't waste all of my time going from place to
place.*"

"*So you've been saying, Boss.*"

"*Yeah.*"

"*For months.*"

"*Yeah. But now it's a bit more urgent.*"

"*Good. Then we should find a place with no problem, right?*"

"*You aren't helping.*"

I hung around the fountain, trying to duck into corners,
while I thought about it. This really was just about the worst
place for me, so close to my old office—

"*Boss, no!*"

"*Loiosh, yes. They'll never look for me there.*"

"*No, because they won't have to.*"

"*It'll work, Loiosh. Have I ever been wrong about this kind of
thing?*"

"*You mean this week?*"

"*And if they do figure it out—*"

"*When.*"

"*It'll still be damned bloody hard for them to get me there. It's
perfect.*"

"*Except that you'll have to leave, and you don't dare teleport.*"

"There's the tunnel, remember?"

"And you're betting everything that no one knows about it?"

"Not everything. Just most things."

"Boss, this is just stupid."

If he was going to be unreasonable, there was no point in continuing the conversation. I took us down the street, skirting the edge of Copper Lane until the old place was just opposite. A deep breath, a careful look around, and then across the street to a little storefront that still sold the "Summer Wind" and "Sweetwater" strains of dreamgrass for the best price in this part of the city.

It was a small place, and the smell would have been pleasant if it weren't quite so intense; but I was only in for the space of a breath before going through the curtained doorway and into the back room with its tables and chairs and cards and sweat and an enforcer giving me a cold stare that looked like it could turn into a glare at any second. I couldn't let that happen, I might not be able to stand it. So with everyone staring at me, I walked up to him and said, very softly, "Tell Kragar that Vlad is here." I smiled at him. "If you don't mind." My hands were well clear of my body.

He hesitated, then looked over at his partner, who hadn't heard me. There was a moment when, I assume, they were speaking psychically, then they both shrugged and the one I'd spoken to turned to me and said, "Wait here."

I nodded and set about doing so. It wasn't that hard, except for the constant itch between my shoulder blades.

I didn't have to wait long. Lord Tough-guy came down and, stepping aside, motioned me toward the stairs up to what had once been my office. I had to walk right past him, giving

him a shot at my back from eight inches. Yes, Loiosh and Rocza
were on full alert; and yes, this operation was controlled by
someone I trusted completely.

But making that walk still wasn't easy.

My courage was rewarded at the top of the stairs by a grin
wrapped around the face of an old friend.

"Vlad!"

"Kragar. I can't believe I can see you."

"Come in! Klava?"

"Klava," I said. "May you dwell forever in Barlen's heaven
of musical jewels."

"Sounds boring."

He led me past a couple of his enforcers and into his office,
calling, "Klava!" as he walked by. I wondered—not for the first
time—if he had trouble with no one noticing the orders he
gave them. He sat behind my—his—desk; I sat facing it, but I
turned the chair so I could stretch my legs out.

"So, how's business, Kragar?"

"Good. Not so much income as when you ran things, but
less trouble."

"No border disputes?"

He smirked. "No one seems to notice my operations."

"Nice."

"And you? Anything new?"

"I think I might have a way to get this matter handled."

"By 'this matter' do you mean—?"

"Yeah."

He whistled. "How can I help?"

"For starters, let me stay here."

"Here? In the office?"

"I'll curl up in a corner."

The klava arrived. I drank some, and the day became better.

"Seriously, Vlad?"

"Seriously. I need somewhere to operate from. Somewhere I know the Jhereg isn't going to be able to get me."

"Here? This is your idea of a place the Jhereg can't get you?"

"Well, yeah."

"Vlad, did you lose your mind on the road, or was it since you came back?"

"Kragar, who hangs out up here in your office?"

"Jhereg, Vlad. You know, people who want to kill you?"

"Yeah, have a lot of them done 'work'?"

"The people in my office? No, but—"

"And do they do what you say?"

"I . . ."

"Yes?"

"If word gets out—"

"As Loiosh says, *when* word gets out. It will. And then they'll have the problem of setting up a shot at me in the worst possible place."

"But every time you leave—"

"Kragar, remember? I know about the other exit."

He frowned, looking pained. "How long?"

"A few days at the most."

He shook his head. "All right. I'll have my old office cleared out. Been using it for storage. However crazy I am for letting you do it, you're crazier for wanting to."

"Thanks," I said.

"You know, I can't believe you haven't gotten me killed yet. Even once."

"Yeah, we'll see if we can do something about that before it's too late."

"Hey, thanks, Vlad."

"What are friends for?"

"How does the thing work?"

"What thing?"

"Your idea for getting out from under."

"Oh. It's complicated. The short version is I've come up with a business opportunity so lucrative, the Demon says he'll clear me if I can prove it'll work."

"Really?"

"So he says. And I trust him as well as I trust anyone in that position."

"What's the plan?"

I hesitated.

"No," he said. "Skip that. What do you need to make it work?"

"Kragar, are you really asking me that?"

"Yeah. I invited you to stay here, and now I'm asking what you need. Tonight, I'm going to drop a rock on my foot, and tomorrow is eat a live teckla day."

"*Hey, now—*"

"*Shut up.*"

"Fair enough," I told Kragar.

"So, what do you need?"

"Any idea where we can find a hawk's egg?"

He frowned. "A hawk's egg. I assume you mean the, you know, the magical hawk's egg, not just the egg of some hawk."

"Right."

"I'd ask Daymar."

"Yeah, I've been trying to avoid that."

He chuckled. "I can understand that. I could look for someone else—"

"No, no. We'll go with Daymar. I told him I'd be needing his help again."

"That makes me feel better. If I have to deal with you, you have to deal with Daymar. More klava?"

"Always."

"Want me to get a message to him?"

"If you would, Loiosh would be grateful."

"Got that right, Boss."

"What should I tell him?"

"Let's say an hour before noon in the back room of Mertun's."

"Will do. Need any money?"

"No, thanks. I'm good."

He gave the orders for the message to be sent, then we sat in companionable silence while we waited for klava, and then again after it arrived. It was good, and I felt some tension drain out of me.

I was going to need a hawk's egg.

Depending on the region, it is known as the thorn-hawk, the gully-hawk, the scatter-hawk, or the brushbird. It is one of 114 varieties of raptors so far identified by Imperial naturalists, all of which are commonly called hawks. The thorn-hawk is ubiquitous in many regions, including the jungles near Adrilankha itself. It makes its nest in thorny shrubs, where the male guards the eggs and the chicks as the female hunts. Many naturalists believe that, long ago, by chance or design, essential material from an athyra was mixed with that of a raptor.

Maybe so. What cannot be argued is that in the normal course
of things, such a creature could not survive in the environ-
ments where it is found without some form of that odd hic-
cuping of nature that we call magic.

As with all magical creatures, it is impossible to say how
much of what it does is natural and how much supernatural.
But there's no doubt that one element is magical concealment
of the nest. That's what makes it so tedious to search through
the jungle, looking at each nest, to find the one egg in thirty
that cries out into the mind as having the peculiar properties
needed.

There isn't much danger in the search; provided the
searcher has a modicum of psychic ability—enough, that is, to
send the cock away while eggs are searched; and enough savvy
to survive in the jungle for the two or three days the search is
liable to take.

I know all of this, because I found it in Jescira's *Birds of the
Southeast* and most of it I just quoted word for word, at least as
well as I can. If it bothers you that I did that, feel free to write
a letter of complaint, fill it with threats and obscenity, and
send it to Lord Morrolan, Castle Black. Let me know how
that works out for you.

"Hawk's egg," Kragar repeated after a while. "I've heard of them,
but I've never been clear on what they are, or what they're used
for. Is it a witch thing?"

"Not exactly."

"Some weird kind of sorcery?"

"In a way."

"Psychics?"

"Kind of."

"Vlad—"

"I'm not an expert."

"I was starting to suspect that."

"Shut up. What I know about the hawk's egg is that it comes from a particular kind of hawk, and it can be used by a witch to simulate the effect of a circle for a short time, and that psychics use it in different ways, and—"

"Circle?"

"A witchcraft thing. Amplifies power."

"So, you're not sure what it does, or what it is, but you know you need one?"

"Yeah."

"Uh, okay. What else do you need?"

I shook my head. "Lots of stuff."

"Then I suppose we should get started."

"I saw the Demon about this."

"Yeah, so you said."

"Before I went in to see him, he tried to have me killed. For an on-the-spot effort with no set-up, it wasn't a bad try. It was close."

"I'm listening, Vlad."

"That was fourth attempt on me in three days."

"Fourth?"

"Yeah. All of them spur-of-the-moment, so I was able to survive, but—"

Kragar looked me over. "You got nailed, didn't you?"

"Pretty bad, but I lived."

He nodded. "All right. Is there a particular point you're getting at, Vlad?"

"I'm saying that there have already been bodies, and there might be more before this is over."

"Just like old times."

"Yeah," I said. "Just like old times."

"Vlad? You okay?"

"With any luck, I will be in a few days."

He nodded. "One more klava, then we switch to wine?"

"Better eat something in between."

"Steamed kethna rolls."

"I just had some bad ones."

"So I'll get us some good ones. I have a craving."

"I like how your mind works."

"More klava, first."

"I'm tempted to ask for a report."

"And then set me to learning an impossible number of things about unknown people in too little time?"

"Exactly."

"Resist the temptation."

"Okay."

Someone poked his head in and asked Kragar if someone with a name full of consonants could slide another week. Kragar said to add another point.

I drank some more klava. Not long ago, that would have been me. It was an odd feeling—mostly relief, but just a hint of nostalgia for seasoning.

"Kind of miss it a bit, don't you, Vlad?"

"Get the fuck out of my head and order some kethna rolls."

"Whatever you say, boss."

"Heh," I said.

He called out for someone to pick up a basket of kethna

rolls and a bottle of Khaav'n. When it was delivered, he told the guy to pick up a pillow and a bunch of blankets. The guy didn't even give him a funny look; just nodded and headed out.

"I never would have thought it, Kragar."

"What?"

"Nothing, never mind."

I had the odd feeling of my shoulders relaxing when I hadn't noticed they were tense. My hand twitched—not like it wanted to go for a dagger, but like it could. Does that make sense?

"Time to pour some wine."

We spent the next couple of hours being lazy: drinking, exchanging stories, reminding each other of the good times and the bad, sometimes just sitting there. Talking about those hours is pretty dull, but it had been years since I'd spent more pleasant time. Yeah, there was a lot to do and this wasn't getting it done. But.

Somewhere in there, a non-magical kind of magic happened. Just that couple of hours did something. Even with half a bottle of wine in me, when I got up my head was clearer; I was more alert than I had been in longer than I cared to remember. I realized how lucky I had been in the fight with the Demon's button-men. I should have seen it coming sooner, and either avoided it, or struck sooner. I hadn't been at my best. I hadn't been at my best for years. I was going to need to be.

"*Glad to hear it, Boss.*"

"*Which part, Loiosh?*"

"*That you know you were off.*"

"*Why didn't you say something?*"

"*I assume that's the sort of thing you mammals call a joke?*"

"Kind of, yeah."

"Boss, you know there was nothing to be done about it."

"That's never stopped you before."

"I'm glad you're back, Boss."

"Thanks."

"At least, partway back."

"Yeah."

Like I told Loiosh; I was at least partway back—back to feeling like my old, competent self.

Yes, I'd have liked to spend time with my boy. And there was an Issola minstrel it would have done me a world of good to have sat around with, listening to her sing, drinking obscure liqueurs and chatting about a Teckla boy we both knew. Other things would have been good. But this was what I needed; I felt it. I felt a stirring of the old optimism, of the feeling that I wasn't just a chip of wood swirling down a creek. I could swim against the current if I needed to. I could maybe even build a dam.

I said good-bye to Kragar, and headed down the stairs, down more stairs, and into the tunnel. It let out in a part of the neighborhood that was relatively safe. There were no signs that I'd been spotted, so I blended in with passing crowds as much as I could while I made my way to Mertun's Fine Wine Sampling House. I'd picked it because it was big, almost always busy, and you could enter it right from the street—in fact, when I was younger, I'd occasionally hang out there just to watch what happened when an obnoxious aristocrat left the place and bumped into another obnoxious aristocrat who was walking by. That's entertainment, you know? Or it was when I was younger. I guess somewhere in there I got old and boring.

"You said it, Boss, not—"

"Shut up, Loiosh."

We went in without bumping into any obnoxious aristocrats. I approached the hostess and passed her some silver and said, "Back room free?"

She looked me up and down disapprovingly. "Help yourself," she said.

I got a couple of glasses instead of cups because I prefer glass when possible, a habit I picked up years ago from Morrolan. I also got a bottle of the house white, which fell short of "fine" but was good and affordable, then I took us to the back room, Loiosh and Rocza making sure no one paid undue attention to us. I poured myself a glass and settled in to wait for Daymar.

"I feel like I should give a speech about how, once we do this, we're committed."

"You mean we weren't committed when you spoke to the Demon?"

"Yeah, we were. That's why I'm not giving the speech."

I drank some of the wine and was pleased that my hands weren't shaking.

Daymar has never been known for punctuality; it was most of an hour before he showed up, as before, floating cross-legged two feet off the floor. I jumped, of course, but was lucky enough not to be holding my wineglass.

"Have some," I said, pouring. "Thanks for showing up."

Daymar picked up his wine and studied it through the glass, holding it up to the light. I've seen Morrolan do the same thing. When Morrolan does it, I get the feeling he's enjoying how pretty the light is through the wine; when Daymar does it, I can't help but thinking he's wondering what sort of prism spell would be required to isolate that color from pure white.

He lowered the glass and drank a gulp like he was thirsty; I'm pretty sure if I'd bought a bottle of the good stuff it would have been the same.

"So, Vlad. What is it you need?"

"How would you go about acquiring a hawk's egg?"

He frowned. "A hawk's egg? Well, I'd find a nest—"

"No, a hawk's egg."

"Oh. Why do you want it?"

I just waited.

"Right. It has to do with what you asked me about before."

"Yeah," I told him.

"I've gotten them before," he said.

"Can you again?"

"Certainly," said Daymar. "It may take some time. Where can I find you?"

"Remember my offices?"

"Yes. Isn't Kragar there now?"

"He's offered me his hospitality."

"Oh, I see. I'll bring it there, then."

"I appreciate it."

"Anything else?"

"Yeah. Ever heard of the Wand of Ucerics?"

His eyes widened. "Why yes, certainly. In fact, it's in my possession."

"Really?" I said putting on a surprised look.

"Indeed."

"Well, that's convenient. Might I borrow it for a few days?"

"It'll take me some time to fetch it. It's in," he frowned, thought for a moment, then continued, "an inconvenient place."

I didn't want to think about what sort of extra-dimensional

or imaginary place Daymar would consider inconvenient. I said, "No hurry. If you can get it to me in the next day or two, that'll be fine."

"All right," he said. "Anything else?"

"Yes. Talk to me."

That Daymar quizzical expression appeared. "About what?"

"Anything. About things that have nothing to do with any of this, with the Jhereg, with hawk's eggs, with, I don't care. Just talk to me."

"Um. I don't know what to say," he said. I wondered if those words had ever before passed his lips.

"Try anyway," I said.

He was quiet for a little longer, then he said, "Could you, um, ask me questions, or something?"

I guess that was only fair. "All right," I said, and considered. "What do you care about, Daymar?"

"Excuse me?"

"What matters to you?"

"Why would you want to know that?"

"Pretend it's important."

"Um." He got a strange expression on his face. "Is it really important?"

"Yeah. Really."

"What I like is learning things."

"What sort of things?"

"Almost anything. Anything that—" He paused.. "Anything that makes me sit up straight."

"I think I understand that."

Daymar nodded.

"So, it's about that moment when you suddenly understand something?"

"Not just that," he said. "It's also about getting there. Gathering facts, and the connections between them. I like that, too. You know I'm a desecrator?"

"No, I didn't know that."

He nodded. "That's what I like about it. Finding pieces of the past and figuring out how things happened."

I asked more questions; he answered them. After a while I said, "That helps."

"Helps what?"

"My project. We talked about it yesterday."

"I remember. But what part of the project does it help?"

I guess his desire to draw conclusions stopped when it was a conclusion about what I didn't want to talk about. Or he didn't care that I didn't want to talk about it. Or he hadn't noticed. All of the possibilities equally likely.

"I need someone to think like a Hawk," I said. "I figure there's more to it than being randomly irritating and profoundly oblivious."

Daymar considered. "No," he said. "That's most of it."

"Who'd have thought he had a sense of humor, Boss?"

"You sure he's joking?"

"Um."

"You've been a lot of help," I said. "Thanks."

The corner of his mouth quirked—such a tiny thing I wasn't entirely sure I'd seen it. "You're welcome," he said, and, without changing expression, vanished with an irritating pop of displaced air.

"So, that was useful, Boss."

"Yes, it was."

"Seriously?"

"Seriously."

"*If you say so. What's next?*"

"*Next I seek legal advice.*"

"*Seriously?*"

"*No. Sort of.*"

"*This will be good,*" he said.

7

MAKING SMALL TALK
OR
MAKING WAVES

It wasn't, really. I mean, it wasn't anything exciting, danger-ous, or even terribly interesting. I made my way to the Palace district and looked up an advocate named Perisil I'd had deal-ings with before. After a few pleasantries, he asked what I wanted.

I said, "I've come up with a way to eavesdrop on psychic communication. I need to make sure it's illegal."

He blinked at me. "You need it to be illegal?"

"If I'm going to sell it to—never mind. Can you find a way in which it's against the law?"

He coughed. "Several, probably."

"Good. I like having options. Run them down for me?"

"This is outside my field."

"I know. But I need help."

We went back and forth for a while, until he said, "I think what you want will be in the Imperial trade laws."

"All right. Can you point me toward an expert on Impe-rial trade laws?"

He shook his head. "There aren't any experts. It's too complicated."

"Then—"

"Here. Let me look something up."

He found a book among his shelves, paged through it, nodded, and showed me a passage.

"Um."

"I'll explain," he said.

He explained about the relationship between Imperial Secrets and commerce, and I nodded. "That'll do it," I said. "Can I borrow that?"

He put a bookmark in the page and handed me the book. I thanked him, and paid him for his time. I'd never before paid so much to sit and listen to someone talk. On the other hand, I had employed tags who made more for that service.

Loiosh and Rocza guided me back to the tunnel into my—that is, Kragar's office.

Kragar said, "Should I order in some food? Sorry."

"Bastard," I said, and sat down again. "Yes. I'll cover it. Jesco's?"

"Someplace you've never eaten. Just in case."

"Good idea."

We ended up with a big bowl of rice with saffron and duck. I'd never had it before, and liked it a lot; Loiosh expressed the opinion that we should never eat anything else ever again. We sat around, ate, talked, and it hit me that I missed the times Kragar and I used to just sit and talk; and that, whatever happened, there wouldn't be many more occasions like this. Then I stopped thinking about it—that's the sort of crap that can get you killed. Kragar came up with a bottle of a white wine from Guinchen that I'd never had before. He put his feet up on my desk.

"We've been through some shit here, haven't we?" he said.

"Shut up."

He looked amused but didn't say anything.

"I need to figure out a way to see my kid," I said.

He rubbed his lower lip. "Shouldn't it wait until this is over?"

"Too much chance I'll be dead by then."

"That doesn't sound like you, Vlad."

"What, fatalistic? I've always been a fatalist."

"No, you've always talked like a fatalist. You've never acted like one."

"Asshole," I said.

He smirked and poured wine, then shut up and let me think.

Every time something in the Jhereg changes, everyone gets nervous and starts looking around. All negotiations come down to a balancing act between making trouble you don't need and can't afford, and looking weak. How much do you let someone push you around? How much pushing do you do? Where do you draw the line? Once negotiations are over and settled, everyone relaxes, because then you can get back to just doing business—until another ripple comes through that means there's more or less of some limited and valuable thing, and everyone has to settle who gets how much.

I intended to cause a pretty big splash.

A little later Kragar raised his glass to me, drained it, and left me to decide on the next step.

Sorry. Left *us* to decide on the next step. Loiosh, as it happened, had a lot to say on the subject, none of it productive.

I'll spare you the details. In the end, we went out through the tunnel and I found Kiera's drop spot, and, as promised, the lockpick was there. It fit neatly into my palm—just a pretty usual-looking hook pick, very small. It felt a little cold, and I might have sensed some magic in it if I weren't wearing the Phoenix Stone. I was sure it would work; I could find my own torsion wrench easily enough. I wanted to take a moment to study it, but I was outside and nervous, so I went back into the tunnel, and emerged once more in Kragar's office.

There were a couple of lounging toughs keeping track of the place. They nodded to me and I nodded back. I turned toward the room I was sleeping in and stopped, staring. After a moment, I said, "Hello, Cawti."

"Hello, Vlad."

"How did you know to find me here?"

"Kragar sent me a message."

"Oh. Where is—"

"Norathar is watching him."

I nodded, then wasn't sure what to say.

She said, "We're going to try to set up a time for you to see him, but I wanted—"

"I understand," I said. "All right. Uh, should we sit down?"

"Probably."

We found a couple of chairs. I was weirdly aware of the distance between us as we carried them into an empty room.

"You had an Imperial Guardsman outside your house."

Her lips tightened and she nodded. "I'm working on that."

"There were also a couple of Jhereg."

"Wait. You were there?"

"Yeah. Three days ago."

"They tried to kill you?"

"Yeah."

"Outside of my house?"

I nodded. "Where my son lives." I released the arm of the chair and flexed my hand.

Her nostrils flared. I could see her register the information—the threat to her, the threat to Vlad Norathar. Her jaw tightened.

I said, "I'm working on it, but—"

I broke off and waited. After a moment, she said, "I'm sorry, Vladimir, but it isn't safe for you to try to see him anymore."

I nodded.

Her eyes were deep-set, and such a warm brown. I said, "I'm starting a project. I need to fix this."

"Is this project related to the rumors I've heard?"

"What do the rumors say?"

"There's a lot of money involved."

After working to get the rumors started, I guess I couldn't complain that they were floating around. "And that's what brought you here?"

"No, seeing you brought me here."

"All right."

"Vladimir, what are you working on?"

"A plan. If it works, it'll get the Jhereg off me. For good."

It crossed my mind that, even if this didn't work, it was worth the effort just for the look on the face of everyone I told.

"Can you do it?" she said.

"I think so."

"Can I help?"

"Yes. Go somewhere safe until this is over. Don't let anything happen to the boy, or yourself. That will take a huge load off my mind. It will help."

I'm pretty sure that isn't what she had in mind when she offered to help, but after a moment, she nodded. "I'll go stay with Norathar."

"Perfect," I said. Then, "How's the boy?"

"As well as he was a month ago. He may be starting to miss you."

I felt a smile grow. "Good."

She gave me that pressed-lip smile that means she's pretending to think it isn't funny. There was a moment, but then I looked away and so did she.

Let's just not dwell on it, okay?

"What else is going on?"

She filled me in on details, mostly antics about Vlad Norathar, which I'd tell you about, because they prove what a remarkable kid he is, but they're private so you'll just have to trust me. Eventually, Cawti said that she should be going.

I nodded. "I'm glad you came."

"Me too," she said.

I avoided watching her walk away, because that would have just made everything worse. After she'd left, I sat there for a while. I could have thanked Loiosh for not saying anything, but it wasn't necessary. Once again, though for different reasons, it took me a long time to fall asleep.

Look at it this way: An organization like the Jhereg operates by supplying things that people want but the law doesn't want them to have, or that are cheaper or better in their illegal versions. The Jhereg has a reputation for using violence casually and effectively. Speaking as someone who spent years providing that violence, I can say that the effectively part is true, but the casually part is a little exaggerated.

There are reasons for the violence, and also reasons for it to be exaggerated. People who break the law every day tend to be a bit casual about smacking someone with the hilt of a dagger or breaking his leg with a lepip. You learn to be casual about it by being around it, or you're around it because you're the sort of person who doesn't mind that, or both. Also, since we—pardon me, they—can't count on the Empire to make sure everyone in the organization follows the rules, they have to do it themselves. Last, on the rare occasions someone not in the Jhereg comes into conflict with their interests, it's useful to have a reputation for ruthlessness. If you scare someone enough, you usually don't have to do the thing he's afraid of.

That's where the violence comes from, and why it serves the Jhereg's interest for it to be exaggerated. But remember that violence costs money—either because you're paying someone to commit the violence, or because the existence of violence is bad for business, or both.

See, what a Jhereg wants is money. Money lets you live better, keeps you safe, and lets everyone know how good or important you are in case that's what matters to you. You need violence—or the threat of violence—to protect the money, but it's the money that matters. That's what I was counting on.

It isn't that simple, though.

Suppose you're running a few gambling operations and maybe a brothel or two and handling some loans. Someone comes into your area and messes up a game, robs a brothel, and threatens your people. If he then comes up to you and wants to make it right by paying you money, you aren't going to be inclined to take it. Money's good, but not if everyone around sees him pushing you around and getting away with it—that sort of thing will see you out of business fast. And maybe out of business in the permanent, embalming-gloss-on-your-skin sort of way.

Of course, the guy might offer you so much money that you'd consider taking it anyway. But it would have to be boatloads of gold. I mean big boats: the real cargo skybenders, not the canal skiffs.

That was, more or less, the position I'd gotten myself into, except that I didn't have big boatloads of gold. Instead, I had something I hoped was just as good.

If I was wrong, I'd find out.

I slept well enough to make me realize that sleep had been rough for the last few years. It was good. I smelled klava, which brought me into Kragar's office, where he grunted and pointed me to a covered glass. It was still hot.

I didn't remember Kragar being unpleasant in the morning, but that may have been because I'd been the boss, or else because he never used to get in that early. In any case, he didn't say a word, so I took my klava off and spent some quality time sharpening my cutlery. When I was done, I practiced a few draws—left sleeve to right hand, left boot, cloak both sides, and right-hand shoulder. I was horribly out of practice.

A couple of hours later I was less out of practice—some things come back pretty quickly. Kragar had a target set up, which let me throw some knives at things that weren't trying to hurt me, and I did all right.

All in all, I was feeling a little better about my ability to survive. I was considering what my next move should be when the Jhereg made it for me.

I mean, as horribly unsafe places go, I figured I was in a fairly safe one: they couldn't get at me while I was in Kragar's office except by buying someone or infiltrating someone. Oh, I suppose they could have staged a military-style assault or blown up the building, but, seriously, they don't do that kind of thing. The Empire gets touchy about it. So, yeah, I figured I was fairly safe, Loiosh's snide remarks to the contrary.

I was pacing back and forth in the room I slept in, talking over details of my plan with Loiosh, when I heard excited voices and heavy boots from just outside the door. I touched Lady Teldra's hilt and ran toward the sounds.

I counted six of Kragar's people standing in front of the desk that Melestav used to sit at before I killed him. Two of them had weapons out, the rest were staring at the floor. There was a lot of blood on the floor. And a body.

"All right," one of them said. "He's safe here. Find a healer."

He?

I started to get closer, but one of the bodyguards gave me a look, so I changed my mind.

I said, "Is it Kragar?"

The bodyguard was a broad-shouldered guy with thin lips and a tall forehead. He hesitated, then nodded.

"How is he?" I said.

"Took one in the back, got his heart. He's still breathing. We've sent for a physicker."

"How did they even notice him?"

The guy shrugged.

"Where did they get him?"

"Malak Circle."

I moved forward; this time he let me.

Kragar was facedown, and, yeah, he was still breathing, but that was a kill-shot. I should know; I've made enough of them. It was just a matter of time, and not very much of it. I didn't think there was anything a physicker could do. It's really hard to get someone with a knife, point-first, one shot, and make it a kill. Just because I've done it so often doesn't mean it's easy. This was done by someone who knew what he was doing.

For a long, long moment I just stood there, paralyzed, staring at him. Then I stirred. Dying, but not yet dead. Maybe, maybe. I drew Lady Teldra and everyone spun to me.

"Don't worry," I said. "Just a precaution. Drop the teleport block."

They didn't look reassured. Or agreeable to my idea. One of them started to speak. I said, "There's no time to argue. Do it."

Still holding Lady Teldra, I slipped the amulet off my neck and put it away. I could hear Loiosh start to say something, and then stop as he recognized the futility.

Yeah, right then, in various places around Adrilankha, sorcerers—and probably hired sorceresses—were going, "Oh, so *that's* where he is."

So what.

I put the amulet into its case and recalled a certain face, and voice, and, above all, attitude. She was short, bad-tempered, very good at any number of things.

"Vlad? I'm rather busy just at the—"

"Aliera, Kragar is hurt. Dying."

"Yes?" she said. *"And?"*

"And I need to save him."

"Best of luck with that."

"Aliera."

"What?"

"It's Kragar."

"I'm glad you understand."

"Aliera, he was hit because he's been helping me."

There was a pause. Then a psychic sigh. "Are you with him?"

"Yes."

The was a pop of displaced air, and she said, "Fine, then. But you owe me."

Before she was done talking, Kragar's bodyguards had drawn their weapons. Aliera gestured, and they all went flying back against the far wall. I don't mean the weapons, I mean the bodyguards.

"It's all right," I told them. "She's here to help. And owe you? What about saving your life?"

"My life is nothing," she said. "This is humiliating."

The bodyguards stood up. They still had their weapons out, and were watching Aliera, but not moving.

"Fine," I said. "I owe you."

She nodded.

"Guys," I said. "Put the weapons away, all right? Seriously. Don't piss off the Dragon. It never ends well."

The bowlegged one with thick eyebrows said, "Yeah, all right," and they made their weapons vanish. Aliera paid no attention; she stepped forward and knelt next to Kragar.

She looked him over, then glanced back at me. "You are paying for getting the blood out of this gown."

I didn't say anything. In particular, I didn't point out that Aliera probably had gotten blood on everything she owned at one time or another. Loiosh did, but only to me.

"Nice knife-work," said Aliera. "And there's a staydead spell on it, too."

"A staydead spell?" I said. "Did you just make that up?"

"The term. Not the spell."

"I kind of like it," I said. "The term. Not the spell. Can you keep him from dying?"

"Not if you keep distracting me," she said.

Her fingers dug into Kragar's back at various points around the knife. Then she slid a hand under his chest, and her shoulders tensed. I felt the swirl of sorcerous energy, which reminded me to put my amulet back on, after which I didn't feel it anymore. I resheathed Lady Teldra.

"Good work, Boss. Now that they already know exactly where you are, you cleverly vanish, and stay right where you were. That'll fool 'em."

I ignored him, Aliera ignored everyone and kept working—pressing her fingers around the wound, mostly; at least, that's all I could see. I unclenched my hands. A moment later I unclenched them again. I kept watching, waiting.

I almost strained my neck trying to simultaneously stay out of Aliera's way and watch what she was doing. It was futile because, from what was visible, she wasn't doing anything. Of course, in reality, she was doing a great deal; I hoped it was enough. Loiosh shifted his weight back and forth on my left shoulder. Sometimes when he does that it means he's nervous; other times it's comforting to me. I'm not sure what the difference is, but he always seems to; on this occasion it was a comfort.

I needed some.

Kragar coughed, which I thought was a good sign until

Aliera said something un-ladylike and muttered about stupid
lungs.

There was a disturbance at the stairway, and lots of weapons were suddenly out—including mine, I discovered. It turned
out to be the physicker, who was summarily sent back to where
he'd come from. We all put our weapons away. Aliera never
stopped working. Or muttering under breath. Her back was to
me, but I'd have bet big that she was scowling.

After about three minutes she stopped and glanced back
at me. "I'm losing him," she said.

"Isn't there anything—"

"Yes, there is. Get everyone out of here."

When Aliera uses that tone, I don't argue. The others
gave her looks, but shuffled out of the room. She didn't seem
to mind if I stayed, so I did. When they were gone, she fiddled
with her necklace and removed a tiny, round stone of dark
blue, of a type instantly recognizable to anyone familiar with
Elder Sorcery. And to me as well. I couldn't help it. I laughed.
"Good thing you had everyone leave, Aliera. It wouldn't do to
break the law in front of a bunch of Jhereg thugs."

She glared at me. "Do you want him saved or not, Vlad?"

"Yes, my lady. Shutting up, my lady."

She turned her attention back to Kragar.

I took a step closer. She put the stone on the small of his
back and as she pressed her fingers into his back, the stone
darkened, some red creeping into it, and light played across its
surface.

Kragar said, "What—" and screamed.

"Lie still," said Aliera. "Better, go back to sleep."

His head dropped back to the floor. Aliera used a term of

strong approbation under her breath. "I'd worry about brain damage," she said, "only—never mind."

Ten minutes later, I made my contribution to the event: I found a cloth and wiped the sweat from Aliera's forehead. Glad to help.

"Death is a process," said Aliera.

"Yeah," I said.

"In some sense, one could say he's dead. But what's really happening is that his heart is unable to pump blood. So I have to artificially force the circulation while repairing it."

The knife rose about an inch. She kept working.

"There aren't many sorcerers who could manage to do that while repairing the heart, keeping the arteries intact, preventing the other organs from shutting down, and making certain the pathways from the brain don't die out before they're needed again. It isn't easy. Just so you know."

"I know," I said.

A few minutes later she pulled the knife out and set it aside. Blood rushed from Kragar's back for an instant, but Aliera ran her finger along the wound and it closed up. Then she placed her palm over it and held it there. A moment later, I noticed that the blue stone had vanished.

Aliera sat back. "Done," she said.

"He isn't awake."

"I used a sleep spell. The screaming was annoying."

"But you can wake him up, can't you?"

"But then he'll say something, and I'll kill him, and all of this work will be wasted."

"Ah. Well, thank you."

She nodded and stood up. She gestured toward Kragar and vanished. He stirred.

"Ouch," he suggested.

"Yeah, I imagine. Be right back. Don't move."

I went into the next room—actually, his office—and let his people know that it was safe to come out. They did, giving me odd looks which I ignored.

Kragar turned himself over, then tried to stand up; failed. A couple of his guys helped him up and assisted him to a chair. He looked very, very pale.

"Remember the part about not moving?" I said. "That was moving."

"What happened?" he said.

The guy with the shoulders picked up the knife and handed it to him. He stared at it, but didn't touch it. After a moment he looked at me and said, "Did they miss?"

I shook my head. "Aliera," I said.

"Really?" He laughed, then winced. "She must have loved that. What did you have to promise her?"

"That she could kill you when you were done helping me."

"Seems reasonable."

"Kragar, how did they notice you?"

"Vlad, you notice me. Sometimes. Eventually. I mean, it isn't impossible. Just tricky."

"Heh. I'd always figured . . . never mind. Does it hurt?"

"Not really. More like a stiff back than real pain. I'm exhausted, though. Did Aliera leave any instructions?"

"No."

He chuckled. "Of course not. Well, if I keel over, I leave you that funny chair you left me."

"Who was it? Who got you?"

"How should I know? It was in the back."

"Other than helping me, have you done anything to piss anyone off?"

"Not that I can think of."

"All right."

"Vlad, it isn't going to help for you to blow your top."

"I'm not going to—"

"How does your hand feel?"

"My—"

I forced myself to relax the grip on my rapier. Now that I thought about it, the hand *was* sort of cramping up. Painfully. "My hand is fine," I said.

"Uh-huh." He grimaced. "So's my back. But there's no point in being mad because they took a shot at me. They know I'm helping you, they want to get you. It's how things work." He punctuated it with a shrug, then winced.

"I'm not mad."

"Or short," he agreed.

I called him a name; he nodded.

"Give me the knife," I said.

He looked at me. "You can find who did it?"

"They don't usually protect against witchcraft. It's worth trying."

"Okay, Vlad. But I don't know what that will give us. It'll just be hired muscle."

"I have some ideas."

"All right. Take it."

"Is my lab still intact?"

"Never touched it."

"See you in a while," I said.

He nodded and closed his eyes.

I started to walk away, stopped, looked at him sitting

there. I had all kinds of thoughts and memories. I don't know how long I stood there.

Eventually, I decided that if he opened his eyes again and saw me there, it'd be uncomfortable for both of us, and Barlen preserve me from ever being uncomfortable.

I walked out and headed down the back stairway.

Back when the office and the area were mine, I'd had a special place in the basement for performing witchcraft, which I called by a traditional Eastern term I don't understand. It was much as I'd left it, give or take a few layers of dust. I stood there for a few minutes, sneezing at old memories.

"Been a while, Boss. Sure you're up to this?"

"This is you building my confidence, right?"

"You're pissed off, and trying to do a spell, that's—"

"Loiosh, I'm fine. You—"

"This is my job, Boss."

After a while I said, "Yeah, it is, isn't it? All right."

"Take some time, Boss."

"Okay. But we don't have a lot—"

"We can take half an hour."

"All right."

So I sat on the dusty floor and leaned my head back and pretended I was trying to sleep. At least they hadn't tried to make it a Morganti killing; that was something. Morganti is ugly. That's how the Jhereg wanted me. Dead, dead, dead: no soul to reincarnate or go to Deathgate, just the end of everything. A big void. I couldn't conceive of it; I couldn't help trying.

I remembered a guy named Faloth back in 241. He was an enforcer with more pride than sense, and when he couldn't pay off his debt, he'd hinted that he'd go to the Empire if he wasn't left alone. Worse, when he wasn't left alone, he actually did. He made a serious amount of trouble for a lot of people.

Turns out, the reason he needed the money in the first place was to buy presents for his lover, a Chreotha who had too-expensive tastes. After the Jhereg had threatened him, he started visiting her at different times, and taking different routes; sometimes even teleporting to be really safe. Only he couldn't teleport, so he had to have it done for him by a sorcerer who lived just one street over from him. I caught him just outside the sorcerer's door. It was very fast. It has to be. I mean, it always has to be fast, because you don't want the target to have a chance to fight back. But with a Morganti weapon, it needs to be exceptionally fast, because anyone can sense the power that comes out of those things. You have to keep it in a sheath with special enchantments, and then draw and use it fast. I had the sheath on my left hip for a cross draw. And I was fast enough, taking him in the left eye and into his brain. He looked surprised. They always look surprised.

I don't know who or what will finally get me, but I'm pretty sure that when it happens I'll look surprised. And, if it's Morganti, after that will be nothing, nothing, nothing.

"Okay, Loiosh. I think I'm ready."

"Let's go then, Boss."

8

Making Waves
or
Making Magic

I emptied the brazier and filled it again from the bucket of charcoal. I found the candles, and placed them, black and white, around the brazier. Then I took the amulet off. I mean, they knew where I was anyway, right?

"*Loiosh, don't monitor the spell. I need you checking for anyone about to show up and ruin my party or anything coming from outside that might, you know, hurt me.*"

"*I can do that, Boss. But . . .*"

"Yeah?"

"*Sure you'll be all right, Boss? It's been years since—*"

"Yeah, I think so. It should be pretty straightforward."

There wasn't all that much in the way of supplies, but a spell like this didn't call for much; I found what I needed and arranged it in front of the brazier.

Since I had my link to the Orb back, I used it to light the charcoal, and then the candles, moving wrongwise around the circle. I took the knife in my left hand, gripping it by the blade, the hilt held over the fire. Fennel and caraway went in, along with a little rosemary just because it smelled good. It's a lot like cooking. Well, no, it isn't at all like cooking, but you use some of the same things.

I sat cross-legged in front of the brazier, watching the coals glow and inhaling the smoke. The knife felt slightly heavy, but that's because I'm a little guy, at least compared to Dragaerans. The blade in my hand no longer felt cold. I was touching Kragar's blood, the smoke was curling around sweat and skin oil of whoever had used the weapon.

My breathing was even and deep: in through the nose, out through the mouth. My breath disturbed the dark gray smoke billowing up, wrapped up with traces of someone, someone who killed for money, just like I do, I mean did, but if you kill, I mean, if you actually go out and just put a knife into someone, does it make that much difference why? There were whys drifting in the smoke, in my eyes. I was no longer in the musty basement, I was gone, lost in my head among a corridor of whys. It doesn't make any difference to the guy you've just shined why you did it. Money. Honor. Duty. Or maybe the pleasure of knowing that, just for a second, you're the most important thing in someone's life. I've known guys like that. Worked with them. Hired them. What did that make me? Bullshit question. I reached to secure the connection to my target, to give it tangibility. Some things you have to do—you either do them, or live with the Empire's foot on your head. I didn't choose to live that way, so I did what I had to. Maybe this guy was like that, too. Or maybe he killed for one of those other reasons. It didn't matter, but then again it did—it mattered because I had to secure him, to bring him to me, to turn wisps of dark gray smoke harsh and burning in my nose, my eyes, in the air, in my mind, floating, drifting, letting it happen, no longer aware of my heartbeat, my breathing, my body, turn

that into who and what he was. Nothing and nowhere, everything and everywhere, and I was studying the image that had
formed in my head before I was consciously aware that it was
there.

No, "image" isn't exactly the right word. It was more like a
feel, or a taste of his presence. Not much, but it was something. All I needed to do was—

Oops.

This was where I turn the sense of presence into a psychic
impression embedded in a crystal. Only I'd forgotten the part
about having a crystal ready. You get out of practice with this
stuff.

I could say that I held the spell together while I tried to
figure out what to do, but that wouldn't give you any idea of
how hard it is to maintain awareness of something as nebu-
lous as another's consciousness while, you know, *thinking*. I
could have dropped the spell and just done it again, but I was
too irritated. I fumbled with the drawstring of my pouch and
managed to find a coin. I used that.

In the end it worked fine, and I let the spell drop, feeling exhausted and embarrassed. Loiosh snickered into my
mind, but didn't say anything. I think it was his sense of self-
preservation.

"Anything, Loiosh?"

"You were spotted, Boss, but no attacks."

"Good, then."

"Uh, going to put that thing on again?"

"In a sec. Might as well save you a trip."

"Make it fast, Boss. They're bound to be setting something up."

"Yeah," I said. "They always are."

I waited a few minutes until the hour. Daymar and I had

left things undecided, but maybe he was opening up anyway. I reached out for him, and yeah, there he was. Without his shields, it's like a fish that goes for your line if it's anywhere in the lake. (Yes, I fished once. I didn't care for it.)

"Hello, Vlad. You require something?"

"If you aren't busy, I need someone located. I have—"

"A psychic impression embedded in a crystal?"

"Actually, in a one-orb coin."

"Oh? Why a coin?"

"An experiment. I've always wanted to try that spell with objects other than crystals, and this seemed like a good opportunity."

"All right. Where are you?"

"My old offices."

"I'll be there."

I was going to thank him, but his presence was already gone from my mind. I put the amulet back on, feeling a certain amount of tension go out of my shoulders.

"Hey, Boss, what about the other spell?"

"The oth—crap. I forgot about it."

"Are you going to have to do this all over again?"

"I don't know. Maybe I'll ask Morrolan for help. I don't want to think about it right now."

He let it drop. I went back upstairs to wait for Daymar.

I checked in on Kragar, who was asleep in his chair, but seemed to be doing all right. His people walked past, checking on him, milling about. I couldn't quite read the looks they gave me, but they weren't openly hostile. But if the only reason they hadn't turned on me before was because Kragar had told them not to, and if he was no longer in shape to tell them not to, and if they realized that it was my fault that he was no longer there to tell them not to, things could get interesting.

That's interesting as in, "Oh, I'm dead now and my soul has been destroyed. How interesting."

The guy who appeared to be in charge was called Sellish. I told him a guy named Daymar might be appearing, that he was with me, and that we were going to find out who wanted Kragar shined.

"Good," he said and seated himself next to Kragar's desk. I'd been impressed with how well Kragar had done taking over the area, but it wasn't until now, when he was laid up, that it really hit me how much in control he was. I made a mental note not to tell him so. But it meant there was a good chance none of his people would betray me, kill me, or do other unpleasant things.

There were a few padded chairs in front of the desk in the other room—the desk that, in my mind, I still saw Melestav sitting at. I indulged in a moment's annoyance about him. I hate it when someone I like . . . yeah, skip it. Moment over. Then Daymar came tromping up the stairs. I heard the footsteps before I knew who it was.

"Hello, Vlad."

"Daymar. Here." I tossed him the coin. He missed it, but levitated it back into his hand before it hit the floor. I suspect he missed it on purpose, just so he could do that. He studied it.

"Hm," he said.

"Can you use it?"

"Oh, yes. It's surprising how well it took the impression."

"Good."

"His name is Havric. Right now he's at a place called the Front Gate in Little Deathgate, having drinks with two other Jhereg."

He waited and looked at me.

"Daymar."

"Vlad?"

"You're very good at what you do."

"I know."

"Feel like a walk to Little Deathgate?"

"Can't we teleport?"

"Not while I wear this thing."

"Um, couldn't you take it off?"

"We've had this conversation, Daymar."

"Oh, right. Walk, then. But what if they see you?"

"Yeah. Mind putting a bit of cloud over me?"

"Sure."

I took the amulet off so he could work. My vision blurred, then cleared. Daymar said, "That's odd."

Okay, sorry, I need to explain something.

The simplest way to not be seen is an invisibility spell, making light bend around you. The better you are, the tighter the bend you can get and so the less chance there is of someone noticing a distortion, but even sloppy it's easy to do and effective. The only trouble is, if you happen to walk by someone with a reasonable amount of skill in sorcery, you're going to stick out like a kethna at court. Even when I'm wearing the amulet, Lady Teldra can identify an invisibility spell in the area if she's paying any attention at all. The best way to deal with that is to plant a field around you that absorbs the sorcerous energy. It isn't easy, because it requires getting into your mind and folding—well, skip it. It's hard. I can't do it. Daymar can.

"What's odd?"

"Your head—there was a wall in it."

"A wall? How could there be—oh, right. Yeah, I don't want to talk about it."

"All right."

I replaced the amulet. We stepped onto the street, and I found myself staring at my left palm.

"I've remembered and forgotten this once before."

"Brought back memories, did he, Boss?"

"Yeah."

"Now probably isn't the time."

"Right."

Loiosh and Rocza were flying above us, keeping an eye out. I walked next to Daymar, making sure I didn't bump into anyone and hoping I was as invisible as I should be but didn't feel. We turned north onto Backin, which was narrow enough that it was tricky not running into people who didn't know I was there, so I stepped behind Daymar.

It felt like a longer walk than it actually was, what with feeling like an idiot walking in Daymar's footsteps. The invisibility was a blessing in more ways than one.

The Front Gate was on top of a butcher's shop. You climb three steps from the street and enter a long, thin room, with a bar running half the length. Rocza flew off to wait, Loiosh hid in my cloak. As we entered, Daymar looked around before my eyes had a chance to adjust and said, "There, in the back."

"All right. Make me visible again."

"Might be more fun the other way, you know."

Daymar was surprising me in all sorts of ways.

"More fun," I agreed, "but less efficient."

"All right," he said, and the air in front of my eyes swirled for a moment. We approached the table.

The three of them were looking at us as we walked up, but no one reached for a weapon. We stopped about six feet away. They remained seated. "Havric," I said.

The one with short, red hair cocked his head and narrowed his eyes. "Something I can do for you, Taltos?"

"A pleasure to be recognized," I said. "Yeah. Who paid you to put a shine on Kragar?"

Nothing. No reaction at all. "I'm afraid you've mistaken me for someone else," he said.

I gave Daymar an inquiring look.

"Got it," said Daymar.

They all looked at him. Loiosh climbed out of my cloak and positioned himself on my shoulder.

"Sorry for the mix-up," I said. I smiled, bowed, and turned around, listening hard for any scary sounds. There were none; we made it out onto the street, Daymar made me vanish again.

"I hope this'll be enough," I said. "We aren't going to be able to pull that off again."

"Enough?"

"I hope the name you got will be enough to get me there."

"Get you there? I have the person who hired him."

"I know. I hope that's enough."

"I don't understand. Isn't the person who hired him what you want?"

"No, I want to know who hired the guy to hire the guy to hire him."

"Seems awfully complicated."

"That's how Jhereg do things."

"Why?"

"Did you know that assassination is against the law?"

He hesitated, considered, nodded.

"The Empire becomes very sad when you kill someone for money. They do all sorts of things to discourage that kind of behavior. This leads to those who want it done taking some pains to be sure that the Empire doesn't know they did it. Am I going too fast for you?"

"No, no. I've got it so far."

"That's why it's so complicated. So the guy who orders it doesn't want it known that he ordered it, so he has someone else get someone else to get someone else to do it."

"Oh." He considered. "Makes sense."

"That's a relief. What name did you get?"

"Yestac. Know him?"

"Yeah."

"Know who he works for?"

"Yeah."

Yestac worked for Taavith, also called "Flatstones." Flatstones had a big section of Adrilankha running from the South Hills all the way to Overlook, and as far inland as the Terrace. He gave a percentage to a guy named Krasno, who was on the Council. I didn't know a lot about Krasno, and I didn't have Kragar to collect information. Bugger. I thought about it as we walked, and for a wonder, Daymar was quiet and let me think.

We made it back to Kragar's place without any trouble. Daymar asked if he could do anything else for me, and I bit my tongue and just said no. Then I thanked him, politely, because that's the kind of guy I am.

I went up to see Kragar. He wasn't there. I was just settling in for a good panic attack when one of Kragar's people stuck his head around the corner and said, "Sellish said to tell you we've taken the boss home."

"His home?"

"Yeah."

"Can I—"

"The boss said you were welcome there, if you want."

My heart returned to its normal speed.

"We could take you there," he said, and I had an image of myself walking down the street to an unknown destination surrounded by guys who could make enough to live in luxury for the rest of their lives just by putting a shine on me, or even stepping aside while someone else did.

"Sure," I said.

He nodded and gathered up three others, and they escorted me down the stairs and out onto the street.

"*For someone worried about the Jhereg, you sure are spending a lot of time parading in front of them.*"

"*I have absolutely no fear. Oh, come on, Loiosh, it wasn't that funny. Last time I was invisible. This time I have protection.*"

"*If you have protection.*"

I had no answer for that.

We didn't have far to walk; in ten minutes we were at a tidy little rooming house on Garshos. We entered the front door, and Sellish went up to the first door on the right. He clapped, then opened the door.

My first thought was, *I wonder what he does with all of his money?* He certainly didn't have any of it invested in his home. He was lying on the bed—one of three pieces of furniture in the place. The others were a single chair, and a table; neither of them looking like they cost more than six coppers.

"I see why you spend so much time at the office," I told him.

"This isn't where I live, Vlad. It's just where I sleep."

I nodded. "Right. The other place is where you stash your various mistresses and the Kathana paintings and the big wine cellar."

He looked over at me, then turned his head back to stare

at the ceiling. He was flat on his back, but his eyes were clear. He gave me an appropriate answer.

"I don't bend that way," I said. I grabbed the chair, pulled it up next to his bed, sat down, and crossed my legs. "So, how are you feeling?"

He used a bad word.

"Good to hear," I said.

"You aren't here to check on my health. What is it?"

"I'm here to check on your health."

"Right."

I shrugged. "I can make something else up, if you want."

"Yeah, I'd like that. It would help my recovery."

"Okay. Can I borrow six tablespoons of Eastern red pepper?"

"No."

"All right."

"Vlad, do you remember when it meant something to be a Jhereg? When there was honor, and—"

"Kragar?"

"Yeah?"

"What are you talking about?"

"Seeing if I could convince you I was dying."

"You had me half convinced you were off your head; does that count?"

"Better than nothing. What have you learned?"

"About what?"

He turned his head to look at me.

"The shiner was a guy named Havric."

"Hired by?"

"How would I know that?"

"Vlad—"

"Yestac."

"Don't know him," said Kragar. "Can't think of anything I ever said about his mother."

"Flatstones," I said.

"Ah," said Kragar.

"Yeah," I said. "That means Krasno."

"No, it doesn't," said Kragar. "It means Terion."

"Huh?"

"Flatstones used to work for Terion, and they're still close."

I opened my mouth to ask Kragar how he knew that, then shut it again. Finding out things like that is what Kragar did before I sort of donated the area to him; what possible reason could he have for stopping?

But. Terion.

Not long ago, during a conflict over South Adrilankha, I'd come close to putting a shine on him. I'd started in to do it, too, only, in the end, events had dictated otherwise. Matters had gotten complex. I'd had to—no, never mind. That really is a long story.

The point is, I'd been running into him for years. We didn't like each other, and we kept getting in each other's way. Now he'd taken a shot at Kragar, and it would have worked if I hadn't known one of the Empire's leading experts in healing magic.

I was suddenly convinced that he was the one who was spending so much money to get me. Because he could. I had no evidence, but I knew I was right.

I was getting tired of the guy.

"Terion," I said aloud. "He really does seem to keep popping up in my life. Is it personal, do you think?"

"Does it matter?"

"It might. Tactically."

He shrugged, then winced; I could see him deciding not to do that anymore.

Terion. The guy kept showing up and getting in my way. He didn't like me. And he could seriously mess up this thing I was working on.

Loiosh spoke into my mind. *"We could, I don't know, kill him."*

. . . *You could always kill someone high up in the Organization.*

Yeah, and then what? Would I have to kill Krasno too, if they were friends? Could I, in fact, kill either of them? And what would happen afterward? Occasionally, killing someone is the natural culmination of a complex series of events; more often it's the midpoint—it has repercussions. Consequences flow out from it. When I was just taking someone's money to do a job, they weren't my consequences, so I didn't have to worry. I was just a tool.

But still, this was different. It was all about me, and anything that happened would be my problem. Killing Terion could, for all I knew, set off a chain of events that would be as bad as . . .

As not killing him.

But I'd already said I needed something to stir up the Jhereg, to distract them.

Well, okay; two reasons to kill him, about ninety against.

"Okay," I said. *"Let's kill him."*

Nothing. Then, *"Boss, you mean it?"*

"Yeah."

"I've been waiting for this day. I'm so proud of you. I knew that eventually—"

"Shut up, Loiosh."

"Shutting up, Boss."

I looked over at Kragar. "Can I get you anything?" I said.

Sellish cleared his throat.

I looked at him. "Sorry," I said.

He nodded.

Kragar said, "It's all right, Vlad. Just don't make any more trouble for me, all right?" He frowned. "No, forget I said that. I changed my mind. Make more trouble. I'm in a mood."

"I can do that," I said.

"Let me know how it comes out."

"Oh, you'll hear," I said, and headed out. The toughs who had escorted me over escorted me back. There was no trouble, but I could see the tension in their shoulders. It was good to get back to Kragar's office, where I felt safe. Safer. A little safer.

"I think I liked Dzur Mountain better, Boss."

"Who didn't? But it's a bit too far from the action."

"What action?"

"Killing Terion."

"Oh, right."

I was sitting there, trying to work out exactly how I was going to do that, when one of Kragar's people came up to me. "Sellish says I'm supposed to ask if you need anything," he said.

A few sarcastic comments came to mind, but he was big and his shoulders were very wide and he was dressed to conceal and I saw no signs that he had a sense of humor.

"What's your name?"

"Deragar."

I nodded. "Ever heard of a guy named Terion?"

He nodded. "I know who he is."

"Can you find out where he lives? Where he goes, and when he goes there? What kind of—"

He was holding out some paper. I took it. Three leaves, closely written, with perfect penmanship. I looked them over. Favorite place to drink and what he liked to drink there. Friends and lovers, where they lived, where he liked to meet them. Who cut his hair, who made his clothes. His bodyguards, and where they lived, and more. Substantially more.

"Yeah," I said. "Like this."

"Anything else, m'lord?"

"How did you know—Kragar?"

"Got the message before you showed up, m'lord."

"Fast work," I said.

"A good number of us on it, in pieces."

"He's gotten good at this," I remarked. Deragar nodded. I didn't say so, but I was also thinking that it was a bit scary, how well Kragar knew me.

"All right," I said. "Let me look this stuff over and get back to you. It was Deragar, right?"

He nodded.

I went into Kragar's office, started to sit behind his desk, then changed my mind and took the chair on the other side. I studied the information Deragar had gotten.

"*What do you think, Boss?*"

"*I wish Kragar were feeling better. Then I'd ask him to talk to Mario.*"

"*That bad?*"

"*Yeah. Bodyguards I can't buy, sorcery protection, he avoids regular patterns. May be open to witchcraft attacks, but it wouldn't be easy because he has psychic protections. Very tough.*"

"*You've handled tough before, Boss.*"

"*I'm out of practice.*"

"*Yeah, you are.*"

I went over the intelligence again.

"*Do you think if I asked Aliera very nicely, she'd put me in touch with Mario?*"

"*Knowing you'd want him to assassinate someone? Not a chance, Boss.*"

"Yeah, I suppose you're right. Okay, next idea: Maybe I can pull the deal with the Jhereg without handling Terion."

"*Maybe*," said Loiosh, sounding deeply and passionately convinced.

"Yeah," I agreed. "Okay, I guess not. But my focus still has to be on pulling off this move."

"*Be harder if you're dead.*"

"Yeah, it—wait. Maybe not."

"*Seriously, Boss? The whole faking-your-own-death thing? Do you really think that will work with these people?*"

"What if it isn't faked?"

"*Boss, what are you—you mean like Mellar?*"

"Yeah."

"*That seems like a really, really bad idea.*"

"Yeah."

Many years ago—seems like lifetimes ago—when everything was simpler, I had dealt with a complicated problem by arranging for Aliera to be killed by a Morganti blade, gambling that Aliera's Great Weapon, Pathfinder, would protect her soul. It had worked. Now I had a Great Weapon, Lady Teldra, and I was thinking that I could do the same thing. Faking my death would buy me time to put my plan into action without worrying about the Jhereg trying to kill me.

I tried not to think about the fact that I would have to kind of let myself get stabbed with a Morganti blade to pull it off. I mean, Aliera had done that without blinking; was she any braver than me?

Yes, in fact. A lot braver. But maybe I could do it. Maybe.

"*You know, Boss. If that will work, then it will work any time. You don't have to go out of your way—*"

"Aliera said she had to communicate with Pathfinder, to prepare her."

"*Boss, can you communicate with Lady Teldra?*"

"Well, no, not exactly. I mean, sometimes it seems like—"

"*Boss.*"

"*You're saying it's a bad risk.*"

"*Boss, even by your usual standards of bad risks, this one is just stupid.*"

Okay, well, the fact is I was kind of happy to be talked out of it. "*Loiosh, I have to do something. This sitting around waiting to be shined, right here in the middle of Adrilankha, is—*"

"*Not much different than it's been for the last several months?*"

I exhaled slowly. "*I suppose you're right. It's just now there's a chance to end it, to get out of this mess.*"

"*I know.*"

I sighed. "*It's the hard way, isn't it?*"

"*Always is, Boss.*"

9

MAKING MAGIC
OR
MAKING TROUBLE

The hard way. Yeah.

The put-it-together-a-piece-at-a-time, taking-my-chances-of-being-shined, and just-fight-it-through way.

All right, then.

"*Let me guess, Boss: You need to talk to Daymar again.*"

"*Soon. I want to make sure I'm clear on what to do next. And I need that hawk's egg. And the wand.*"

"*For what?*"

"*The egg? I don't have enough power for the spell—the eavesdropping spell. I need a burst of psychic power.*"

"*And the wand?*"

"*One way things might go down involves a sleep spell. The wand will prevent several of those from working.*"

"*'Several of those,'*" he repeated. "*And the others?*"

"*Koelsch leaves.*"

"*Oh.*"

"*Also, when we take the next step, things are liable to start popping. We won't be able to control the pace.*"

"*Right, Boss. Because, up until now, we've had perfect control of everything.*"

"Shut up."

So, okay: I had enough clinking stuff, and the lockpick, and the hawk's egg and the wand should arrive soon. I opened up the book of Imperial trade laws (volume nine, it said) I'd gotten from Perisil, and went over the significant passage again. It was not exciting.

I was still doing that when I received word that Daymar had arrived in the office, and would like to see me. I offered up a silent prayer of thanks to Verra and told them to send him in.

Daymar entered, ignoring the various tough guys standing around, and walked up to me. He declined refreshment, and placed a brown egg, mostly round, and about a quarter of the diameter of my palm, on the table in front of me.

"That's it?" I said.

"No," said Daymar. "That's a wood carving of a dragon, actual size."

"*Wow, Boss. Sarcasm from Daymar.*"

"*I know. My whole view of the world is turned on its head.*"

I picked up the egg and studied it. It was warm, reminding me of Loiosh's egg, so very long ago. It was almost weightless in my hand, and felt fragile; like I might break it if my finger twitched. I set it down again.

"*Loiosh, can you feel anything from it?*"

"*Oh, yes.*"

"*You can feel a lot of—of whatever it is? Energy? Latent psychic power?*"

"*Yeah, Boss. A lot.*"

"It won't retain its potency more than a few days," said Daymar.

"That'll be enough," I said. "Um. Any chance you got two? I'd like to practice this spell."

"How soon?"

"A day?"

He shook his head.

"Okay. It should work. Thanks."

"Is there anything else I can do for you?"

"The wand?"

"I ought to be able to get, uh, to get it by tomorrow. I didn't forget about it. Is that all?"

I hesitated, wishing I'd remembered to do the spell when I had the amulet off. I could remove the amulet yet again, or I could ask Morrolan to do it.

But Daymar was here, and—

"I'm not sure if this is something you can do," I said.

He an arched an eyebrow at me.

"I mean," I said, "that it's a witch thing. It's the sort of thing witchcraft is really good at. But I can't do any because of this amulet."

"You took it off a few hours ago," observed Daymar.

"Yeah, I was mad."

"Oh. Couldn't you have done this other thing then, since you had it off anyway?"

"No, it would have been an inauspicious time, because of the mystical fields of, well, it's an Eastern religious thing."

"I see. Well, what would you like me to do?"

"Exert a subtle influence on someone, without his being aware of it."

"Ah," said Daymar. He considered for a moment. "Just invade his mind enough to help him make a decision the way you want?"

"Sort of. To come up with an idea and make him think he thought of it."

Daymar looked intrigued. "I think I can do that. Who is it you want it done to?"

I reached in my pocket and handed him the handkerchief I'd stolen from the Demon's desk. He studied it. "What idea do you want him to have?"

"There's a building right at the point where Kieron's Watch used to be. It would be the perfect place for him to meet me. Think you can suggest that without alerting him?"

Daymar looked directly at me. "Vlad, I think I can do it, but I'm not sure. I'd really appreciate it if you'd let me try. This is, well, this is exciting."

I *did* kind of owe him.

"Of course," I said.

About two minutes later, Daymar went out the way he'd come in: walking, just like a normal person. I wondered if that annoyed him. I hoped it did, at least a little. Yeah, I'm a bad man.

"*All right,*" I told Loiosh. "*Let's assume it worked. Time to visit the jeweler.*"

I declined the offer of an escort, and took the tunnel. I made sure my rapier was loose, and checked a couple of the unsurprising surprises I keep around me, then waited just a bit longer to let my eyes adjust. Loiosh and Rocza flew out, reported that everything looked all right, and I stepped out once more onto the busy, dirty, terrifying streets of Adrilankha. I cut

across a street, down an alley, then left, then right a good distance, and stepped into a storefront shop in the middle of a
row of cheap yellow brick rooming houses.

Athek is and always has been a dealer in high-end stolen
merchandise, especially jewelry. I know it, the Empire knows
it, and I'm sure the dirty kids playing bones-and-muffins on
the street outside know it. And he knows me; Kiera introduced us years ago. He wasn't her favorite fence, but he was
close to my office. Which was not, in fact, why I was there
today.

"Lord Taltos," he said, looking nervous enough to confirm
that he knew I was marked for a shine. He was a Jhegaala,
with a full head of white hair and a permanent squint.

"Close up," I told him.

He nodded nervously, and walked around the counter to
the door, locked it, and went back to the counter, sort of edg-
ing past me as if I were a poisonous reptile. Of course, I did
have a couple of poisonous reptiles on my shoulders, which
might have had something to do with it.

"My lord?" he said.

"I need a plain unadorned, platinum ring."

"Yes, my lord. I have—"

"No, I need a particular one," I told him, and watched his
expression carefully.

On the third floor of the Imperial Wing of the Palace is a
dusty room in which, by tradition, ancient Imperial relics are
stored. Three doors lead out of it. One is the hall; one is a closet
where janitor's tools are stored; the other is to the tiny room
where, once a year, the Master of Upper Repositories spreads

out the paperwork that corresponds to the relics, and makes sure that it does, in fact, correspond to the relics on hand.

The rest of the time, that room is used by a small group of Imperial operatives. The leader—whose identity is kept strictly secret—reports directly to Her Majesty. The group carries no identification, except that each wears a simple, unadorned platinum ring on the middle finger of his left hand.

The rings have no special magic on them except for a unique, imprinted identification mark. The spell was designed and each ring treated personally by Kosadr. According to the best arcane knowledge, there is no way to duplicate this spell. When I first learned about them—that's its own story—I asked Sethra, and even she agreed. I don't know about you, but I find that convincing.

On the first Homeday of the month of the Vallista in the two hundred and fifty-first year of the reign of Zerika the Fourth, Lord Bristoe-Camfor, House of the Dzur, of the Third Floor Relic group, was found dead behind a pawnshop a mile and a half from the Imperial Palace. A dagger had been driven up under his chin into his brain. Other than the wound, he had not been disturbed, except that his ring was missing.

Third Floor Relic carried on its own investigation, as did the Special Tasks group (commanded by a guy nicknamed "Papa Cat," an old acquaintance who didn't like me much). As usual with such matters, each group was more worried about the other group finding it than they were about not finding it themselves. It took several weeks, but the trail being followed by Third Floor Relic eventually led to the Jhereg owner of the pawnshop. Fittra of Third Floor Relic knew that it was unheard-of for a Jhereg to knowingly kill an Imperial operative. Furthermore, no Jhereg would ever let a body be found near his own place of business if he had anything to do with it. All of which, taken together, meant that something else was going on. Meanwhile, at this same time, Special Tasks bowed out of the investigation.

Maybe the Jhereg hadn't known he was an Imperial operative. Maybe someone else had arranged the whole thing, using the Jhereg as a tool. Maybe.

But when one of their own is killed, the Empire is not fussy about who gets hurt during the investigation. In this case, a lot of people were hurt, starting with the owner of the pawnshop.

Eventually Third Floor Relic got its answer: Bristoe-Camfor's future brother-in-law killed him in a dispute over table settings for his sister's upcoming wedding. The ring, they assumed, had been taken from the body by a passing stranger, and there was nothing to be done except wait and hope that it would turn up somewhere.

Now, here's what really happened: The business with the Dzurlord's future brother-in-law was nonsense. The murder and robbery had, in fact, been planned and executed by a Jhereg—one of the very rare instances of the Organization killing any Imperial representative of any kind. There were personal motives involved, and special circumstances that I won't go into, and, though some years ago I did learn of the whole thing, there were a lot of details I never discovered, such as exactly how they managed to conceal it from the Empire.

I learned about it at all because I know Kiera, and Kiera knows everything. The point is, the ring had vanished, and, while the Jhereg were happy to have it remain missing, it didn't matter, because no one knew where it was.

Well, not *no* one.

He turned a little pale. "I—"

"Careful, Athek. If you lie, I'll be unhappy."

He swallowed, and shut up. He looked like he had no intention of speaking. Ever again.

"Obviously," I said, "you know which ring I'm talking about."

He nodded.

"And obviously," I went on, "since everyone knows it's on the waves, you have some idea which wave it's on."

He hesitated, then nodded again.

"And for one last obvious statement, you have a reason for not wanting me to have it. Perhaps, if you tell me what that reason is, we can work something out."

I gave him my warmest, friendliest smile.

"My lord," he said, which was respectful but not responsive.

"Go on," I suggested.

He seemed incapable.

I said, "Did someone tell you not to give it to me?"

He shook his head.

"Did someone tell you to keep it hidden?"

He shook his head again.

"Go ahead, Boss. Ask him if it's physical, magical, or spiritual."

"Shut up, Loiosh."

"Is it being held by someone you're afraid of?"

He nodded.

"Yes for a copper."

"Shut up, Loiosh."

"Is it a Jhereg?"

He nodded again.

"Yes for two—"

"Loiosh!"

My next question was, "Does this Jhereg scare you more than I do?"

He had to consider that. It took him some time. I started to feel a bit jealous.

"No," he said at last.

"So, who has it?"

He clamped his mouth shut, as if daring me to pry it open. I considered doing just that.

I had to decide carefully what to do next. Putting too much pressure on Athek would piss people off; but, to the left, how much more could they do to me than they wanted to already? I thought it over, while he stood there, waiting to see what I'd do.

I knew very well that mere possession of the thing was a capital crime. So did he, and, maybe, so did the person who had it. I know you're asking yourself why, if the thing was so dangerous, and if Athek knew who had it, did whoever it was let Athek live? I asked myself the same question. I mean, it's true: You don't go around casually shining people like him—they always have protection or they wouldn't be in business. But still, this was a dangerous secret.

Unless the guy who had it didn't know Athek knew he had it.

Yeah, that would account for everything. Well, for him not wanting to tell me and him still being above the Falls, at least. So, someone who might have it, someone scary, someone Athek would know had it, someone who didn't know Athek knew he had it. . . .

"So," I said. "The Left Hand of the Jhereg puts in an appearance, does it?"

He didn't answer; but the look on his face was answer enough.

Yeah, had to be the Left Hand: the sorceresses. They wouldn't know how Athek operated, about his contacts among all things jewelry-related. They'd see him as merely a corrupt merchant. And he, of course, would be terrified of his own knowledge—afraid someone would let it be known that he had information that could get him killed.

And here I was, right on schedule.

"Who in the Left Hand?" I said. "Now that I know, you might as well—"

"I don't know," he said.

"How did you find it?"

"The Imperials questioned me, made me look for it."

"Sorcery?"

He nodded. "I have a thing for jewelry. I can find it when no one else in town can. I could find a—"

"Yeah, I know. So you found it?"

"I found it. Got a face and a location. I didn't get a name, but I recognized her as Left Hand."

"Then why didn't you tell the Imperials?"

"It didn't seem safe." He sniffed. "And besides, I didn't like how they asked me."

I nodded. You don't survive as a cleaner for the Jhereg if you're weak.

"I can't protect you from the Left Hand," I said.

"I know."

"But they can't protect you from me, either."

He considered that for what seemed a very long time. I let him think. At last he said, "All right. Make me an offer."

"Twenty."

"Thirty."

"Done."

I passed him over enough money to keep a family eating well for several months, and he said, "Unless they've moved it, it's in the back room of an inn at the very end of Western, in the false back of a three-shelf bookcase."

Well, that ought to be precise enough. "Any traps or wardings on the false back?"

"None that I saw, but I wouldn't recognize any."

"Yeah, all right."

Loiosh and Rocza checked the street, and I went back out there and down the street to the tunnel into Kragar's office, where I found Deragar hanging around.

"Need something?" he said.

"There's an inn at the tail end of Western."

He nodded. "Black Rose," he said. "It's a Left Hand place."

"Yes," I said. "Can you check it out for me?"

"What do you want checked?"

"How hard would it be to get me a minute alone in the back office?"

He nodded. "There's going to be sorcery."

I fished out my purse and handed him fifteen gold imperials. "That'll do it," he said. "Should I have some food sent in before I go?"

"That'd be great."

"See you soon, then."

Half an hour later there was ginger-roasted kethna, wine, and Forbidden Forest soup, and I was feeling fairly good about life.

"*So, you trust this guy, Boss?*"

"*You think I've been poisoned? I feel fine.*"

"*Oh, now is a good time to ask.*"

"*Kragar trusts him.*"

A couple of hours later Deragar was back. "You get it?" I asked him.

"When it's open or closed?" were the first words out of his mouth.

"Whichever is easier."

"Open, then. That gets rid of everything at the entrances and windows, and eliminates the passive sorcery detection."

I nodded. "I'm listening."

He unrolled a piece of paper, and held it spread open on the table in front of me. It had a detailed drawing of what I assumed was the inside of the Black Rose. "The two Xs are sorceresses, keeping a watch on the office door at all times. There's no window into the office, so the front and back doors are your only way in. The back door is locked and sealed—sorcerous seal and alarms—except for deliveries and special requests."

"Two sorceresses," I said. "Are you sure you didn't miss one?"

He looked at me.

"Good answer," I said. "All right, go on."

"The door into the office has what's called a Ferni Seal. A Ferni Seal—"

"I'm familiar with it," I said. It was serious security.

He nodded. "Also, the knob on the door has a ten-candle alarm tied to a bell in the bar, and something inside the office; obviously, my sorcerer couldn't tell what."

"Right. Understood."

"That's it," he said.

"That's plenty," I said. "Good work."

He nodded. "Any kethna left?"

"Help yourself."

He did, while I tried to figure out a way in. The sorcery was no problem—I had a Great Weapon called Lady Teldra, which meant I still had, albeit in a different form, what had once been a gold chain I'd called Spellbreaker. The trouble was the sorceresses. They weren't going to just stand there while I walked into the office to look around; not to mention whoever worked in that office.

"You're sure open is easier?" I said after a while.

He swallowed a mouthful of kethna and wiped his lips on the back of his hand. "Two more in the office, one more in the bar, plus more sorcery."

Plus the fact that even walking in would be a signal to start the mayhem. I could maybe take them all out, but right now was not when I wanted the Left Hand after me as well as the Right. "Yeah, okay," I said.

He went back to eating.

"*I can't wait to hear your plan for this one, Boss.*"

"*Shut up.*"

I considered. "*Okay, we walk in and ask to see the lady in charge. They—*"

"*Identify you and kill you for the reward. With you so far, Boss. Then what?*"

"*I was more thinking they let me in to see her.*"

"*I wouldn't have thought of that, Boss. Bet they won't think of it either.*"

"*I could use a disguise.*"

"*First thing they'll do when you ask is check you for sorcery and find your Phoenix Stone.*"

"*I could take it off.*"

"Oh, then the Jhereg would kill you instead. Good plan."

"All right, smart guy. What's your idea?"

"Mock you mercilessly until you think of something better."

"Does that usually work?"

"Yes."

I didn't have an answer for that.

What I wanted to do was charge in, kill everyone in sight, then search the place. Even without the benefit of Loiosh's penetrating insight, I understood that wasn't practical.

Of course, there was the fallback position: ask Kiera for help. Again. I hated the idea of running to her every time I needed to steal something, but I was willing to do it if there was no other way.

"Yeah, Boss. Now is exactly the time to be too proud to—"

"Shut up."

Maybe some capers are out of the reach of a lone Easterner. Maybe. Can't say as I liked the idea much.

"You don't have to like it, Boss. It's the only thing that makes any sort of—"

"Loiosh, if you can't be useful—"

I broke off and started chuckling.

"Boss? Boss, what's funny? I don't like the sound of that."

Three hours later, he was telling me it wasn't funny.

I said, "Go," and opened the door. He and Rocza flew into the Black Rose. I counted to ten, then followed them in, hugging the wall. There was the sizzling and popping of spells, and people moving everywhere. Lots of people; twenty at least. The sorceresses were having trouble hitting the jhereg without hitting the customers. The door to the office opened as I was approaching it. I pressed myself against the wall. A woman came out; when she was past I slipped in behind her, and there I was.

There was a three-shelf bookcase, just as promised. There were, supposedly, sorcerous alarms on it. There was an easy way to disable them: draw Lady Teldra, strike at it, and let her handle the rest (handle, you see, is kind of a joke, because Lady's Teldra's hilt, you know, *handle*, was really Spellbreaker, which—this is dumb, right?). The trouble was, once I drew that blade everyone in the other room would know instantly, and they'd lose interest in chasing jhereg.

So instead I leaned in and gave that bookcase a big hug. In case you've forgotten, I was wearing a Phoenix Stone amulet.

Then I pulled books off the bottom shelf, carefully, keeping them in neat stacks. I spotted the compartment built into the back of the shelf, studied it, flipped the catch, and looked inside. Hoping I'd disabled everything nasty, I reached in and took the ring. My hand came out with as many fingers as it had gone in with, and I had the ring. I closed the compartment and replaced the books.

Then I slipped out of the room, hugging the wall again.

"*Okay, Loiosh. Out.*"

"*We're no longer speaking, Boss.*"

"*Yeah, yeah, whatever. You know you enjoyed it.*"

I made it out onto the street. I walked for a quarter of a mile or so, then Loiosh and Rocza landed on my shoulders. Loiosh bit my ear, but not very hard. I patted my pouch.

"*Well, you got it,*" said Loiosh.

"*Yeah.*"

"*Is that about everything?*"

"*No,*" I said.

He didn't say anything; he didn't have to.

He and Rocza left my shoulders and started circling above

me. I made it back to Kragar's office, inspected the ring, and wondered if I'd been played. It really did look like a plain, unadorned platinum ring. No marks, nothing.

I shrugged. I'd find out eventually.

I put the ring back in my pouch; with any luck, the same amulet that kept anyone from finding me would keep anyone from finding it. With no luck, I was dead anyway.

I found a chair, sat down, and stretched out.

"You see, Loiosh, here's the thing you don't get. All—"

"This is going to be good."

"Shut up. All of those Jhereg bosses—all of them, every one as long as the Jhereg has existed—what they loved was building their organization. Becoming more powerful. Becoming more secure. Becoming more wealthy."

"I'm missing something, Boss."

"Becoming, not being."

"Oh."

"The trick is, I'm not sure if the Demon sees that; it might matter a lot."

"Is that what you meant about making the Jhereg see things like a Hawk?"

"I keep forgetting you pay attention," I said. "Yeah, I need the Demon to focus on the details, and miss the big picture."

I picked up volume nine of the Imperial trade laws and tried to read them, but I couldn't concentrate.

"What is it, Boss?"

"Kragar."

"Yeah, I know."

"It was a close thing. I could see from Aliera's face how close it was."

"You should eat something, Boss."

"Just did."

"That was hours ago, before the excitement."

"Not hungry, Loiosh."

"All right."

I hadn't admitted to myself how scared I was when I saw Kragar lying in a pool of blood; or when I saw the way Aliera looked at him. There's no point in dwelling on that stuff. I picked up the heavy legal book, again tried to concentrate, again put it down.

Too much on my mind, I decided. Too much at once. It wasn't just how seeing Kragar like that had affected me; it was also the fact that I was involved in two major projects at once: killing Terion, and getting the Jhereg off my back. When I'd taken on projects in the past, I mean big projects, like an assassination, I'd only done one at a time. Now I was finding out why.

"We should get something to eat, Loiosh."

"Good idea, Boss."

An hour later, Deragar was back with bread, cheese, wine, and river-fried herring, which I gobbled down furiously. He joined us, and looked pleased when I complimented him on the cheese selection. He talked about it for a while, but I don't remember what he said.

As I ate, I studied him. He had broad shoulders, a square head with barely a noble's point, and astonishingly thick wrists. He looked like someone who could break any bone you cared to name with his bare hands. In a strange way, he reminded me of a guy named Sticks I used to know. Not physically, but in the sense of always having a sort of half-asleep look that I knew was deceptive. He also reminded me of someone else, but I couldn't quite figure out who.

"Deragar," I said. "Did you ever work for me, a few years ago? I don't remember you."

"Not directly," he said. "I was collecting for Gasto until, you know."

"Yeah, I know. So, how did you end up with this job? I mean, helping me."

He looked at me.

"Oh," I said. "Right."

"The job is keeping an eye on you."

"Of course."

"For your protection, I mean."

"Yeah. What happened to Gasto?"

"Throat cut first, then—"

"No, I don't mean that. I mean, why? Who'd he piss off?"

"I don't know. Maybe just a power struggle. Might've been personal. Never heard."

"All right."

Around then one of Kragar's people came in and handed me a sealed piece of paper. I looked at him and waited. "Just delivered," he said.

"From?"

"A messenger."

"Uh. All right."

On the outside was written "V. Taltos" in expensive blue ink. I broke the seal, unfolded it, and read: "Come. I can help." The signature was a stylized dzur. I'd seen it before.

"*Trap, Boss?*"

"Nope."

"*How can you be—*"

"Loiosh. No one, I mean, *no one is going to be so stupid as to fake this.*"

"*Uh. Yeah.*"

If I knew anything, I knew the note was real.

Leaving me only the problem of figuring out how I was going to make my way to Dzur Mountain, the home of Sethra Lavode.

10

Making Trouble
or
Making Progress

Teleportation was the obvious choice, and only required doing what I'd been doing an awful lot lately—removing the
amulet that kept me invisible to any Jhereg looking for me,
and immune to anyone trying to cast a spell on me. Now, admittedly, I also had Lady Teldra to protect me from random
spells meant to kill me from a distance. Still, if I kept taking
the amulet off, someone was going to come up with a way to
sneak past her. Which meant I needed to be wearing that
amulet. And I was beginning to get irritated about the whole
thing. I very much wanted this plan to work, if for no other
reason than I could get rid of that bloody damned amulet.
Even having it hanging around my neck was starting to annoy me.

I came up with several ways to reach Dzur Mountain
without removing the amulet; unfortunately, they required
between three days and three weeks to work. Deragar said he
hadn't made much progress on finding how to take a shot at
Terion, but had left some messages and hoped to be getting
word. I grunted and continued trying to figure a safe and fast

way to get to Dzur Mountain, which was tricky because there
was no such thing.

Oh. Unless—

I smiled. Why not?

"Deragar," I said. "Feel like teleporting to Castle Black?"

"Not really," he said. "I prefer my skin whole."

I removed a ring from my pouch—no, not the ring I'd just
acquired, the other ring: the one with my seal as an Imperial
nobleman—and handed it to him. "Show them this. It's proof
you came from me."

"And that will matter to them—why?"

"Trust me."

"All right. Then what?"

"Then get a message to Lord Morrolan."

He listened; I told him the message. He looked confused,
but repeated it to make sure he had it right. "Anything else?"
he said.

"When you're done, ask him to teleport you back here.
It'll be less traumatic that way."

"I can trust him to bring me here, and not to somewhere
a mile deep in the ocean-sea?"

"Yes," I said. "Probably. Almost certainly. Yeah."

He looked doubtful, but nodded and headed out. I settled
in to wait.

"*Okay, Boss. Not bad.*"

"*Glad to hear it.*"

You see, the Lord Morrolan e'Drien, who is such an ar-
rogant little shit that he calls his home Castle Black, has a
tower full of windows, and each window can be a doorway
to wherever he wants, including to some places that don't
exist in the same reality as the rest of us—and don't ask me

what I mean by that; I'm quoting the Necromancer. The point is, it isn't teleportation, it isn't even sorcery. It's something else. I'd used those windows before. And Morrolan, for whatever reason, was usually inclined to help me out when I needed it.

It was less than half an hour after Deragar had left that the air in front of me started shimmering. In a few seconds, there was a man-sized ring of golden sparks in front of me. I stepped into it.

Yeah, remember the part where I said it couldn't be a trap? What happened next will take some explanation.

The point is, I stepped into the shower of golden sparks and then things happened fast. Too fast for me to react to. Even too fast for Loiosh.

I hate it when that happens.

Here's what I figured out later: Picture, if you will, this idiot Easterner stepping through a necromantic gate, mind in the clouds, no weapons ready. My first warning was that unmistakable feeling that indicates the presence of a Morganti weapon. If you've never felt it, you're lucky. It's like a horrible, gray oppression settles over you; but that isn't right, it doesn't settle, it smacks you down, it beats at you. There isn't anything else like it.

At the same moment, Loiosh screamed, "*Boss!*"

But of course, by then, it was already too late.

Apparently, some bright fellow had figured out that if I wanted to travel without removing the amulet, a necromantic gate would be the only way to do it; confirmed that Morrolan had such a thing; and decided, correctly, that sooner or later I'd use it. I had one thing right: No one had forged a note from Sethra. Instead, they'd watched Morrolan's tower, waiting for a gate to open between there and Kragar's office. Then they opened their own gate over it, and I stepped into it.

Well, it isn't that simple, really. It required a skilled necromancer. I hate to think what it had cost. But it was money well spent, in the sense that when I appeared, there was a guy with a Morganti sword, and he was in a good position to put a permanent, final, all-done-with-it-forever shine on me.

I had enough time to see the sword, and to get a vague impression of someone tall, dressed in gray and black.

I had enough time to see the blur as he took a step in toward me and swung, cutting down and to the left.

I had enough time to realize what was about to happen.

I had enough time to feel terror such I had never before felt in my life—the kind of terror where, however much practice you've had, you freeze. Your limbs lock, you can't breathe, and you can't even formulate the wish to be elsewhere; but you have the strong desire to be curled up on the ground.

It's strange how, at moments like this, you seem able to experience so many different and contradictory emotions at once. And while you don't have time to move, you have time to be aware of each emotion you're feeling.

There was terror, of course, like I said.

And anger right next to it—at the Jhereg for killing me, and at myself for getting caught, and, stupidly, at Morrolan for having had the means whereby I was set up.

And, most peculiarly, a sense of calm that was so strong it washed over everything else, and seemed as if it came from a place inside of me that I'd never been aware of before. I had time to feel a certain relaxation steal over me before—

The stupid little blade—a longsword in form, but tiny in

essence—is rushing at me, its greed and hunger a wave of red, but the change to the pale green of fear is so abrupt I'm tempted to laugh, though of course I do not. I brush it away and for a long, long quarter of a second I fasten myself around its metaphorical throat, just to show it what I can do. There is a shapeless, pulsing mass of life behind it, and I admit to myself that it tempts me—I am still weak from my recent exertions—but HE was upset the last time, so I let the hunger pass over and through me and I move just a little, and a coolness washes over me; I feel good about what I have done, and what I have refrained from doing.

And time holds still; time doesn't breathe. There is no motion, no sound—everything is holding, there is a waiting time as if waiting were the only existence, as if the universe itself were nothing but the space between events, and would last forever that way. And in this waiting time there is an adjustment that is not physical, or emotional, or spiritual; it is an adjustment in mood and in the way sensations might be experienced. The timeless time reforms itself, and I am here and there, and HE is there and here, and we are forever separate, unique, apart—and one being at a level too profound to express. It is our very inseparability that makes us forever distinct; the uniqueness of our beings that keeps us together. And with that realization, motion starts up again, slowly, grinding, unsure of where to go.

At that moment, a thought forms, as if in words; directionless, though the mind behind the voice is an old friend: Sethra sends her regards, it says, and pleasure washes through me that I have not been forgotten.

I swung Lady Teldra to point to the sorceress who stood, frozen, behind and over the body that still clutched the Morganti longsword in its lifeless hands.

"What foul sorcery is this?" she said.

"Pretty standard foul sorcery; nothing special."

"Okay," she said. "Just checking."

"There's blood on my boots," I said. "Do you know how much I hate blood on my boots? It really, really pisses me off. Scrub, scrub, scrub, that's what I'll be doing. Or I'll just have to get new boots. Days waiting for them. You just *had* to get blood on my boots, didn't you? Oh, and did I mention that I hate getting blood on my boots?"

"You picked the wrong line of work then," she said. "Are you going to use that thing, or just keep it in my face for the next week?"

"I'm still deciding," I said.

Okay, I admit it: I was impressed. Acting brave when someone might be about to kill you takes something. The same act when someone is holding a Morganti blade takes a lot more. And to pull it off when staring down the pointy end of a Great Weapon is, well, I couldn't do it.

Okay, maybe I kind of did it once, but I was really mad that time. In any case, I was impressed.

"What's your name?"

"Disaka."

"Was this what it seemed? You were hired by the meat? A straight-up business deal?"

She nodded.

"When?"

"Apparently they took a shot at you a few days ago that didn't work. After that."

"How did you do it?"

She opened her mouth, closed it again, glanced at Lady Teldra, then shrugged. "He told me about Morrolan's windows, so I set up a necromantic illusion, and redirected the energy for the transfer spell to myself."

"Must have been a hell of an illusion."

"It's why I had to be here to maintain it."

"You were just waiting for the windows to activate?"

"Yes. For the last two days."

"What did he pay you?"

"A lot."

"Where are we? I mean, physically."

Her brows furrowed for a moment; the "windows" vanished, replaced by dark wooden walls, full of knots. The room narrowed, and there was a table pushed against the far wall, chairs stacked beside it. "It seems familiar," I said.

"Back room of the Blue Flame."

"Ah, right."

She stared down the length of Lady Teldra. My arm was getting tired, at which point I realized that she had shaped herself as a significantly heavier weapon than I usually use. I lowered her. "All right, go," I said.

She nodded, and managed to keep the relief off her face, and even to turn her back to me as she left the room. If she was anything like me, she'd go off somewhere private and have a good, long breakdown. She was certainly entitled.

I sheathed Lady Teldra.

"*Boss.*"

"Yeah?"

"*That was scary.*"

"Yeah."

"*What happened?*"

"*What did it look like to you?*"

"Like you moved faster than it is possible for anyone to move. Like the sword was drawing your arm. How did it seem to you, Boss?"

"Like—I don't know. Like I was someone else. Like I went somewhere else."

"You did, Boss. For a minute there, I couldn't find you. I didn't much care for it. Can you not do that anymore?"

"I can't promise that, Loiosh. I was me and talking to me, and I was her."

"Her? Who her?"

"Lady Teldra. The one who used to be a person. The one who was killed."

I opened the door. Rocza flew out, then back to me. I walked through the Blue Flame, ignoring the stares from patrons and staff. At the door, Loiosh and Rocza both flew out, and, on their word, I stepped out and walked back toward Kragar's office.

"So, do we try again, Boss?"

"Yeah, I think we should—"

I stopped, right there, and leaned against a wall. I didn't lose my last meal, but I felt like I was about to. Then I started shaking. Then I cursed, silently but with great sincerity, about standing there out on the street unable to move.

I felt Loiosh, on full alert.

I knew from experience that the more I tried to rush through the shaking horrors, the longer they'd last. I stood there on the street and waited it out, trusting to luck and Loiosh. People—that is, Dragaerans—walked around me, carefully not looking at me.

After what felt like longer than it probably was, I was able to walk again. I got back to Kragar's office, keeping my pace steady and my face expressionless as I made it back into the space set aside for me, then collapsed against a wall, sat on the floor, and did some more shaking.

You know. Like you do.

It went on for a while. Then I walked out, found Deragar, and asked after Kragar. He was mending. As we were talking, someone I didn't know came up and said, "Lord Taltos, there's a Dragonlord requesting to speak with you."

"A . . . did he give a name?"

"Morrolan."

"All right. Invite him up."

"I did. He declined."

I nodded. "Of course he did. He'd never walk into a Jhereg office. Unless he felt like it. All right. I'll go down."

"Boss, are you sure it's really Morrolan?"

"Yes. Lady Teldra recognizes Blackwand."

"Lady . . . all right."

I headed down before Loiosh could think of questions I wouldn't be able to answer.

"I waited for you, Vlad," were the first words out of his mouth. I suddenly wanted to laugh, but I fought it down, because once I started I'd probably become hysterical.

"Yeah," I said. "Sorry. Something came up."

He looked like he was about to ask what, but instead his eyes flicked over me; I'm not sure what he was seeing, or concluding from what he saw, but he said, "The Jhereg took a shot at you, Vlad?"

"Yeah. They tapped into your tower enough to direct me somewhere else when I tried to use it. They were waiting for me."

"They used my tower?"

"Yeah. Rude of them, don't you think?"

"Who?"

"He's kind of dead now."

"The sorcerer?"

"No, I let her go."

"Who is she?"

"No idea."

"Vlad—"

"She said her name was Disaka, but under the circumstances, I doubt she was telling the truth."

He glared at me. Then, "I can trace it. Or have the Necromancer trace it. How did you escape?"

"The Necromancer," I repeated.

"What?"

"The Necromancer. The Warlock. The Sorceress in Green. The Blue Fox. All of these people with a name that starts with 'the.' It isn't fair. Why don't I get a name that starts with 'the'?"

He suggested one.

"Now, is that nice?"

"Vlad, how did you escape?"

I touched Lady Teldra. "She woke up," I said.

His eyes widened. "Are you sure?"

"Yeah," I said. "On account of, you know, when dealing with weapons that are more powerful than the gods, and that involve a destiny tracing back longer than the Empire, and when you learn things with vague impressions of half-memories in the middle of almost having a Morganti sword shoved into your vitals, it's easy to be sure of things. Why do you ask?"

"Vlad—"

"I think so," I said. "I gave her a message from Sethra and it felt like she heard it, all right?"

"All right."

I couldn't tell what he was thinking or feeling; my guess is he didn't know himself. I said, "Maybe we should go somewhere else?"

Morrolan looked around, his lips curling with distaste. "Yes," he said. "You wanted to go to Dzur Mountain, yes?"

"Yes."

"I'll accompany you."

"All right."

Once more the shimmer of sparks, and we stepped through, and then there was a window in front of me, and I walked through that, and we were in Dzur Mountain. We had arrived just inside a door I recognized as opening out onto the western slopes. From there, I could, if I wanted, get a distant view of Adrilankha on those nights when the Enclouding was high and there were a lot of lights in the city. I'd done that before, just looked.

Morrolan led us in the other direction, and I followed.

I think I'll have to live about as long as Sethra to learn the insides of Dzur Mountain. The odd thing is that, as you negotiate the short, narrow corridors and the unexpected stairways and the back doors to rooms that look like they should only have one door, it always seems as if it's such a small place—as if you should be able to learn it all the first time you're there. It isn't until your third or fourth visit that it starts hitting you how big the mountain is, and the fact you're crawling around inside of it.

I guess Morrolan has a better head for that sort of thing than I do; he took us to a small sitting room where Sethra's servant, Tukko, was stretched out on a sofa. Tukko opened an eye as we came in, saw me, saw Morrolan, and pulled himself grudgingly to a standing position. Then he bowed a little to Morrolan and said, "I'll let her know."

Morrolan nodded and found a chair; I found another.

We sat there, saying nothing, for about five minutes. Then I heard Sethra's voice: "Well, Vlad. What have you done this time?"

I rose, bowed, and said, "It's more what I'm going to do."

She sat down and so did I. Tukko set a glass of wine next to Morrolan, then gave me one. He looked at Sethra, who barely shook her head; then he twitched and shuffled out.

"All right," she said. "Let's hear it."

I told her pretty much what I'd told Kiera about my plan for the new business deal for the Jhereg, and eavesdropping on psychic communication. She listened intently; Morrolan shifted back and forth a few times as I spoke, and made various sounds that could be interpreted as disgust, disbelief, or disdain. When I'd finished, he said, "Not a bad idea."

I studied his face to see if he was just messing with me. He looked like he meant it.

I told Sethra, "You said you could help."

She nodded. "What do you need?"

"Um," I said. "I hadn't exactly thought about it. You said you could help—"

"I can. But what do you need?"

"First of all, a good night's sleep."

"I can help with that," she said, smiling a little. "What else do you need?"

It was, I suddenly realized, another one of Sethra's maneuvers. She wanted me to think of something, because anything I figured out on my own was going to stick with me better than stuff she just told me. She was right, as usual, and it irritated me, as usual.

I ran down the list: Kiera's lockpick, the passage from the book on Imperial trade laws, a hawk's egg, the ring, the euphonium, and the other stuff. I went through the whole plan in my head, piece by piece. It took a while, but they were patient.

"Not seeing it," I told Sethra eventually. "How about, you know, a hint?"

"Vlad, do you think I'm playing games?"

"Of course you're playing games, Sethra. You're always playing games. Everything you've done as long as I've known you has been a game of one sort or another. You've been around so long, the only way to keep yourself from going crazy is to make everything into a game, and then play the game as if it were life and death. I get that. I don't mind it. That doesn't mean it isn't serious. Now, how about a hint?"

For a second I thought she was going to blow up at me, but then she frowned. "You may be right."

"Yeah, that'll happen from time to time. Now, as I said, how about a hint?"

She smiled. "All right. A hint, then: What's the part of your plan that's still vague and unformed?"

"None of it. Oh, except right. How to get back up if I go over the cliff. How can you help with that?"

"I know an artificer who can show you how to build what you need. Or a stonecutter, if that's how you want to go."

I stared at her. "Sethra, how could you know about that? I haven't told anyone—"

"I wasn't sure until now. But from knowing how you

think, and from the rumors I've heard, and then with what Daymar told me, well, it just seemed likely."

"Wait, with what Daymar told you? When?"

"Today. He was very excited about that bit of work you had him do. So I put that together with—"

I swore. "Any idea who else he's told?"

"No one. I impressed upon him the need to not talk about it to anyone but me."

"Oh. Well, good. Thanks."

"You're welcome."

"But even knowing that, you had to guess—"

"Why you wanted that location? Yes. As I say, I wasn't sure until now."

"You're looking smug," I said.

"And with reason, don't you think?"

I shook my head. "You continue to astound me."

"I'll be sad when I no longer do," she said.

"Yeah, because it'll mean I'm dead. Well, thank you."

"Which way are you going?"

"Stonecutter."

She nodded, found paper and wrote, then handed me a small note with a name and an address on it. Then she said, "There's something I need from you."

I nodded and waited.

"Okay, not true. Something I want from you."

"A subtle distinction, but important. All right, I'm listening."

"I want to try something with Lady Teldra."

I studied her pale, angular face, framed in dark hair. Sometimes, like now, her eyes appeared to absorb light, rather than reflecting it; it was sort of creepy.

"Try what?"

"Reaching her."

"Um. May I ask why?"

"Because Iceflame is bound up with the fate of the Empire, and Lady Teldra is bound up with the fate of the gods, and it will be useful for me to have a hint about how those will interact."

"Do I want to understand that, Sethra?"

"No. But you do want me to try reaching Lady Teldra."

"Not without me there," I said.

"Of course. You can continue holding her. In fact, it'd be much better if you did."

"All right, then. Oh, and I delivered your message."

"Good."

I took a deep breath and let it out slowly. "Now?"

"If you would."

I stood up and drew her; she took her original form—a long knife with too small a crossguard, and a hilt that was too light to balance properly; a knife that felt absolutely right in my hand for no reason that I'd ever been able to figure out. I suppose Great Weapons are like that.

Sethra also stood, and drew Iceflame. Morrolan tensed a little, and I wondered how Blackwand was reacting to all of this.

I'd been in the room before when Iceflame was taken from its sheath. I remember the feeling—like standing unarmed in front of a dzur whose hot breath and huge, sharp teeth were right in your face, and who gave every sign of being extremely displeased with you. Okay, well, no, I've never been in exactly that situation with a dzur, but you get the idea.

The point is, this time was different—like being twenty feet from a dzur who was sleeping. You don't want to move, you wish you didn't have to breathe, but you feel like maybe, if you're careful, you won't die right now.

Lady Teldra, that was the difference.

Sethra approached and extended Iceflame. "Cross the blades," she said.

"Look," I said. "I mean, I know you're you, and I'm only me. But—"

"Yes, Vlad, I know what I'm doing."

"All right."

I glanced at Morrolan, hoping to judge something by his expression. If he was looking terrified, I'd feel my own nervousness was more reasonable, I guess. In fact, his expression reminded me uncomfortably of Daymar when confronting something that promised an interesting result. The association didn't help, so I turned my focus back to Sethra. She was waiting patiently, Iceflame held out in front of her, not quite in a guard position, but close.

I took in a breath, let it out, then touched Iceflame's blade with Lady Teldra's.

Sethra picked herself up from the far wall.

All around me, the mountain shook, and I was convinced that I'd have fallen over if I'd had legs.

I felt awful. I mean, really really awful, in both senses of the term.

"*I didn't mean to do that," I said.*

She picked herself up, wide-eyed, and said, "Vlad?"

"Sethra," I said. "What happened?"

"I was going to ask you that. Did you just go flying across the room, and did the whole mountain tremble?"

She seemed shaken; seeing her shaken shook me. We both looked at Morrolan, who said, "Yes."

"That's what happened, then," I told Sethra. I could hear my own voice quivering, so I decided not to speak any more. I wondered if my legs would support me yet.

"Boss?"

"You can't blame me for this one, Loiosh. It was Sethra's idea."

"Sethra," I said, "what did you expect to happen?" So much for not speaking any more.

"I was hoping to get a feel for Godslayer."

"Her name," I said, "is—"

"Lady Teldra," she said. "I'm sorry."

I nodded.

Sethra said, "When you said you didn't mean to do that—"

"I didn't."

"I believe you. But—"

"No, I mean, I didn't say that." I got to my feet and made it to a chair.

"Oh," she said. She sat down next to me. "Interesting," she added, which has to go down as one of the great understatements of all time.

Yeah. Interesting.

I put Lady Teldra into her sheath.

I didn't want to think too much about what had just happened, or about how I hadn't died earlier, or, well, I didn't want to think about much of anything except the task I'd set myself. It seemed like the universe wanted me to be thinking about other stuff.

"The universe," I told Sethra, "is welcome to commit various improbable sexual acts on itself."

"What?"

"Nothing."

Morrolan coughed, and we both looked at him. "Yes?" I said.

"I wish to suggest," he said, speaking slowly, "that whatever you did that flung you both against opposite walls and made the mountain shake, you not do again."

"Good thinking," I muttered.

11

Making Progress
or
Making Threats

"I don't have to," said Sethra. "I got what I wanted."

"Thrown against a wall?" I said. "I could have done that."

"No, you couldn't."

"What did you get?" said Morrolan.

Sethra looked at him, and her eyes were glistening. My heart suddenly started hammering as if I were in danger. I had never seen Sethra Lavode with tears in her eyes, nor had I ever thought to see such a thing, and it shook me like the mountain just had.

Morrolan met her eyes.

If at that moment someone had asked me what I wanted most in the world, getting out of trouble with the Jhereg would have been my second answer; my first would have been to not be in the room. But standing up and walking out felt a little too awkward.

"Teldra is really in there," said Morrolan.

Sethra nodded.

"We knew that already," he said.

"I know, but . . ."

"All right," said Morrolan, and looked away. It seemed like he was working very hard not to look at me, and I was fine with that. There was a silence that I have to record as among the most uncomfortable ten seconds of my life—and remember that I've died a couple of times.

"Okay," said Morrolan at last. "I'm sorry. It just hit me."

"I know," said Sethra. "Me, too."

I thought the wall at the far end of the room was distressingly bare. It needed some art. What sort of art would go there? Maybe a ship at sea. Storm-tossed. Yeah, that would be good.

"All right," said Morrolan, and I could see him put the whole matter on a shelf in his mind for later consideration. I wish I could do that. I guess I can do that. He said, "Let's talk about Vlad's problem."

"Are you planning to help me too?"

"Of course not," he said. "Now, what do you need?" There was a smirk hanging around the edge of his lips, but he kept it under wraps.

"As I said, I need rest. I have everything else pretty well covered. Especially now that Sethra's pointed me to an artificer."

"You have everything else you need for whatever it is you're going to do?"

"No, not quite. I've been working with Daymar to collect things."

"I'm sorry."

"Thanks."

"What else do you need?"

"Something to make a thick cloud of smoke that doesn't get blown away by the first gust of wind someone conjures up."

"How big an area?"

"Not big. Diameter of forty feet should do it."

"What form?"

"Something Loiosh can drop from a claw."

"How long do you need it to last?"

"As long as possible."

"Anything more than a couple of minutes would be difficult."

"That'll have to do, then."

"Mind telling me why you need it?"

I shrugged. "Doing the spell is hard, but I should be able to manage it with the hawk's egg and the sorcerous euphonium. But—"

"The which?" said Morrolan

"Never mind. Another thing. But there are ways things could go wrong, and I'm trying to come up with a means of staying alive if they do. Having a big cloud of smoke at hand might be useful."

"All right. I can get that."

"Thanks."

"What else?"

"A cloak."

"But you have—oh. What's special about this one?"

"It needs to have a stiffened frame."

"Vlad, if you're trying to fly without sorcery, I can tell you—"

"Not fly; just not land so hard if I jump off a cliff. I probably won't need it. I have an enchanted lockpick, and I can't think of any way this will play out that I'll need both of them; but I'm trying not to take chances. I'd rather not say more because if I tell you, you'll laugh at me, call me an idiot, and refuse to have anything more to do with it."

"All right," he said. "A cloak that will slow a fall. All you need is a cloak with reinforced hems and throat closure, and a little padding or stiffening around the neck."

"All right."

"Does it need any other special features?"   ·

He was asking about places to conceal weapons, and as he didn't approve of concealing weapons, I allowed as to how that wasn't important in this.

"I'll take care of it," he said. "I know someone."

"Thank you."

"When do you need it?"

"Soon. Tomorrow or early—what day is it?"

"Farmday."

"Or early Endweek."

He nodded. "That won't be a problem," he said.

"Thanks," I said.

"Anything else?"

I shook my head.

"*Boss?*"

"*There's nothing else I'm willing to ask Morrolan for.*"

"*If you say so.*"

"Vlad," said Sethra.

"Yes?"

"Are you going to survive this?"

I hesitated, and decided she deserved an honest answer. "I need to be out and about to set this thing up, and there are a lot of Jhereg after me. For the most part, the ones who know enough about me to be a threat aren't the ones who are willing to take any shot that presents itself; and the ones who are willing to take a shot, I can catch by surprise. But I don't know how long this state of affairs will hold. I need a day or two. I think I have a pretty good chance."

"You know, Vlad," said Sethra, "one of us could hang around with you. Sort of help keep you alive."

"There are things I'm doing that I couldn't do if you or Morrolan were there."

"All right. Is it really better than running, Vlad?"

"Obviously, I think it is, Sethra."

"All right."

Morrolan shifted uncomfortably, but didn't speak.

I told him, "Yeah, I know. I'm being stubborn, and I'm being stupid."

"You're being an Easterner," said Sethra.

"A Dragaeran wouldn't do that?"

"A Dzurlord would," said Morrolan. "Or a Dragonlord."

I said, "If you're saying I'm failing to behave like a Teckla, that isn't a good way to change my actions."

"I'm not sure I want to change your actions," said Sethra.

"So, you like the idea of trying to end this?"

"If there's a reasonable chance of it working."

I didn't ask her to define "reasonable."

She chewed her lip. After a moment I said, "Well? What is it?"

"I wish I could help more," she said.

I stood up and walked to the far end of the room, then came back. On a shelf to my right was a display of ceramic goblets of many colors, from many cultures, all of them imprinted with a symbol I'd never seen before. No doubt it was important and significant for something. I studied them for a little while. I noticed that I was drinking out of one of them now—a sort of deep purple mug, slightly tall and thin, with an elaborate handle.

I drank some more wine and turned around. Sethra and Morrolan were having some quiet conversation that didn't concern me. I yawned. It hit me around then how very, very long it had been since I'd slept in a place where I was both comfortable and safe at the same time. It had been a long while. And I was more tired than I had any business being.

Aloud I said, "About that room—"

"Of course," she said. Then, "Tukko, show Lord Taltos to a room, please."

He didn't look at me; just turned and led the way. He shuffled rather than walked, and didn't appear to be hurrying; but I never had to wait for him. We walked down several short hallways, and eventually came to a door. He opened it and grunted at me.

I said, "I've never quite figured it out. Do you prefer to be called Chaz, or Tukko?"

In a voice like gravel, he said, "Depends who you're talking to."

"I mean, you."

"They're both me."

"I don't get it," I said.

"I know," he said, and turned back the way he came. I stepped out of his way, but a little too slowly, and his shoulder brushed mine. Lady Teldra twitched in her sheath—I mean, really twitched; it wasn't like she was trying to leap free, it was more like the whole sheath jumped and twisted against my leg. At the same time, Rocza leapt from my shoulder, flew a few feet behind me, then came back. Out of the corner of my eye I saw that her head was moving and swaying furiously.

Tukko took a step back, his beady eyes wider than I'd ever seen them before. Rocza settled down on my shoulder with a halfhearted hiss.

"Who *are* you?" I said.

"Rest well, Lord Taltos," he said, saying my name as if it were vaguely distasteful. I watched him as he shuffled his way down the hall.

"*Boss?*"

"*I have no idea. What was up with Rocza?*"

"*I don't know. It isn't something she can communicate about.*"

"*What can you get? It may be important.*"

"*Just that she felt like something hit her.*"

"*Physically?*"

"*No.*"

I went into the room. Last time I stayed there, I was dead; or rather, had been recently. I looked around. The water pitcher was a blue and white mosaic, and the jhereg in the painting was still holding its own against the dzur. I have to assume I got undressed and climbed into the bed, but I don't remember anything about it.

I woke up and the bed was soft and warm. Very soft, very warm. I didn't know what time it was. I didn't care. With a happy sigh, I went back to sleep.

The second time I woke up I felt just as good—you need to go for years sleeping on the ground, or in flophouses, or on a pile of bedding in the back of someone's office, to appreciate just how good a bed can feel. If I'd stayed there another five minutes, I might have stayed there forever, so I got up.

The triumph of willpower: let none say I am weak.

Sometime during the night, someone had crept in and filled the basin with water, and put an enchantment on it to keep it hot. And brought a chamber pot. There was also soap—a very unusual, soft, pleasant soap—and a towel. Life was as close to perfect as I could imagine it being just then.

"It was Tukko."

"What?"

"Who came in with the water and the soap."

"I'd have been happier not knowing he was in my room while I was asleep."

"Sorry, Boss."

I got dressed, and spent some time making sure various knives, darts, and shuriken were where they were supposed to be, by which time Loiosh had breakfast on his mind. So did I, for that matter.

I opened the door, and there was a note pinned to the wall just opposite it. *Vlad*, it read, *there's breakfast set out in the small dining room. Sethra. P.S. Turn left, then take the first right, and it's the first door on the right. S.*

I did those things, and found bread, cheese, a bowl of apples, and a pitcher of iced sweetened coffee. I sat at the small table and had breakfast, feeding cheese to the jhereg from time to time. I wondered how I was going to get back to Adrilankha, but I didn't worry about it a great deal; Sethra would have arranged something.

As I was considering that, Morrolan walked in and tossed me a bundle of cloth. I opened it up and looked at it. There was a glass bulb wrapped up in it.

Some things just naturally lend themselves to sorcery. There's stuff I don't know—there is a *lot* I don't know—but if you want to make a lot of smoke, that's pretty easy. Start a fire, get it smoking, direct it into whatever object you want to use to store it, and seal it.

It gets harder if you want the smoke to expand a certain amount, then stay there in spite of any breezes. I have no idea how to do that, but I'm told it isn't difficult.

It certainly wasn't difficult for Morrolan.

"That was fast," I said.

He nodded.

"Can you show me how the cloak works?"

He did, and I got it, and that's about all the time I'm going to spend on it, because, in the event, I might as well not have bothered. I'm including it, because it may matter to you that Morrolan procured it—it matters to me—but I never actually used it.

"Were you up all night?"

"No, my tailor was."

"And it's even Jhereg gray."

He smiled. "Seemed appropriate."

"I owe you," I said.

"You say that as if this is the first or only time."

"Bite me."

"Would you care to return to Adrilankha?"

"The windows?"

He nodded.

"Yes, please. Unless you want some breakfast first."

"No thanks. I've vowed that food shall not pass my lips until this matter is ended."

"What?"

"I said I've already eaten."

"Okay."

A necromantic gate outlined in sparkling gold appeared before us. Morrolan vanished into it, and, a few seconds later, so did I.

We didn't hang around his tower. He indicated the window that showed my temporary quarters in Kragar's office and said, "I'll be in touch, Vlad."

I nodded and stepped through, and this time there were no surprises. I prefer it that way.

I went out and looked for Deragar, but he wasn't in yet. There was someone sitting at the desk I still thought of, a little sadly, as Melestav's. I asked the guy at the desk how Kragar was, and he grunted something generally positive-sounding. There was no klava, but someone had brought in a steam-jug of coffee, and there was honey for it. I drank some and missed my klava.

I had another glass in spite of everything, and while I was drinking it Deragar came in. I led him into the little storage room I was using, and we pulled out a couple of chairs.

"You made it back, I see."

"That time." He passed me back my signet ring.

I nodded. "Figure anything out?"

"About what?"

I looked at him.

"Yeah," he said. "The key is a guy named Chesha."

"He's handling Terion's security?"

Deragar nodded. "He could set him up if he wanted to."

"Any reason to think he wants to?"

"Maybe. I know a guy who knows a tag who thinks Chesha might be wanting to make a move of some kind someday."

"Would you mind being a little more vague?"

"Sure. I might know a guy—"

"Shut up."

He smiled; I guess my impression that he had no sense of humor was wrong. I had mixed feelings about this. He said, "Did you learn wisecracking from the boss, or did he learn from you?"

"We both learned from an ancient Serioli master. Anything else? Any other weak spots?"

"Not that I saw."

"Well, okay. See if Chesha is willing to meet with me. Try to convince him."

"Do you have a preferred method?"

"Use your powers of persuasion."

"If I do that, he won't be in any condition to help us."

"Not those powers of persuasion."

"They're the only ones I have."

"Tell him someone wants to meet with him, discreetly. Tell him it may be to his advantage, and that we'll make sure it's safe."

"Safe for him?"

"Safe for us both."

He frowned. "That's hard to do."

"I know."

"Got any ideas for it?"

I shrugged, thought about it. "He picks the place, you pick the set-up, he decides on the amount of protection, you pick where they are."

He nodded. "Yeah, he might go for that."

"If not, we're up for any reasonable alternative."

"Reasonable alternative," he repeated, as if the words tasted funny. "Where did an Easterner learn to talk so good?"

"I have a lot of smart friends. They made me read books."

"What do I tell him about why you want to meet?"

"You don't tell him it's me; you tell him it's your principal."

"My principal."

"Yeah."

"And when he asks who that is?"

"Be mysterious."

"And when he asks what it's about?"

"Be even more mysterious."

"And if he insists on knowing?"

"Give him an evasive answer. And twenty gold."

Deragar whistled.

"The mystery should intrigue him. And the gold will help. If the gold turns out to be unnecessary you can keep it."

"And if it is necessary?"

"We'll work something out."

"All right. Do you need any lead time?"

"No. If he wants to meet in an hour, I can do that. But it needs to be in the next day or two. I'm kind of on a deadline."

"I'll do what I can."

"Good enough."

"Smart friends, huh?"

"Yeah."

"Books."

"Yeah."

"Got it."

He left the room, closing the door softly behind him. I squeezed my eyes shut and leaned my head back, opened them again and exhaled slowly.

Then I waited.

I bantered with Loiosh a little, let him and Rocza out for a late-morning fly, let them back in, waited.

A couple of hours had gone by when Deragar came back. "You know," he said, "if you didn't have all that stuff blocking psychic contact, my feet wouldn't hurt so much."

"I'll calculate that into your bonus."

"Good answer."

"What did you find out?"

"He'll meet with you."

"Good answer. When?"

He paused, presumably to check the time. "An hour and twenty-three minutes."

"What are the arrangements?"

"Three each. One outside, two inside at a table just outside of the private room. Same table for all four, so we can have a good stare-down. We're doing a little dance to make sure everyone follows the rules."

"Outside the room. He must be confident he can handle himself."

"Well," said Deragar. "He can."

"I know. Where is it happening?"

"A place called the Frozen Globe, just north of the docks."

"I know the area. All right, good."

"Should I find some people?"

"Yeah."

"How many?"

"You and two others. We're playing this straight."

"Think he will?"

"No idea."

"What if he doesn't?"

"We'll improvise."

"Improvise."

"Yeah."

"Books."

"Yeah."

"All right."

"What about us, Boss?"

"What about you? You're why I can risk playing it straight."

"No, where do you want us?"

"Rocza outside, you with me until the meeting starts."

"Then?"

"You wait outside the door."

"Boss—all right."

Deragar collected a couple of toughs and gave them a meeting place not far from where the secret passage let out. I went through the tunnel, met up with them, and we walked down the street, a little parade of Jhereg, looking all, you know, tough and like that. In that area, we didn't call much attention to ourselves.

"Boss?"

"Yeah."

It was about a half-hour walk, so we got there early. It was a nice-looking place—I'd have guessed wheelhouse Orca or higher. Deragar waited with me while his people went in and looked around. They came back out, nodded, and we entered; one of them remaining outside.

Eventually a couple of Jhereg walked in, looked around, saw us, nodded, walked out again. Apparently, he'd sent his people in early. There's so little trust in this world.

I sat down at a table with Deragar and the other guy, whose named turned out to be Nesci. He didn't say much. Neither did Deragar or I, for that matter. I bought us a bottle of wine, but didn't drink much more than half a cup of it.

After a while, I saw Deragar's eyes narrow a little. He was watching the door. He said, "They're here," at the same time Loiosh said it into my mind. I resisted the temptation to turn around. Loiosh said, *"He's talking to the hostess now."*

"All right."

"She's going down the hall, now she's unlocking a door. He's going in."

I stood up, turned around, and followed him into the room. There was a table there of dark wood that had been polished until it gleamed. The hostess lit a fire, though it wasn't all that chilly. The Jhereg glanced at Loiosh, and shook his head.

"Boss."

"Go."

He flew out of the room. Then the hostess left, leaving me alone with the Jhereg seated across the table. He looked at me, and his eyes narrowed. There was only about four feet between us—he really did think highly of himself.

"Lord Chesha?"

"You're Taltos, aren't you?" He pronounced it Tahltoss, and I somehow didn't think he'd much care that he was saying it wrong. From the sound of his voice, he wasn't all that pleased to discover I was the one he'd come to meet. I tried not to be hurt.

"Yeah," I said. "I want to talk to you about—"

"Can you come up with any reason I shouldn't kill you?"

"Well, at least one. You don't have a Morganti blade on you, and without that, you won't get paid."

"You sure I don't have a Morganti blade on me?"

"Well, most people don't, you know, just carry them around as a matter of course."

"You do."

"Yeah, but I'm special."

"What did you want, then?"

"I want you to leave Terion open for me."

"That's not going to happen," he said.

"Well," I said, "let's talk about it."

"There's nothing to—"

"Oh, nonsense. There's always something to talk about."

"I don't talk with—"

"Don't say it. You'll just piss me off. I assume you don't care about gold, or you'd have listened sooner. I assume you aren't personally loyal to him, because no one is. That leaves me wondering just what it is."

"Maybe you should just walk away, right now."

"Or? Do you really want to throw away an opportunity before you even know what it is? Of course, I'm worth a lot of gold, but to collect it, you'd need a Morganti weapon, and we've already established that you don't—"

He reached into his cloak, and, very slowly, removed a long, slim dagger. I knew it was Morganti before it was in sight.

"*Boss?*"

"*I got this.*"

"Of course," I said aloud, speaking to both of them at once, "I might be wrong."

He didn't lunge, he didn't even point it at me; he just held it and said, "Get out of here."

"Or what?" I said. "Or you'll use that? Here and now?" With my left hand, hardly moving, I pulled Lady Teldra about an inch from her sheath. "Because if you want to do it now," I said, "I'm fine with that. Let's get it over with, this terrible thing you're going to do to me."

He caught my eye and held it; I waited.

"Or," I said after what seemed enough time. "We could talk a little first. After a bit more conversation, if you'd like, you can still do those awful things that you have contemplated, and that I can do nothing to prevent, helpless son-of-a-bitch that I am, oh, woe is me."

He held my eye a little longer, then grunted and put the knife away. I pushed Lady Teldra back into her sheath.

"So," he said. "It's true. I'd heard that you had . . ." His voice trailed off as he gestured with his chin.

"Yeah," I said. "Now. What is it that makes it so out of the question for you to leave Terion open?"

"Because," he said, "I don't like you."

"Yeah, I get that a lot. What else?"

"I don't trust you."

"Then you haven't checked up on me as well as I've checked up on Terion. Or you, for that matter."

He stared at me as if his eyes were weapons, which they weren't. I've been glared at by experts, and, whatever else he was good at, his glaring powers didn't come up to scratch.

"All right," he said. "I'll give you one minute. What do you have?"

"What Terion has."

He kept staring.

"You get his area, his connections, his—"

"What makes you think I couldn't have all that if I wanted, just by taking him out myself?"

"Because then everyone would know you had. You'd be that guy who betrayed his boss to get his territory."

"And this way I wouldn't? How do you figure that?"

"You leave me an opening. I take it. I don't take his area. You're positioned to move in. And it doesn't trace back to you."

"How do I leave you an opening without it tracing back to me?"

"We need to work that part out," I said.

He arched an eyebrow and gave me a look in which skepticism was about equally blended with disdain; and I didn't care, because I knew I had him.

"What do you get out of this? You just don't like him?"

"That's part of it. He's been a hole in my boot for a long time, and I'm tired of it. And he just tried to shine a friend of mine. But more important, I'm working on something, and he's liable to get in the way."

"What are you working on?"

"I'm trying to set up a store to sell baskets of none-of-your-fucking-business at wholesale prices."

His lips twitched. "All right."

"So, how does it happen?"

"Is it true what they say? That you have a pet jhereg?"

"I wouldn't call him a pet, exactly. He works with me. What's your point?"

"One of the regulars has a terror of the things; just have it show up, and he'll collapse."

"And the guy who works with him?"

"Can be gotten to."

"Money?"

He shook his head. "I have something on him."

"And making sure it doesn't blow back on you?"

"I'm going to put it on the guy I have something on."

I worked that out. "You were going to shine him anyway, weren't you?"

"Sooner or later."

"Personal?"

"Yeah."

I nodded. "Then we're in?"

"When do you need it."

"In the next day."

He stared at me. "Look—"

"Maybe two."

He continued staring at me, then frowned and said, "Actually, that works out. Can you do it tonight?"

"Tonight?"

"Yeah. This evening."

Served me right, I guess. If I was going to rush him, it was only fair. I took a deep breath and let it out slowly. "Yes," I said.

He nodded. "How do I reach you?"

"Deragar, the guy who set this meet up, will be around. Get him a message and it'll get to me."

"Where?"

"Do you know the Blue Flame?"

"The place where they make the pepper sausage?"

It was almost enough to make me like him. "Yeah," I said. "He'll be there."

"All right. Anything else?"

"No. Want me to leave first?"

He nodded. I stood up and, my shoulder blades only twitching a little, I opened the door and walked out. I made myself walk slowly, both to reassure his people, and because, well, you know, you just don't let on that your shoulder blades are twitching.

12

Making Threats
or
Making Connections

Loiosh flew onto my shoulder, and Deragar, Nesci and the other guy, whose name I never learned, flanked me.

"Rocza says we're clear, Boss."

We stepped out the door, and turned back toward Kragar's office. The return was scarier than getting there, I suppose because I had less to think about. We took the secret way in, in spite of my discomfort at letting others in on it; I just didn't feel like walking back into the front of the office was a good career move at that moment.

As soon as we were back, I told Deragar he needed to head to the Blue Flame and wait until he got a message.

"It's a good place," he said.

I nodded. "Yeah, and order something good. On me."

"I'll be in touch," he said.

"Don't get killed," I told him.

He nodded and left. Not even a smart remark; where was Kragar finding these people? Speaking of Kragar, once Deragar was gone I asked about him. I was told he was doing all

right. I asked if he was out of danger, and was told, "probably."
I loved that.

"*So, what do you think, Loiosh?*"

"*About?*"

"*Will he go through with it, or is he setting me up?*"

"*Fifty-fifty, Boss.*"

"*I think we're a little ahead of that. Not much, maybe. But he
wants the area, and this is his chance to get it.*"

"*If he can trust you enough.*"

"*Yeah.*"

I retreated to my corner and sharpened my knives, just to
be doing something. I suggested we eat something, and Loiosh,
shockingly, agreed. That "shockingly" part was a joke. One
of Kragar's people went down the street and came back with
goose soup. I mean, it was called soup, but there wasn't much
broth in it—mostly goose and vegetables and some really sharp
spices and noodles that stayed crisp in spite of the liquid.
Loiosh expressed strong approval, although he let me know
that Rocza was a bit uncertain about the spicing. I said she
was just weak, but I don't think Loiosh passed that on.

I finished the soup and fought off the desire to take a nap.
It became easier when Deragar came back.

"All right," he said. "It's set."

I nodded. "What do I need to know?"

"Do you know the corner of Undauntra and Paved Road?"

"Yes."

"There's a place there, on Paved, second door in from Un-
dauntra. It's a brickstone building with a cherrywood facade.
Two flats. In the lower one, on Farmdays, there's a low-stakes
Shereba game he likes."

"I remember. Isn't there a big range on when he shows up?"

"After the seventh hour, before the tenth."

"That's a pretty wide window."

"I know."

"And he doesn't always go."

"He'll be there tonight."

"All right. I know the area. It could be better, but I think it'll do. It won't be crowded, anyway."

"I checked over the place. Alley next to it, alley across the street, the building to the north is tall and there's a big cistern in front of it. Big enough to hide behind. The alley is eight paces from the door, the alley across the street is twenty, the cistern is twelve."

"Your paces or mine?"

"Yours."

I mentally increased the amount I was going to pay him.

"What color is the cistern?"

"Sort of a dull silver."

"Good," I said.

"Lord Taltos, do you want me to do this?"

I hesitated, considered. Then I shook my head. "No," I said. "I've got it."

I hoped I had it. I'd put a lot of shines on a lot of sons-of-bitches over the years, but this one was going to be different.

I stretched my legs out, tried to relax, and thought about it, considering this, that, and the other. In a few hours, I was going to—finally—get that asshole Terion out of my life, either by killing him, or by, well, no longer having a life. The good news was that, unless he was carrying a Morganti weapon, losing my life would also be cheating the Jhereg.

Although there had been an appalling number of Morganti weapons around of late. The Empire should really do something about that. I considered writing a letter to the Empress and filling it with threats and obscenity. Maybe next week I'd see how that worked out for me.

We went out the secret exit and took a slightly circuitous route, so it was around the fifth hour when Loiosh, Rocza, and I got there—I'd declined Deragar's offer of company, because some things I just feel are personal. I looked around. Deragar's description had been good, except that he hadn't mentioned how exposed the closer alley was—it was more like a narrow street than an alley, and there was nothing in it. The building was made of that horrid stuff where they carve rocks to look like bricks, and someone had stuck some wood in front to make it look better. There was nothing there to hide behind, though. But the cistern was there—taller than me, wider than me, pump and spigot on the street side. I stood behind it and eyeballed the distance I'd have to cross. Loiosh and Rocza flew in gradually widening circles overhead.

There was some street traffic, but not a great deal, and I can blend in pretty well. The grayish color wasn't necessary, but it didn't make things harder.

Usually, I liked to have days or even weeks to put things together; to pick an exact time and place, decide on the weapon, and have the approach and escape down precisely. This time, it would need to be half improvised, and I didn't care for it.

But I'll tell you something. One reason you go to all the extra trouble, pay so much attention to detail, and plan everything so carefully is that, every once in a while, there's a situation where you'll have to just do the best you can, and all the extra work you did the other times makes it a little easier and more natural to make the right move. It's like a catchback player who uses perfect form on the easy balls: He's the one more likely to make those sensational unlikely catches that make bookies scream and tear their hair out.

The weapon up my left sleeve was about my favorite for this sort of work: a long, slim stiletto. Remember when I was talking about how hard it is to kill someone with a stab wound? Well, it's another matter if you know how—if you can get to the guy's heart in one shot like the guy who nailed Kragar did; or get to his brain in one shot, like I can.

I drew the knife and studied it, then swore under my breath because I hadn't coated it with anything to reduce the glare. I resheathed it. Then I realized that getting him in one shot was unlikely. I just didn't have the level of detail I usually need to be able to find an exact place, an exact angle of attack. Too much was unknown. I didn't know if there would still be daylight when he showed, and, if not, what the lighting around here would be like. I knew almost nothing. The idea of taking him with one perfect shot went from seeming unworkable, to plain ridiculous. I was going to take this on like an Orca thug earning ten imperials from a guy he met over wine at a dock-side tavern.

Well, all right then. I did have some advantages over the hypothetical Orca thug: Loiosh, Rocza, knowledge of my target, and the fact that I was much, much better than any of them were.

I looked around, considering.

The thing about merchants—even those at the upper end of the class—is that they're predictable. If they don't live behind or above their shop—which most of them do—then they get done with work around six hours after noon, go home, and usually stay there. Sounds dull to me, but I guess they like it. And this was an area with a lot of merchants, which means by the time darkness began to fall, the street was nearly empty. Other than really, really crowded, empty is best for my business.

The night descended gradually. The weather was cold but muggy—a trick Adrilankha would pull every once in a while. I drew my cloak around me to warm up, then started sweating. I was beginning to develop a bad mood. I hoped killing Terion would help. Killing someone doesn't usually put me in a good mood. The set-up and planning do though, so that's something. As for the killing, well, it doesn't usually seem to affect my mood at all. Maybe this time would be different. I hoped so.

"Boss, when have you been so worried about mood? Who are you turning into, and how do I stop it?"

"If I can pull this thing off, that should fix it."

"Yeah, and if you can't, it won't matter."

"I was about to say that."

Adrilankha hissed, moaned, thudded, and murmured around me, and I waited.

You know, with all its ugliness and stench and irritations, I really love this city.

A wind came up and my hair got in my eyes; something else I'd forgotten. I tied it back. What else had I forgotten? Rocza settled back on my left shoulder.

This guy, Terion, had annoyed me for a long time. Also scared me, and hurt me. I wanted him gone. And now he'd tried to put a shine on Kragar. That I wanted him dead didn't mean I was any more prepared to kill him; that I wasn't really prepared to kill him didn't mean that I didn't want him dead. Like that.

Time dragged just like it does—did—for a more standard job, like the kind I used to do and get paid for, when I was living a life that, in retrospect, seems simpler, even though it didn't seem simple at the time and there was probably not much difference. But waiting was part of the job; you even factored it in. As the waiting time expired, as you got close to the moment to move, you got a little more excited, and a little calmer at the same time—everything got sharper and cleaner, and when it came you were utterly and completely ready. Back then, I'd never work with a three-hour window; I'd find another time, another place, another way.

I wiped the sweat from my palms.

I considered a stiletto again, but then rejected it and drew my rapier. This was not going to be clean. And making sure he couldn't be revivified might involve severing his spine; that wouldn't be clean either.

I kept the rapier down by my side.

Terion showed up a few minutes before the eighth hour, as near as I can tell. He was flanked by a couple of toughs, who seemed to be doing their job.

"All right, go," I said, and Loiosh and Rocza left my shoulders. I remember distinctly feeling the wind from their wings on my ears as they flew toward the target.

And now I'd learn if Terion had been set up, or I had.

Turned out he had, and all was well.

Is that too perfunctory? Do you want to know what went down? I don't want to tell you. It wasn't pretty, it wasn't elegant, and it wasn't clean. It wasn't like all of those times when the set-up was prearranged and perfect, with nothing left to chance. It wasn't like that at all.

I'll tell you, if it helps you sleep nights, that as soon as Loiosh and Rocza appeared, one of the bodyguards screamed and ran and that the other stepped back out of the way, so Loiosh and Rocza were able to concentrate on Terion, whom I caught completely off-guard. He never had a chance. But it still wasn't clean.

He recognized me, and when the killing blow hit, he looked surprised.

Here's a thing, if you're taking notes: One indicator of how well you've done your "work" is the amount of blood on you when it's over. If you do it right—one thrust straight into the eye is my favorite—you'll hardly end up with a drop on your hand, because avoiding it is part of the planning. That's important, because in case you get stopped on your way back from committing an antisocial act, the lack of blood might be enough for the Phoenix Guard to overlook you.

But sloppy work is, well, sloppy.

And this was sloppy.

When it was over, I didn't hang around. I cleaned the blood from my rapier on my own cloak, because why not at that point. I kept the weapon with me, too; he had a weapon out, and if this was investigated and my name came up, I'd be able to make a case for defending myself.

I hugged walls and I used alleys. I hardly passed anyone, and none of them looked at me. Loiosh was quiet. I reached the secret entrance to Kragar's office. I went past my old lab, and up the stairs, and into the room where I was staying. I realized that I was shaking with exhaustion.

Deragar came in and looked me over. I leaned against the back wall.

He said, "Where do you get your clothes?"

I became aware that all I had with me were some extra-warm things that would make me miserable in Adrilankha, so I told him. He asked for my measurements and I told him what I remembered, and I gave him an imperial. He nodded, and headed out. I'd never cleaned the blood off my boots, which was just as well, as I'd just have to do it again anyway.

I slumped down onto the floor.

"You all right, Boss?"

"Not sure."

"You should eat something."

"My stomach wouldn't hold it. In a bit."

Terion was gone. Just like that. The guy who'd been tormenting me for so long was now a useless pile of meat and bone. I wasn't sorry; I mean, of the things I was feeling, regret was so far away from any of them that you couldn't find a rider to carry a message there. But it felt odd. It felt like it should somehow have been harder, or more significant. I tried to figure out why I felt that way, and it hit me that this had never happened before. That is, I've never gone after someone because I wanted him dead. I'd killed cold because I was paid to; I'd killed hot because I was furious; I'd killed desperate because I was attacked. But I'd never just gone after someone for personal reasons, set him up, killed him.

Laris, for all I'd hated him, had forced it on me. Mellar, who had maybe come closer than anyone else to finalizing me, had been "work." And Loraan had first been an accidental casualty, then had come after me. Ishtvan forced it on me. Boralinoi was going after Cawti.

And so on.

It was strange.

I closed my eyes, took a deep breath, opened them, and noticed there was something neatly folded in the corner: the cloak of Jhereg gray Morrolan had given me. And sitting on top of it was a small box that held a ring and a hawk's egg and an enchanted lockpick. Yeah, things were coming together.

"Okay, Boss. Now what?"

My heart gave a little thump as I realized I was actually starting to get close to what I needed.

"Now I wait for clean clothes, because standing around in this is making me crazy."

"Actually—"

"Shut up, Loiosh."

I went out and found a closet that, years before, had held what I needed next; I was pleased to find it still did, all together in the same metal box I had always kept it in. I brought the box back to what I was now thinking of as my room. I took out what I needed, and carefully went to cleaning the blood off my boots.

My mind wandered while I worked, but nowhere that matters, and nowhere I want you to go with me. By the time my boots were clean, I was a little more settled down and ready for what came next.

"What comes now, Boss?"

"A nap."

I never quite fell asleep, but it did feel good. I'd been resting less than an hour when Deragar came back with trousers and a shirt that didn't have blood all over them. I changed, and managed to make them fit well enough.

"What next?" he said.

"Hang around for a bit. I'll have another errand."

"Oh, good," he said, and left me alone.

I looked at the stuff he'd gotten me. A bit more stylish than I was used to, with black seams on the trousers and a hint of ruffle at the sleeves, but I didn't mind. I spent some time transferring my hardware. If you're good at concealing things about your person, you can not only get at what you need quickly, but they don't feel as heavy as they should. I used to be good at it.

I tried a few draws with this and that, made sure I remembered where that and this were, and nodded. *"All right, buddy. Let's get on this."*

What came next was, maybe, the scariest part of the whole operation, just because I had to put myself in someone else's hands—in fact, in the hands of a stranger.

I arranged for a message to be sent to the stonecutter Sethra had told me of, and an hour later he arrived, a husky-looking Vallista with thick fingers that didn't look like they'd be capable of fine work. But if you judge by appearance, you're an idiot.

I told him what I wanted, and where, and when. He allowed as to how constructing a stairway, or more precisely a ladder, would be pretty easy. I gave him a lot of money. Then I explained to him, as politely as I could manage, that if he told anyone about this, Sethra would be very angry. He seemed to believe me, and I wasted about ten minutes listening to him declare, swear, promise, and protest that he would never, ever do anything that made Sethra mad at him, even if he had any reason to, which he didn't, and, well, on like that for a long time. I shouldn't have brought it up.

When he finally left, I felt exhausted. It was getting late; I slept.

My eyes were barely open when Loiosh said, *"What are we doing now, Boss?"*

"Can you guess?"

"Klava?"

"Good guess."

"After that?"

"You did so well with the klava, I'll bet you can guess that, too."

"Fluffy kitten tea party?"

"Done that already."

"Boss, you have a hawk's egg, a cloak with reinforced hems, a ring, and an enchanted lockpick. And you want me to guess what comes after that?"

"I also have my sword sheath."

"You always have your sword sheath."

"True. And you heard what I asked that guy to do."

"How can I possibly, oh, right. The sword sheath."

"Yeah."

"You can't be planning—"

"Guess."

"I'd rather not."

"Do it anyway."

"A rusted boat anchor."

"A rusted boat anchor? Why do I need a rusted boat anchor, Loiosh?"

"You don't need a rusted boat anchor. You need to get a rusted boat anchor."

"Oh." I laughed. "Nice. That's better than anything I'd come up with. A rusted boat anchor. Lovely."

"So this is what you've been planning, Boss?"

"Don't ask rhetorical questions."

He shut up.

I considered a little more, then said, *"There is a piece of good news."*

"And that is?"

"We don't need Daymar for this part."

Adrilankha Harbor (or Port Adrilankha to the older folks, or Port Kieron to the very oldest) is wide, extending from the mouth of the Adrilankha River a little bit east and a considerable distance west. The farther west you go, the smaller and less important are the crafts at the piers, docks, or at anchor. The naval vessels are to the east, the big merchant ships in the middle, and the smaller crafts and fishing boats (gradually diminishing in size) are to the west.

The western end is marked by the place where a jutting section of cliff called Kieron's Watch fell into the ocean during the Interregnum. There in the water is a mass, effectively a small island, of brutally sharp rocks that used to be up above. They are called, with the imagination typical of Dragaerans, Kieron's Rocks.

There is something of a game played by the smaller fishing boats (except for the very smallest, of course, the one- or two-man vessels, which are pulled up onto the shore). The object of the game is to find a place to anchor as far from Kieron's Rocks as possible. The better you do, the less you have to worry about the winds shifting or the waves breaking wrong; the losers, in the worst case, lose their boats.

This has been going on for something like four hundred

years. So, even though only a few boats are lost each decade,
there is, by now, quite a collection of them.

And, naturally, when the boats sink, their anchors are
lost. And by lost, I mean, they sit on the floor of the harbor
and rust. If you want to get one of those, for some strange
reason, all you need to do is offer a few coppers to one of the
urchins who inhabit the western area of the docks, and who
are very good at salvaging from sunken hulks.

I sent Deragar to find the boy I'd saved, Asyavn, who had no
fear whatever of being in a Jhereg office. I told him what I
wanted. He looked at me like I was an idiot. I told him what
I'd pay for it. He took off like he was afraid I'd come to my
senses.

A few hours later he was back with just what I wanted—a
rusted boat anchor.

I pulled out a purse, weighed it in my hand. "How did it go?"

He shrugged. "Easy enough, m'lord."

"Easy? How did you get it?"

He blinked at me. "I dived down, m'lord, with a rope.
Found one, tied it, then came back to shore and pulled it in."

"You can dive that deep?"

"M'lord, it's only about eight feet, in front of the rocks."

"Oh. Hmmm. I'd thought it was deeper."

I tossed him the purse. "I'll be in touch if there's anything
else," I said.

He bowed and left—very polite. I studied the rusted boat
anchor now sitting on the floor of the room I'd been sleeping in.

Deragar looked at it and said, "I'm not going to ask what that's for because I'm afraid you might tell me."

"Wise," I said. "How is Kragar?"

"He sat up on his own today."

"Good!"

Deragar nodded. "Anything else?"

"Not right now."

"I'll be around," he said.

"Okay, then, Loiosh. On to the next item."

"Do we need Daymar for this?"

"Depends which one I want to go after."

"I think you should get the hard one out of the way first, Boss."

"So you don't have to go find Daymar?"

"And you don't have to deal with him."

"Well argued."

I put the special cloak on, not because it was special, but because it was the only one I had that wasn't covered with blood. It felt sort of weird, but I stood in front of the mirror in my old office, and it looked okay. I picked up the bloody pile of clothes, shook them to make sure I hadn't left any hardware in them, and made my way down the stairs. When I passed through my lab, I took the opportunity to burn them before continuing out onto the streets of Adrilankha, where waited death and, you know, stuff like that.

There were Teckla and tradesmen and an occasional noble wandering through what had once been my area—stopping to gossip at the Malak Circle Market, laughing and throwing copper pennies at a street jongleur, hurrying to an appointment with a lover or business partner. For just a moment, I felt a bit wistful, then I hurried on.

The cloak didn't move like my usual one, and it was a bit heavier, and made noise when I moved. I didn't anticipate needing to be quiet, however, so that was okay.

And people passed me on the street without paying special attention to me.

And Loiosh and Rocza flew overhead, in careful sweeps, looking for anyone paying attention to me, or moving with me.

And all was just as it had been.

And Terion was dead.

I reached down and tapped Lady Teldra's hilt with my right forefinger; I'm not sure why. I guess it made me feel better.

Nearby was a small shop I'd never been in before, but I knew the type, and I knew it would have what I wanted. I stepped inside, and there was cinnamon, thinleaf, garlic, and several other things all competing for the attention of my nose. I took a moment to enjoy. It was a sort of hybrid shop of a type unknown in South Adrilankha, but not uncommon in the City. It combined the grocer's trade with the ironmonger's; or, at least, that portion of the ironmongers that had to do with cooking. It's the sort of place where I can spend way too much time and money if I'm not careful. This time I was careful. I wished I still had my own kitchen.

"*Boss, don't tell me you're going to stop in the middle of this and cook something.*"

"I'm not."

"*Well, good then.*"

"This is for, as the Shereba players say, the endgame."

I bought an orange and a hollow-blade knife small enough to conceal in my pouch. Then I looked around only briefly, smiled, and made one other purchase.

There is a tree that grows between the Adrilankha River valley and the desert of Suntra, where it was first brought, I'm told, by Pilmasca the Explorer (who might never have existed) from somewhere in the East I've never heard of (and which might also not exist). From the tree grows a bean that has some complex name derived from Serioli, even though everyone is convinced the tree came from the East originally.

This bean can be fermented, roasted, ground (I'm not sure in what order), and, I don't know, have other things done to it to produce a harsh, bitter hot liquid called chocolate, which can then be sweetened in various ways, or used unsweetened if you'd like.

There are lots of things to do with it, and it is very much a part of many Eastern cultures—even those that are nowhere near where the trees grow. There's this thing called "trading" that happens, and, apparently, chocolate is one of the things that gets traded a lot.

One thing that happens with it, is that it gets blended with honey and a clear distilled alcohol, and maybe some other flavorings, and left to sit, and it turns into a delightful, sweet concoction. It is just the thing to offer your guests to go with the fruit course, or even to replace it. Those who know how to brew it up—if they're good at it—can make a pretty reasonable income selling it to Dragaeran food and cooking stores.

I smiled when I saw the bottle, nodded, and said, "That will do very well."

"*I'm not seeing it, Boss.*"

"*You don't need to, Loiosh.*"

"*But—all right.*"

Onward, then.

The last thing I bought was a small flask, suitable for carrying a small quantity of chocolate liqueur with me. That done, I overpaid and bid farewell to the proprietor.

13

MAKING CONNECTIONS
OR
MAKING MUSIC

There are various reasons for preferring a delivered message to psychic communication. The three most usual reasons are: that a piece of paper signed by a witness is more official; that you don't know the other person well enough to communicate psychically; and that if you remove the amulet you're wearing that prevents psychic communication, the Jhereg will know where you are, and it will thus be easier for them to plunge a Morganti weapon into some appropriate portion of your anatomy. This last reason, I would guess, is less common than the other two.

Dotted throughout Adrilankha are small "offices" (sometimes nothing more than outdoor stands) marked by a yellow stripe. Here you can find a runner who will, for a small fee, deliver a message anywhere in the city. Rumor has it that the original owner had a gambling problem, followed by a not-paying-his-debt problem, followed by a someone-now-owns-half-your-business problem. If true, whoever the Jhereg was has to be pretty wealthy by now, because the business keeps growing, with more and more of these places appearing all the time.

The nearest one was a quarter of a mile away. I went there, composed a message addressed to Lady Saruchka, care of the Ball of Yarn Tavern and Music Hall, and sent it on its way.

Back in the office, I had a quick meal of bread, cheese, sausages, and Loiosh complaining about eating the same thing all the time. I went through the list of what we'd eaten lately, but those were only facts, so they didn't impress him. I told him we'd have a good meal when this was all over. He pointed out that I'd likely be dead. I suggested that would be fine, and asked if he would be willing to deliver his complaints then. He gave me an evasive answer.

Then he said, *"Next we get in touch with Daymar?"*

"I think we're out of excuses."

I reviewed the list. I had the cloak, the ring, the lockpick, and the wand was coming—almost everything.

My heart gave a thump. It had been doing that a lot lately. I wished it would stop. I mean, stop giving random thumps, not, you know, stop.

I wrote a note and gave it to Loiosh. He sighed and flew off to deliver it to Daymar. I picked up the book on Imperial trade laws just to make sure that I knew the relevant section well enough. I tried reciting it from memory; succeeded. Tried again, succeeded again. I took out the koelsch leaves Auntie gave me, found a bowl, and used the pommel of a dagger to pound them into a powder.

I heard a commotion out in the office, and decided that Daymar was there. Someone stuck his head in and was probably about to tell me so when Daymar brushed past him. In his hand was a tube about four inches in diameter and maybe four feet long. And my heart thumped *again*, because he had what I wanted, which meant, on the plus side, that I was closer to being ready, and on the minus side, that I was closer to being ready.

He handed me the tube.

It is said that before the arrival of Men or Dragaerans, so long ago even the hills have forgotten, in secret caverns deep in the mountains, an ancient race called the Serioli constructed artifacts of breathtaking beauty, profound subtlety, and unimaginable power.

All of which is true, but has nothing to do with this. The object called the Wand of Ucerics was made by a Hawklord in Adrilankha about two hundred years ago. The creation of powerful magical tools, generally, is the result of one of three things: the desire to impress a lover; an accident while trying to create something else entirely; or a side project created to assist while working toward something considered more significant by the creator. This was the third.

Ucerics had been taken with the notion that it should be possible to teach a wounded or diseased body to heal itself, something sorcerers had been working on for more than ten millennia. Ucerics's notion had to do with stimulating the nervous system in combination with the knowledge contained in the body's cellular structure, and, from hanging out with Aliera, I almost know what some of that means. Ucerics made the wand to visualize cell structures, and, just for convenience, added in an enchantment to help keep him awake while he worked.

When he passed away from acute exhaustion, malnutrition, and sleep deprivation, the wand, with all of his other possessions, went to his only surviving relative: his nephew, Daymar. I found out about it many years ago, and wondered, even then, if it might be useful someday.

One end of the case had a cover. I removed it, and slid the contents out: a narrow rod that appeared to be made of glass, though it wasn't.

"That's it, Vlad."

"Yeah."

"Do you know how to use it?"

I nodded.

"Why do you want it?"

I looked at him. That look was sending a message, a reminder, that I had already told him all that I wanted to tell him. The message, as it happened, didn't get through; he waited.

I sighed. "Why do you think?"

He shook his head. "I've been trying to imagine. With that amulet on, you won't be able to detect anything."

"I know."

"Will you take the amulet off?"

"No."

He frowned. "Are you going to make me guess?"

"No."

"Good."

"You don't have to guess."

"Unless you worry about falling asleep suddenly."

"Yes, I do. The fear of it keeps me awake at night."

He nodded, then frowned. "Ah, I see. Yes. The fear of falling asleep keeps you awake, so you aren't worried about falling asleep. Yes. That's why it's funny. I see what you did there."

"Thank all the gods for that."

"And you still won't tell me?"

"When it's all over, I'll tell you."

"What if you're dead?"

"Then I won't tell you."

"No, I suppose you won't."

"Thank you for the loan," I said. "I should be done with it by nightfall tomorrow, one way or the other."

"All right. Is there anything else you need?"

"A good night's sleep."

"Yes, well, good luck with that."

"Thanks."

"And with, you know, the other thing."

"Thanks."

He turned to go, and I said, "Daymar."

He turned back. "Hmmm?"

"Thanks."

He nodded and walked out, shoulders a little stooped, his tread heavy. I wondered if I'd ever see him again.

"Cut it out, Boss."

"What. I'm in danger. I could be killed. I can't even look on the bright side?"

I sat down, leaned against a wall, and closed my eyes. A last meal at Valabar's would be nice. A last talk with my son would be even nicer. And Cawti. What was I—no, stop it, you idiot. All of those are out of the question anyway. Just think how good it'll be when that becomes your biggest problem, Vlad. So forget the crap and make things work.

Heh. Now Loiosh had me so well trained I was doing it myself.

I went over it all in my head, yet again, looking for things that might go wrong and figuring out what to do about them; or as many of them as possible.

And, you know, it wasn't that bad. Yeah, there were places I was playing probabilities instead of near certainties, but I had contingencies for most of those.

"I think we have a shot, Loiosh."

"I think so too, Boss. But I don't like it that I'm not in the room."

"Actually, that works out better for us."

"Yeah, you said that before. But I don't see how."

"It means you can be where I need you to be."

"Yeah, I know. But where is that, and why?"

"Outside. Holding that, and being ready to use it."

I pointed to the neat little clear ball that Morrolan had given me: a standard, military-issue smoke bomb, only mildly sorcerous, and very reliable.

"So you're afraid of an attack from outside the room?"

"Exactly. And if that happens, I'll be climbing up a cliff on a ladder built into the rock, and be in no condition to defend myself."

"Got it," he said.

Deragar clapped and opened the door. "Lord Taltos, someone is here to see you."

"The most stunningly beautiful Issola you've ever seen?"

He nodded. "Expecting her, huh. Well, my opinion of you just climbed a few notches."

"Good. Now I can sleep nights. So I don't need the wand."

"Wand?"

"Never mind. Send her in."

"I will."

I stood up. "Hello, Sara," I said. "Thank you for coming by."
She wrapped me in a hug, then kissed the top of my head.

I've heard a lot of people say music is magical, and a few say magic is musical. I don't know. Both sound like the sort of clever things people say to make their listeners nod wisely, but when you pick it up to look at it, it crumbles. Or maybe I'm wrong; that isn't my area.

But it is true—or at least, Sethra told me, and that's close enough to true for most purposes—that music was one of the first things that magic was applied to, and that the magical arts have been enhanced by music for almost as long. By now, some have even gotten pretty good at it.

So, yeah, even if you don't buy into stupid aphorisms, there are a lot of enchantments for music, and a lot of musical instruments that carry enchantments. Most Issola had a few, and Lady Saruchka was no exception. She had mentioned the ensorcelled euphonium as an instrument she had no use for: no interest in playing it, nor in being in the sort of orchestra that required one. For the most part, she played instruments that permitted her to sing at the same time, and I'd never known her to play with more than four other musicians at the same time. She'd told me once that it wasn't the number of musicians that mattered, it was the size of the stage; she liked what she called intimate venues, which I guess means small.

The most basic enchantment that can be put on a musical instrument is, of course, the ability to play it. As I understand it, the more musical skill you have, the better it works, even more if you already know how to play that particular instrument. Or something like that.

And, since we're doing the whole balance thing, the better you are at playing an instrument, the better you can use any spell that uses the instrument to enhance sorcery, the better your sorcery will work; and the better you are at sorcery, well, you know.

Sara had acquired—she was a little vague as to how—a euphonium that did both; it had a spell that permitted anyone to play it competently, and it had an enchantment that permitted fine control of psychic phenomena; and I imagine that now you're getting an idea of why I wanted it.

When you don't have the skill you need, you hire someone who does; and when you can't do that, you find a way to fake it. Some days I think that explains most of my career.

"You're welcome," she said, handing me an instrument case. "Here is what you asked for."

I took it, but didn't open it. "Have a chair."

She did, and looked around. "This is where you're living now?"

I sat down facing her, relaxed, and crossed my legs. She sat upright, but on her it looked relaxed. "I'd put it as staying, not living. Just for another day."

"Oh?"

"Then I should have things settled."

"What things?"

"If it works, I won't have to run anymore."

"Vlad, really?"

"Yes."

"You might get out of trouble with the Jhereg?"

"There's a good chance."

"What are you going to do?"

"You mean, afterward, instead of running? Well, I thought—"

"You know very well that isn't what I meant."

I sighed. "It's complicated, and involves some internal Jhereg matters, and arcane magic that I don't understand, and Imperial trade laws that I understand even less."

"You said if it works."

"Yeah."

"What if it doesn't."

I didn't answer.

"Oh," she said.

"Like I said, I think I have a good shot."

"And you need the ensorcelled euphonium?"

I nodded.

"For something mysterious and arcane."

"Yeah."

"I thought you couldn't perform magic with that amulet on."

"I'm taking it off."

"Is that safe?"

"No. But I've reason to think I'll be able to get away with it."

"I hate it when you're mysterious. It means you don't want to tell me the details because I'll know how idiotic it is."

I tried to keep my face inscrutable. I didn't do well. She studied me carefully, then said, "All right."

"Have you heard from the Teckla boy?"

"Last month. He's still improving. He's able to do his chores, and some of his lessons, and he even talks a little around the dinner table sometimes."

"Good."

"Maybe, if this works, we could visit him."

"Because I'm so well-loved around Smallcliff?"

She smiled. "We'll see."

I cast my mind back to that time in that little village. It's strange. I know I was almost killed. I know that it took everything I had, plus a lot of luck, to get out of that mess. But somehow, looking back, I couldn't understand how I could have even been worried about it. It's like everything then was so easy, so simple. Someone wanted me dead, I had to fight him. I did. I lived. Simple. I know that isn't true; it's the sort of trick your mind plays on you in retrospect. But it sure seemed like it.

"Vlad? What is it?"

"Yes. If we can manage it, after I've had some time to catch up with my son, I'd very much enjoy going back to Smallcliff."

She smiled. "It's a plan then."

"Boss?"

"Yeah?"

"You told her you were going to remove the amulet."

"Yeah."

"You told Daymar you weren't."

"Yeah."

"Which time were you lying?"

"Maybe both."

"I hate it when you try to sound mysterious," he said.

"That's not the only reason I do it, you know."

"I'm reassured."

By now, Sara knew me well enough to recognize the signs of a conversation with Loiosh she wasn't privy to. She smirked a little, then turned serious and said, "What can I do to help?"

"The euphonium is a great help."

"Do you know how to use it?"

"Um. I thought it did that by itself."

"Mostly. But the more you can play it, the more—"

"I can't play at all, Sara."

"I can show you how to hold it, at least. That will help."

I nodded. "Good. Everything I can do that will—yeah, you know."

She nodded. "Open it up."

I managed that part. It was shiny and made of brass and looked like a thick tube twisted around and around itself, with knobs here and there. It was the sort of thing that looked like there couldn't possibly be a comfortable way to hold it. It wasn't as heavy as it looked.

"Pick it up," she said. "Hold it in your lap. Let me—"

She stood up, walked behind my chair, and adjusted it in my lap.

"That's rather distracting," I said.

"Work on concentration."

"Um, yeah."

"No, more like this. Your mouth goes there. And your right hand there. No, turn your wrist more, like that. Try pressing down on the valves."

"That isn't comfortable."

"It isn't supposed to be."

"And it is very distracting."

"Think about the discomfort. This arm holds the instrument in place, and your fingers rest there."

"Is my missing finger going to be a problem?"

"It's usually just used for support, so just put the next one through that loop. Yes, that's right. How did you lose it, any-way?"

"A dzur wanted my hand for a snack and mostly missed."

"All right. Now, make your mouth do this."

"Seriously?"

"Yes. When you want to play, you don't just blow into it. . . ."

The following half an hour was bizarrely irritating and pleasant, but by the end of it, I was making sounds come out of the thing without the help of spells.

They weren't terribly good sounds, mind you; nothing I'd be inclined to call music. But Sara was very kind about it, and even told me that the weird ache I was feeling below my ears meant I was doing it right. That was sort of a disturbing thought. We spent a little more time on it, so I could at least sometimes hit the right "valves" as she called them. She said that would help with the spell.

"Not bad," she said.

"You're a good teacher."

I thought about trying to kiss her right then, or at least asking her if I could; but things were complicated. For one thing, we were different species and I wasn't sure how she felt about that—I wasn't even entirely sure how I felt about that. For another, I wasn't over Cawti, and she knew it. And for another, I might be dead in a day or two. Plenty of time to decide about that sort of thing if there was plenty of time; not very nice if there wasn't.

Or, I don't know; maybe I was just worried about being em-barrassed if she said no. I put the instrument back in its case, which required a lesson in itself, but let's not dwell on that.

"Is there anything else I can help you with?" she asked, breaking what was about to become an awkward silence.

I shook my head. "No, this is good."

"You'll get hold of me, once this is over?"

"First thing," I said.

"Thank you," she said, and stood up. "I should be going."

I nodded.

"Vlad—" she said, then shook her head and didn't finish.

"Yeah," I said. "You're about to say good luck."

She gave a sort of smile. "Yes. Good luck."

She gave me a kiss on the top of my head and walked out of the office.

"Boss."

"Yeah, I'm over it."

"I don't believe you, but all right."

"Heh."

"Okay, now what?"

"Now we get a message to the Demon and have him set a time for tomorrow."

"Then we're ready?"

"Not really, but we're going to do it anyway."

"Tomorrow!"

"Yeah, that'll be a busy day."

"We should eat something."

"I need sleep more than food. But we have to go out again. Dammit. A long walk this time."

"Important, I take it?"

"Well, everything depends on it, if that's what you mean."

"In that case, we really should have food first."

"Oh, all right. Food first."

"You know, Boss, I'm not used to doing all these things that *make me happy. Getting out from under the Organization, killing Terion, and now food."*

"*Don't worry, I won't let you get used to it."*

"*This is my surprised wing-flap."*

Deragar was willing to get some food for the mere price of a share in the meal. He retrieved some baked felua in coriander-plum sauce from a place called Jarad's, because I'd been in a mood for flying things for a while. Loiosh commented on it in terms I don't feel like telling you about. The food was good, even though Jarad's was far enough away that it wasn't quite as hot as it should have been. Deragar also picked up a bottle of Descani, which reminded me of the evening all that time back that, in some sense, had started this. More important, however, was that it was a good wine and treated the felua well. I wondered if Deragar knew more about wine than most Dragaerans, or had just gotten lucky. There was no polite way to ask him, however, so I didn't.

We ate in companionable silence. Deragar kept watching Loiosh and Rocza eat, but he didn't say anything about it, and neither did they.

When we'd finished eating and had quite demolished the wine, I gave Deragar a little money, and asked him to buy me a wheelbarrow and some clothing appropriate for a peasant. I also gave him a message for delivery to the Demon; tomorrow would be the day.

Deragar gave me a raised eyebrow that suddenly reminded me of Kragar, and headed out.

I sat in an uncomfortable chair and crossed and re-crossed my legs and stretched and got up and sat down again until he came back. It wasn't long, maybe half an hour.

"This is bound to be good," he said.

"Not as exciting as you might think."

"Can I watch?"

"No, not for this."

He shrugged, reminding me of Kragar again. "All right."

"Where's the barrow?"

"Downstairs."

"Good."

"Boss? Why do we need a wheelbarrow?"

"To complete the peasant disguise."

"Really? That's all?"

"Really. That's all."

"Even though it's empty?"

"When's the last time you noticed whether a wheelbarrow was empty?"

"Um. Okay."

I transformed myself into a lowly peasant Easterner. I'm glad I didn't have a mirror. I threw some dirt on myself and rubbed it in a bit, just to put the final touches on.

Then I collected Rocza, Loiosh, and Loiosh's attitude, and the four of us snuck out of the tunnel once more, complete with wheelbarrow. For once I wasn't too worried about an attack, since no one would imagine I was, you know, me. It's the sort of thing you can get away with for a while, if you're willing.

Wheelbarrows are, no doubt, fine machines; but they're still machines. And as far as I'm concerned, mechanical devices have no reason to exist except to do a bad job of something sorcery can do a good job of. There must be more to it than that, or there wouldn't be all those mechanical devices. I mean, would there? Yeah, okay, so maybe not everyone is good enough at sorcery to pull it off, or rich enough to pay someone else to. I've also heard the argument that some things are just easier and more natural when done the hard way; I'm just not sure I buy it.

If I had had any idea how hard it would be to keep wheeling that thing through the streets of Adrilankha, I might have changed my mind about the whole plan. And when I reflected that Teckla usually had something heavy in one, my opinion of Teckla went up; I made a mental note to tell Cawti that when I could. If I could. The good part was that inside of ten minutes I was as filthy and stinky and sweaty as any peasant, and I felt safer than I had in some time. Though if the choice was to live like this or face soul-death, I'd go for the soul-death. No I wouldn't. Yes I would. Maybe.

Glad the situation hasn't come up, though.

Amazing how loud those things are, too.

14

Making Music
or
Making Bargains

After trudging along Lower Kieron for longer than I want to remember, I was in an area where it was both safe and possible to leave the wheelbarrow, so I did and continued on to Kieron.

It was much easier after that, which is just as well because I had to go a long way, which would have been impossibly long if I'd had to push that thing up and down hills. The area went from poor, to affluent, to peasant (which is like poor but with less trash and more space), and then there were a couple of castles off in the distance and one very large single-story building directly in front of us.

I should explain about that building.

I'd found it a short while back, led there by someone I trusted. The details aren't important. But I'd been inside of it, and had the chance to get to know it pretty well. It was first built by a Vallista named Tethia as, so she told me, "an experiment," which is what people say when they do something that makes everyone laugh at them. There's a story there, too.

It was big, it was empty, and there was a room in it that held a long table and a lot of comfortable chairs. The building was rented out every now and then by groups of merchants or nobles who wanted to solve matters in a less violent way than is usual for the people I know. If you ignore the rest of the structure (and you should if you don't want your head exploding), that room is pretty comfortable. On the south wall are several large windows of glass that were treated to prevent breakage. The glass looks out over the ocean-sea, just where Kieron's Watch used to be. It is, in fact, a spectacular view.

It was night when I arrived, and there were no lights to be seen anywhere; the place was empty. It was usually empty. If it hadn't been deserted this time around, I'm not sure what I'd have done—left town? killed everyone in it? sat down and cried? That had been one of the few things I had to trust to luck on; and so far, luck was with me.

Time to get to work.

There were enough wards and spells and devices on the doors and windows of the place that breaking in would have been a major enterprise. I could have done it, especially with Kiera's help, but there was no need.

"Anything, Loiosh?"

"No one anywhere near, Boss. You're good."

"All right."

"What if your memory is off? I mean, what if you don't recall the inside as well as you think you do?"

"I'm going to look first, Loiosh. As in, look inside. Through the windows. Glass windows. They work both ways, you know. Glass. It's this thing invented by people with oppos—"

"Shut up, Boss."

We went around to the side of the building, my back to the ocean-sea far below me; I could smell it, and hear the waves crashing on Kieron's Rocks. I looked through the window, did a quick calculation, then did it again to be sure, and made a note of the spot.

"*You know this is crazy, right, Boss?*"

"*Not if it works.*"

Glass windows are a sign of wealth. Not so much because they're expensive—a good sorcerer with access to sand can, I'm told, create any size and shape window with a bit of time and effort—but because they *break*. That's what glass does. And then you have to replace them. And after a few times, the cost starts building up, so you have to not care.

Or you spend even more on enchanting the windows so they don't break.

I gave the window an experimental smack with my fist. It hardly even vibrated.

"*All right, so—*"

"*Watch and learn,*" I said.

I ran my fingers over the place where the window was joined to the wall—a wood frame had been set into the stone, and ingenious slots cut into it to hold the window in place.

Those of us in the business call that a "weak spot."

The process was a lot longer and slower than I had expected. For one thing, there was this strange glue-like substance between glass and wood that I had to scrape away. Every time my knife tapped the window it made a ringing sound that was not unpleasant but made me worry about breaking it until I remembered that it was unbreakable. Which was the reason for doing this, after all.

But in the end, it was done—the window would come out with a good push, and from there I'd be just a few feet from the cliff, and there were stairs cut into the cliff.

"*Sleep now,*" I said.

"*Yeah, after a long walk back into the City.*"

"*Who's whining now?*"

It was, indeed, a long and wearying walk, but we made it back, using the tunnel again. I said not a word to anyone; I just trudged into the storage room I was using, threw myself onto my pile of blankets, and went to sleep.

I had an intense dream that night—or rather, morning—but I don't remember much about it except that there were wheelbarrows, and I don't see how it relates to anything, so skip it.

I woke up with one of those surges of adrenaline you get on the day something big is going to happen—you know, you gradually wake up to a certain point, and then, *This is the day. Here we go.* I heaved myself up to a sitting position without even a grunt, and found Loiosh looking at me. He said nothing into my mind. I felt his fear and anticipation—a reflection of mine, and yet still his own—echoing back and forth.

I pulled myself up. I cleaned up in Kragar's private washroom (that used to be mine) and got dressed. No, my hands weren't shaking, and yes, my palms were dry. I went through every weapon I had, carefully, checking the edge, and that it was just where it should be, and that I could pull it cleanly. From time to time, I tapped Lady Teldra's hilt, which was going to become an annoying habit if I let it; but it was very reassuring.

"*Food, Boss?*"

"*Oh, yes. And klava. I'm going to have a full stomach and be wide awake when, you know.*"

"*Good plan.*"

I went out into the office, hoping Deragar was there so I could get him to bring food and klava. He was there, and so was Sellish, but they weren't alone.

"Kragar!"

"You see, you noticed me right away."

He looked pale and fragile, but he was sitting upright in Melestav's old chair.

"How are you?"

"Not ready to fall over dead quite yet. How about you?"

"Probably closer than you are."

"Probably."

"You didn't have to agree so fast."

"How's your problem?"

"Nearing a solution."

"I heard that Terion had an accident."

"Yeah, I heard the same thing."

He nodded.

"Deragar's been great," I added.

"Aw, shucks," said Deragar.

"Yeah, I raised him right," said Kragar.

"You—"

I looked back and forth between them.

"Oh," I said.

Kragar smirked.

"How about you get him to bring us breakfast and klava while I recover and try to adopt this into my view of the universe."

Kragar and Sellish nodded solemnly. "We were just waiting for you. Though it'll be lunch for us."

Deragar rolled his eyes, reminding me more than ever of Kragar. "What, then?"

"Just some rolls, and a lot of klava, for Vlad. For me, you know what I like. Get something good," said Kragar.

"Hot sweet rolls?" he asked me.

I nodded.

"All right. I'm including myself in the list, though, and you're buying."

"I'd expect nothing less," said Kragar.

Some coins changed hands, and Deragar left. Kragar started to stand up, failed, looked disgusted and gave me a glance. I helped him up. He hissed with pain, and I guided him to his own office. As he sat down, I said, "You sure you're out of danger?"

"How do you mean that?"

"I mean, are you about to fall over dead from the wound? I didn't intend to ask if the world was a safe place for Jhereg bosses, so don't even start."

He chuckled and said, "I saw the physicker this morning, and he says I'm doing all right. And he seems to think Aliera is some sort of god."

"So does Aliera."

"Yeah. But she does good work. Don't tell her I said so."

"Of course not; she'd pound me into dust."

"She would at that. I wish I'd been able to hear the conversation when you convinced her to save me."

That was a good time not to say anything, so I gave him my best inscrutable smile and let it drop. Instead, I asked him a few more times about how he was feeling until he started to get annoyed, then I let that drop, too. He wanted to talk about my plans, and if he could help, and I didn't want to and he couldn't—at least, any more than he had by loaning me Deragar. He looked like he wanted to argue about it, and I understood how he was feeling, but he just shut his mouth and nodded.

Deragar came back, with klava that made life possible, and some sweet buns that made it worth living. No, sarcasm aside, life is always worth living. Even when sometimes it seems like more trouble than it's worth.

Oh, who am I kidding? It's when it seems like more trouble than it's worth that I want it the most. I mean, isn't everyone like that? No, I suppose not. Some people just seem miserable all the time, even when they have no reason to be, and my attitude is to just let them stew in it, as long they stay clear of me. That is, unless it's someone I know, then it's different.

When have you ever heard me claim to be consistent? Or, for that matter, claim there was any virtue in consistency? I'm just telling you what happened, and what I was thinking, because that's what I'm being paid for. Don't read too much into it, all right? There's one good thing about needing to devote all of your energy to staying alive: It doesn't give you a lot of time to waste on crap that isn't worth thinking about.

Fresh rolls and klava, now—there was something worth thinking about. Sellish took his away because he had stuff to do. The three of us enjoyed the rolls and klava in silence.

When we'd finished, I asked one question: "What is the time?"

"It's an hour before noon," said Kragar, giving me a significant look. "What time do things get started?"

"I should find out within the next two hours."

"You didn't make firm arrangements?"

"I left the exact time and place open, so the client would feel more at ease."

He rubbed chin with the side of his fist. "So you can't make any real preparations."

"Yeah, I've already prepped the place."

His eyebrows asked me a question.

I said, "I just sort of somehow know where he's going to pick."

"You're sure?"

I shrugged. "Nothing is sure in this, but that isn't one of the parts I'm most worried about."

"I'd ask," he said, "but you wouldn't tell me."

"Correct."

"And I loathe giving you another chance to display your wit."

"Have you been reading books?"

"What?"

I shook my head and wiped my fingers on my shirt. We had more klava, and I don't remember what we talked about, but I'm sure it was terribly important. Just about exactly noon, a messenger arrived with a note for me from the Demon.

I read it, nodded, folded it up, and tapped it against my hand.

"Well?" said Kragar. "Is that it?"

"Yeah."

"And?"

"Good and bad."

"Hmmm?"

"It's where I wanted, but not for another six hours. What am I supposed to do for the next six hours?"

"Yeah," he said smirking. "You've already eaten."

I suggested he perform a rather disgusting quasi-sexual

act; he allowed as to how that would pass the time, at least. Deragar tried not to laugh.

Loiosh sat on my shoulder, shifting from foot to foot; he was nervous too. Kragar pulled out a set of s'yang stones. I shook my head; he shrugged and put it back.

"Well," he said, "any pieces of it you want to talk about? Holes you want to fill in? Really stupid parts I can laugh at?"

"Loiosh is handling that," I told him. "The laughing at me, I mean."

"So, business as usual."

"Pretty much."

"What are you going to do if it doesn't work? I mean, are you going to just die? Do you have a backup plan?"

Once more, I thought about just taking Lady Teldra and killing as many of them as I could before they got me. But . . . "No," I said.

He waited.

"Kragar, what are you really asking?"

"If there's some reason to believe I didn't go through all this for nothing."

He looked unusually serious.

"I can't promise that. But you'll know within a few hours, one way or the other."

"Yeah, but Vlad, has it occurred to you that, if they kill you, I'm probably next?"

"Uh, no. Why do you think that? If they've left you alive all this time—I mean, I know Terion tried not to, but—"

"It's not Terion, Vlad. Think about it. I was your number two. I've been helping you. Why am I still alive?"

"Because you're very hard to kill."

"They could manage."

I bit my thumb and thought about it. "You think they're deliberately keeping you alive because they think you'll lead them to me?"

"That's my guess."

"Why are you only telling me now?"

"I hadn't thought about it until I was lying on my back unable to move. Amazing what it does for the brain."

"Yeah," I said. "I know."

His eyebrows looked a question, but I didn't answer.

"The Demon," I said, "agreed that it would be over if this all works out."

"Yeah," said Kragar. "So you said. For you. Not for me."

I made a theologically improbable suggestion. Then I said, "I never thought about that."

"Me neither," he said. "Until today."

I noticed I was biting my lower lip and stopped.

"Don't get me wrong, Vlad. I don't mind risking my ass for you. I've been doing it for almost fifteen years now. But I like to have some idea of what it's about."

I looked for something to say, came up empty. "Okay," I said. "I've been collecting—"

"Wait a minute, Vlad."

"What?"

"I didn't mean you actually had to unreel the whole thing for me."

"Oh. Well, you made a pretty good argument for it."

"I just want to know how you're so sure the Demon isn't going to sell you out."

"Oh, that."

"Yeah, that. I mean, that's sort of the key to the whole thing, isn't it?"

"What I know about the Demon is that he's going to want the process, because there's just an absurd amount of money in it. I don't believe he's capable of passing that up."

He shook his head. "I just worry that you're too trusting."

"That I'm—what?"

"Too trusting."

"Kragar, who have I shown misplaced trust in as long as you've known me?"

"Melestav," he said.

I winced. That one still hurt. "You know, Kragar, of all the things I've been accused of over the years, I never expected to hear that I was too trusting."

"Don't see why not," he said. "You are. And everyone in the world can see it except you." Deragar watched us go back and forth like someone watching kittens play—with a sort of tolerant amusement that I'd have done something about if I hadn't been busy.

"Too trusting," I said. "Yeah, that's my problem." I rolled my eyes. "I admit, I trust people to be true to their nature. So far, that's worked out pretty well for me."

"Okay, Vlad. Let's look at the facts."

"Facts? You must be really desperate if you're resorting to facts. All right, I'm listening."

"First of all, you trusted me."

"It seems like—"

"You trusted me a long time before you knew me enough to."

"What did I trust you with? I mean, early on?"

"Almost everything you were doing."

"Such as?"

"The name of your contact with Morrolan's security forces.

That you'd killed Loraan. That you'd personally killed Laris—the Empire would have loved to hear about that. That—"

"Did you really consider telling them?"

"Of course not, Vlad. That isn't the point. The point is, you're too trusting."

"I was young, then."

"And now you're not? You're still under five hundred. If you weren't human that would mean you're young."

"Heh," I explained. "What else you got?"

He continued giving examples of my supposed over-trusting nature, some of which may have been valid, and I continued arguing until I finally got tired of it and said, "So, Kragar, because of this, you're convinced the Demon—or someone else in the Organization—is going to put a shine on you as soon as this is over?"

"I didn't say I was convinced, Vlad."

"But you think so?"

"Most likely not."

"Wait. You *don't* think so?"

"Not really."

"Why?"

"I've been too good an earner. If I go down, everyone up the ladder from me loses."

"Well then, why have you been—wait. You've just been doing all of this to take my mind off the six-hour wait, haven't you, you asshole?"

"It's not six hours anymore." He smirked.

"C'mon, Boss. It was well played. Admit it."

"You knew what he was doing the whole time, didn't you?"

"Nothing good can come out of me answering that question, Boss."

"Suddenly," I said, "I feel like killing someone."

"You'll probably have the chance," said Kragar.

"Probably."

"Hungry again?"

"No. How much time did you manage to kill?"

"A couple of hours."

"It'll take me an hour to get there."

"Going to arrive early?"

I shook my head. "Just exactly when I'm expected."

"How trusting of you."

"Kragar, you weren't serious, were you? I mean about— quit laughing. Jerk."

Still smirking, he made a gesture to Deragar with his eyebrows, and the latter went out, then returned with a bottle of Piarran Mist.

"What?" I said. "Some sort of last-drink ritual, so if I die, I'll have had the good stuff? Seriously, Kragar?"

"Shut up and drink it, Vlad."

"Whatever you say, boss," I told him.

We drank, and didn't talk about old times, or new times, or anything at all. However much I may laugh at stupid rituals like that, it was very, very good; it went over my tongue like clear water, but left a whole symphony of flavors and hints of aroma that gave me something to think about instead of whether I was about to die, and, more important, how much I hated waiting.

Kragar seemed to appreciate it as much as I did; Deragar might have, too, but if so he hid it well.

I stopped after two cups, because having my mind foggy wouldn't be a good idea. Then I stood up. "Okay," I said. "I'm heading out."

"It's still pretty early," he said. "I mean, if you really are planning to get there exactly on time."

"I have a stop to make on the way."

"All right," said Kragar. "Good luck."

I took most of the coin I had left and set it aside with a note telling Deragar it was his. It was a lot, but he'd earned it. And soon, I'd be able to get at my own bank account. Or not.

I slung the euphonium case over my shoulder.

I made sure the lockpick was where it should be, and that I had the flask, the orange, the ring, the hollow knife, the glass ball, the wand, and the egg. I was wearing the cloak. I went through every weapon I was carrying, again, one at a time, to see they were accessible and that I remembered where they were.

I took the secret passage for what would almost certainly be the last time, and I didn't let myself think a good-bye to my old lab as I passed it by.

If I lived through this, I decided, first order of business was going to be some new clothes—something that fit better, and looked better. Yeah, that's what I'd do.

No, a good meal first. Maybe Valabar's. Certainly Valabar's.

Focus, Vlad. Task at hand and all that. Worry about later, later.

It was afternoon, just making its way toward evening, but the light was still good. There were lots of Teckla in the market, wearing bright blue, and yellow, and red, and sometimes disregarding their House colors entirely. I wondered why it was only the Teckla who felt so free to ignore their House colors, and why I'd never noticed before. Do most Dragaerans wear their House colors because of tradition? A social obligation? Just feels right? I don't know; I always wore the gray and black because everyone else in the Organization did; I'd never questioned it. If I'd thought of it, I'd have asked Kragar—it was just the sort of thing he and I could talk about for hours over wine and biscuits. Well, too late now.

Stop it, Vlad.

Vlad. I was Fenarian, but had been given a name—Vladimir—imported from a neighboring kingdom. Cawti had always called me Vladimir. There was something caressing about the way she'd said it.

Cawti.

Sara.

I let out a breath between clenched teeth and continued. As I passed a market, I thought I saw Devera, Aliera's daughter, looking at me. I almost stopped, but when I looked again she was gone, so I decided I was either imagining it, or she didn't want to talk to me. She is a very unusual child, but I guess now isn't the best time for that conversation. I put it out of my head and kept walking until I reached the Imperial Palace.

I'd allowed a lot of slack time in my schedule, but if no one on the list of people I could call on was here, I might be in trouble. It would not do to be late to my own meeting.

There were a pair of guards blocking my way into the Dragon Wing. The expressions on their faces were not encouraging.

I showed them my signet ring, and they weren't entirely sure how to handle it. While they were deciding, I said, "Count Szurke requesting an audience of Lord Khaavren. If he isn't available," I added, "any of his subordinates will do."

They let me pass.

The Dragon Wing of the Imperial Palace is nearly as confusing as Dzur Mountain, but there are more people to ask questions of, and some of them are willing to answer. I made it to the captain's office, and was informed that Khaavren would be willing to see me at once, no doubt on account of me holding an Imperial title and all. It was good for that. Also good for having the Empress send someone looking for me when I was almost dead, and saving Orca kids from arrest. I wondered how far I could stretch it.

There's a lot I could tell you about Lord Khaavren, called Papa Cat behind his back, as I happened to know. But most of it is beside the point. What matters for now is that he wears at least two different cloaks within the Imperial Hierarchy, and both of them involve giving orders to people who have the right to perform violence with Imperial sanction. The office I found him in had to do with his role as Captain of the Imperial Guard, as opposed to the much more interesting one.

He was seated behind a desk, just like I used to be. He stood up and gave me an exactly correct bow. "Count Szurke," he said.

"My lord Captain," I said.

"May I offer you something?"

"Please. Hot water, a fine-mesh strainer if you have one, and two glasses."

An eyebrow went up. "Will I enjoy whatever it is you're about to share?"

"Sorry. No. It tastes like—it doesn't taste good at all, but I wasn't offering to share it."

"All right," he said, obviously intrigued.

He gave the orders, and the two glasses appeared. I dumped the ground koelsch leaves into one, poured hot water over it, then strained it into the other and drank it. I guess it didn't taste all *that* bad; it was a bit like if it stopped trying so hard to be a bitter tea, it'd be a fairly effective bitter tea, if that makes sense.

"I assume," he said, "that the beverage isn't why you're here."

"Oh, right," I said. "Sorry." This may be the first time in my life I've apologized to a Dragaeran twice in a single conversation.

"So, how may I be of service?" he asked.

"That must have been painful to say."

"I've survived worse."

"I'd like something from you."

He shifted in his chair and studied me through narrowed eyes. "It seems to me, Lord Tal—that is, Count Szurke—that I have paid that debt."

"No argument."

"Then give me another reason to help you."

"Political infighting."

"Go on."

I hesitated. I hadn't figured out how to put this so I could get what I wanted without pissing him off; and I should have. I spoke carefully. "If there were some department, say a law enforcement unit within the Empire, that wanted to get an edge over a rival department within the Empire, it would seem worth a little effort on the part of the captain, wouldn't it?"

He didn't speak, or even move, for what seemed like a long time. Then he said, "What sort of edge, what sort of effort?"

I stood up, took the platinum ring out of my pouch, and set it on his desk. He picked it up and looked at it, then at me. "How did you get this?"

"I didn't kill anyone for it," I said, answering the question he hadn't asked.

"But you know who did?"

"No, just where it ended up. I got it back."

"All right," he said. "You have my attention."

"I want to report a crime," I told him.

Part Three

TALONS AND BEAK

15

Making Bargains
or
Making Tests

We saluted each other, and I headed out of the Palace, which took quite a while. From the Street of the Dragon, I cut across on Twohills so I could pick up Kieron Road near the edge of the city. Where they joined was a good place for an ambush, so I took my time and was careful. Loiosh let me know it was safe.

I continued the journey. As close to the Orb as I'd been in the Imperial Palace, I knew what time it was, and I was doing all right. I checked my weapons again, focused only on the destination, on getting there safely. One step at a time, that's how you do these things. Make sure you're putting all your effort into whatever the current task is, because if that fails, you'll never get to the next one. And, just now, the next step involved many steps. Walk, walk, walk. While hoping not to be spotted. Being killed now, right before—no, I'd hate that.

Adrilankha proper had vanished behind me, and I was still alive. So far, so good, as the guy who'd fallen off the cliff said halfway down.

"*Okay, Loiosh. Up now, and keep a good eye.*" I turned off Kieron and climbed an empty, rocky hill to my right.

"Boss?"

"Too many Jhereg know where I'm going. I'm going cross-country from here."

"Good thinking. But won't we get lost?"

"Probably. But I've allowed time for that, too."

"Have it all figured, do you, Boss?"

"I hope so," I told him.

I got to the top of the hill and started across rocky hills and through occasional sparse woods. Fortunately, in all of my wandering, I'd become an expert in this and it no longer bothered me and that was two lies in one statement.

For a wonder, I didn't actually get lost. I ended up on a low hill, crouched among rocks, and staring down at the building where, in a short time, we would be settling some important issues. Important to me, at least.

I opened the pouch and took out the small, clear bulb. I set it on the ground next to me.

"Loiosh?"

"Got it, Boss. You're going to tell me when—"

"Yeah."

I waited for a while—a long while, thinking about nothing in particular. I took the opportunity to relieve myself; not that I especially needed to, but I had learned early on that having a full bladder when everything in the world is happening at once was just an annoyance I could do without.

Time passed. I stood up to pace, changed my mind, sat down again. Several times. You take your excitement where you can get it.

Below, four men in Jhereg colors appeared in front of the door. I recognized one as the Demon. I also wondered who knew this place well enough to teleport to it, and if that would be a problem. I still don't know, and no it wasn't, so never mind.

I stood up, brushed myself off, and walked down to meet him.

Of course, one of the Demon's people spotted me and said something I was too far away to hear. The Demon stopped, looked around, saw me, and waited.

"Good precaution," were his first words after I was in earshot.

"It disturbs me how well you know me."

He shrugged. "I've been trying to kill you for several years, you know."

I nodded. "True enough. And you, m'lord, are punctual as always."

"Shall we?" he said, then politely went in first, and even more politely had his bodyguards go in front of me, thus sparing me a lot of itching between the shoulder blades. It didn't actually prove anything, but, like I said, it was polite.

"Okay, Loiosh."

"Boss—"

"See you in a while."

Loiosh and Rocza left my shoulders and flew away.

I followed the Demon into the place. We stepped into a long hallway. The first door on the right was to an antechamber with an oversized fireplace and a door. Past the door was the room we were to meet in. If you're paying attention, you've noticed that, with windows facing the ocean-sea, the antechamber should have been on the *left*. Sorry, can't help you with that.

The Demon opened the door and went into the antechamber, while his bodyguards took positions against the wall

opposite the fireplace. If there were as many bodyguards coming as I expected, or even half as many, it was going to get
awfully crowded in there.

The Demon cleared his throat.

"Right," I said. I flipped the cloak aside and moved my
arm out of the way, hating it. But if that's what it took, that's
what it took.

One of the bodyguards pulled out what looked like a piece
of silver cord, and approached me. He licked his lips. I suspect
he wasn't enjoying this much more than I was. He glanced at
the Demon, and I could see him brace himself. I could also
see him reminding himself of how much extra he was getting
for this.

He wrapped the cord around Lady Teldra's hilt and
around my belt, and made a tight knot. Then he made a gesture, and backed away quickly. He stank of fear, which I admit
gave me a certain satisfaction.

I didn't feel anything, except that, maybe, there was a
vague sense of something missing, as if I were in a room in
which the light was just the tiniest bit dimmer than it had
been a moment before. Only it wasn't sight, it was, well, something else.

"One hour," said the Demon. "As agreed."

"As agreed," I agreed.

I followed the Demon into the room itself.

"Anyone else here yet?" asked the Demon over his shoulder.

"I don't think so, m'lord. But I wasn't waiting that long."

That earned me a quick glance. I looked back at him, and
he barely shrugged.

The room we were in was the one I'd picked out—the only one possible. There was a long, lacquered table, set with several more chairs than we'd need. One thing I hadn't been able to determine in advance was where I'd be sitting, but I'd decided it shouldn't matter too much. Or, at any rate, I hoped it wouldn't.

The Demon indicated that I should sit at the head of the table, and he put himself by my right hand. I wondered if it were a courtesy, a gesture of respect, or if he just wanted to be able to reach my right hand quickly. Maybe some of all of those. But it put me with my back to the window, and it couldn't get much better than that. If things kept going like this, I might actually survive the day. I removed the euphonium case from my shoulder, set it next to me, and sat.

Poletra came in next, nodded to the Demon, looked at me, then gestured with his head to his bodyguards, who were standing outside the doorway. Poletra sat down almost across from the Demon, on my left, but with a chair between us. He looked around. He had this long, skinny neck, so when he looked around, he reminded me a little of a lizard. I tried not to let the thought form so Loiosh wouldn't be insulted.

"Nice place," said Poletra, looking around.

I said, "Are we getting the whole Council here?"

"No," said the Demon. "Just enough of us to make a decision."

"How many is that?"

"Six. Three members of the Council, and of course we have each hired our own sorcerer. Not, you understand, that we don't trust each other."

I chuckled a little because it was expected. "And these three can speak for the Organization? You'll forgive my being a little nervous on the subject, but it is the whole point of the exercise."

"Is it?" he inquired. "I had thought the point was to get me money, and that part was just a convenient bonus."

"Sorry to disenchant you. Figuratively, I mean."

A woman came in, alone, nodded to Poletra, and bowed respectfully to the Demon, who rose and returned the salute. *Three sorcerers,* he had said. He'd neglected to mention that at least one was from the Left Hand. But if I'd been paying attention, I'd have assumed it. The Jhereg—that is, the Right Hand—had precious few of them.

This particular sorceress looked at me and nodded as well, politely. Having a Dragaeran, not to mention someone in the Left Hand of the Jhereg, act polite toward me makes me suspicious, in spite of my too-trusting nature. But I nodded back anyway.

"This," said the Demon, "is my lady Radfall, sorceress."

I decided that saying, "Never heard of you" would be a bad idea, so I contented myself with one of those gestures between nodding and bowing your head that I'd practiced in front of a mirror back when I was young and forcing myself to learn to be diplomatic instead of being, you know, me. She returned the gesture exactly; maybe she had learned to not be her.

She said, "This room is enchanted."

The Demon looked at me, eyebrows raised. I kept my face neutral, and he turned back to her. "What sort of enchantment?"

"It's subtle. It's part of the room. Anyone in this room is

less inclined to act, more inclined to cooperate. There's a sort of lethargy."

"Can you get rid of it?"

She frowned, then closed her eyes. "Done," she said.

"Nice try, Taltos," said the Demon.

I shrugged.

The next to arrive was someone else I didn't recognize; a compact guy in Jhereg colors who reminded me a lot of Shoen, even to the slicked-backed hair. He wore several rings, and at least three chains about his neck holding things that vanished under his jerkin. He stopped just inside the door and his eyes narrowed—at Radfall.

"Well," he said, before any introductions could be made.

Radfall, who had sat facing the door a couple of seats away from Poletra, stood up and glared back at him. "Illitra," she said, like the name was a curse.

"What," he asked, "are you doing here?"

The Demon coughed. "I hadn't realized you two were acquainted."

Illitra answered him without taking his eyes off Radfall. "We've met," he said.

"Yes," said Radfall. "Murdered any children, lately?"

"No," said Illitra. "Why? Did you have some suggestions?"

Radfall sniffed disdainfully, something it seems everyone in the Left Hand gets training in.

"Tell me," said Illitra. "Do you still—"

"That will do," said the Demon quietly.

Illitra shrugged, something it seems everyone in the Right Hand gets training in.

"This is Lord Taltos," said the Demon.

Illitra twitched a little, I suppose at the "lord." It made me want to shove something big and dull into a small orifice, but I did my best to hide it. He did his best to hide his warm and affectionate feelings toward me, and he was good at it.

Three Jhereg walked in about then, and they may as well have had "muscle for hire" written on their foreheads. They looked around, one glanced back and nodded ostentatiously, and a Jhereg I didn't know, wearing clothes of an expensive cut, came in and took a seat.

He smiled to the Demon, and either he actually liked him, or the guy was a good actor. The Demon introduced him as Farthia, and he was kind enough to bestow a quick glance on me. I felt all honored and shit. He had to be one of the sorcerers, because he couldn't be on the Council, though I'm starred if I can tell you how I knew that. That meant the bodyguards weren't actually with him, but with the next guy to show up. They walked back out. I waited.

The other two sorcerers continued glaring at each other, but Illitra added a sneer, so I thought he had the edge. I didn't know which sorcerer worked for whom, but I didn't need to know. The point is, this really wasn't a trick. It was going to have to work. I was going to have to do what I claimed. A shame I hadn't been able to actually, you know, test it or anything.

"How many more are we waiting for?" I asked.

"One," said the Demon.

He arrived just about then. Jhereg tend to be as punctual to a business meeting as a Dzurlord is to a duel. This was someone else I'd never seen before. He was one of those older, quieter Jhereg who made you think that he lived a sedate life in a little barony where all the Teckla were always cheerful and the fishing was good. So far as I know, those places don't exist, but he looked like he belonged there. The Demon introduced him as Diyann, and he nodded gravely to me. You couldn't imagine him ever being unpleasant to anyone.

Jhereg like that scare the shit out of me.

He sat down next to the Demon. No one's bodyguards were in the room. My heart thumped as it hit me yet again.

It had been so long. And now I was close. So close. All this had to do was work, which I was fairly certain it would. I looked at the others in the room. How would it come, and from which direction? Had I made the opening to my heart as I thought, or had I made the worst—and last—miscalculation of my life? Still, no point in worrying about that; hadn't been for a few days now. I had committed myself with the visit to the Demon. Now it was just a matter of playing out the scene.

Oh, and not fucking up.

The Demon was looking at me. I caught his eye. "Nervous?" he said.

"Why would I be nervous?"

He let a smile almost appear. I tried to decide whether I was glad no one had brought wine, or sorry. It would go down well, but I didn't think I'd be able to drink it without my hand visibly shaking.

This wasn't like waiting for the perfect moment to strike. This wasn't like anything I'd done before.

"A lot of that going around, Boss."

I didn't reply, but having him speak to me right then, even from outside, was just what I needed. I felt my shoulders dropping, my back relaxing.

The Demon turned to the rest of the table.

"Here's the deal," he said without preamble or greeting.

"First, to restate, as of right now, until we're done here, no one kills or injures Lord Taltos. Are we all clear on that?"

Several very high-powered Jhereg said they were clear on that, and I felt myself relaxing maybe just a little more.

The Demon nodded and said, "All right. We give him an hour to prove his idea works, and works consistently, and is practical enough for us to make a lot of money on. If it is, the contract on him is off, he gets to keep his soul and his skin, and, if he keeps his bread buttered from here out, no one comes after him. Are we all clear on that?"

There were nods.

"And you can all answer for your people?"

There were more nods.

"No," he said. "Sorry, but I need you to state your agreement."

They each allowed as to how they would abide by the terms as he'd stated. Then he turned to me. "And together, we speak for the Council. Good enough, Lord Taltos?"

"Yes," came out of my suddenly dry throat.

"Then you may begin."

I stood up. "All of you have someone prepared to send you a message?"

There were nods from the the three bosses. The sorcerers—two of them, at least—managed to pull their dislike from each other and redirect it my way. "Presumably," I said, "you took precautions to make sure I couldn't hear what was said by any mundane means. It should also help that, except for my lord the Demon, I didn't know who was going to be here. You sorcerers will be monitoring the spells used, and thus be able to describe and duplicate the technique."

I stopped and sized them up. I had everyone's attention,

even the sorcerers'. Diyann had no expression, but you could
see the flicker of greed in his and everyone else's eyes.

"Any questions before I start?"

"Yeah," said the sorcerer called Farthia. "When you do
this, how far into the boss's head do you get?"

"I don't get into his head at all," I said. "Or rather, just the
very, very surface, enough to become aware that he's receiving
psychic contact. But even if he were to concentrate really
hard on the name of his first mistress, I couldn't tell you what
it was unless he actually sent it to someone. Assuming he remembered."

There were a couple of obligatory chuckles, then he said,
"What if you're lying?"

"You're going to get the technique, so you'll know yourself. If I'm lying about that, the deal is off."

He grunted and nodded.

"Anything else?"

There wasn't anything else. Except, of course, still another of those thumps my heart had been giving since I
started in on this whole thing.

I pulled out the wand and set it on the table. Then I
picked up the euphonium case, opened it, took out the instrument. I kind of wanted to go through an elaborate ritual of
tuning it, just for effect, but I didn't even know how to pretend to do that, so I skipped it. No one made any remarks
about having a concert, though I'm sure a few of them wanted
to; that's how we work.

I took the egg out and set it next to the euphonium.
"These things should not be necessary," I said, "for those of
you with stronger brains than I have, but you know us weak-
minded Easterners." I kept talking before anyone could say

anything. "The point is, the egg will increase my mental strength enough for me to cast the spell. This device," I indicated the wand, "will turn the psychic energy into a form I can use for the spell, and this—" I nodded to the euphonium, "has been enchanted with the necessary spell itself. I'm sure you sorcerers will get the gist of it once I start going, otherwise I'm not sure why you're here. But my object is to show you that you can accomplish the same effect without these tools. Or, rather, for you to detect it on your own."

Oh, just to be clear: That was all true, except about the wand, which was there in case someone cast a sleep spell at me, which was one of the more likely ways things could go down.

"The idea is, each of you—that is, you three gentlemen, not the sorcerers—is to receive a message. You don't know what it will consist of. I don't know who you arranged to have send it to you. Once we've done that, each of you will receive a second message from someone else. Finally, each of you will send a message to someone. By this time, your sorcerers should be able to assure you that they can duplicate it."

The one called Farthia said, "How did you come across this?"

"I know a Hawk," I said. "He told a story about hiding from the Orb. It occurred to me that, if you can use psychic power to hide from the Orb, and if you can use the power of the Orb to enhance psychic ability, then . . . um.

"Okay, let me put it this way. Some communicate with psychic ability, most use sorcery. But I wondered if very subtle psychic control couldn't be used to detect the sorcerous channels."

There was some stirring, and I could see the sorcerers were becoming intrigued.

Farthia said, "But then, you require a lot of natural psy-chic ability and training."

"Unless you have aids," I said, pointing to the devices in front of me. "Only I'm betting you can duplicate the effect us-ing sorcery. In other words, sorcery duplicating the effect of psychics duplicating the effect of sorcery. That's what you're here to observe."

No question, I had their attention; I could see the wheels spinning in their sorcerous little heads.

"Any more questions before I begin?"

When no one said anything, I nodded. "All right. One at a time, please. Who's going first?"

The Demon shrugged. "I may as well."

"Remember, tell him to wait for ten seconds or so before he sends the message. I need a little time to get the spell work-ing." *Always assuming it works.*

He nodded.

I removed the amulet from around my neck, put it into its adorable little teakwood case, and I could tell what time it was again.

So, yeah, there I sat in a room full my enemies, plus a sorceress of the Left Hand, and I had just removed the thing that had done the most to keep me alive for the last several years. I felt fine, thanks. Why do you ask?

I picked up the wand, brought it to life, and set it down again, and no one had killed me yet. I felt it swirl around in my head; strange, but not unpleasant. My toes and fingers were tingling. I was suddenly very alert and focused.

I picked up the hawk's egg, crushed it.

Daymar once "observed" me performing a witchcraft spell, realized it was just psychic energy I was playing with, thought he'd "help" by giving me some extra energy, and he about burned out my brain. It was also like that first rush I'd gotten this morning, realizing this was the day, only it was all in my head; I felt powerful, like I could knock things over just by thinking about it. And I could, too. I felt bigger, tougher, like I could kill with bolts of lightning out of my eyes, and, hey, for all I know I could have done that, too.

Also, I got runny stuff on my palm and wondered if the thing would work if I'd hard-boiled the egg first. Probably not.

I had an instant of almost panic realizing that this effect wouldn't last, and here I'd been sitting around thinking aimless thoughts, and the guy was going to deliver the message, shit, I'd probably already missed it—

No. My time sense came back. It had been maybe a second since I crushed the egg. All was well—in a scary, head full of power, surrounded by enemies, hoping I'd outguessed or outplanned everyone because if not I was dead, kind of way. But I'm sure you've been there, too.

I picked up the euphonium, my hand still smeared in egg goo, and, without preamble, blew into it. I started moving my fingers, too, and then I wasn't controlling my fingers at all, or my breath, and music started happening. It was surprising— for an instant, I almost panicked again, and the whole spell nearly slipped. I hadn't been able to practice this part, and of course, it's the thing you can't practice that screws you up, no matter how much other preparation you've done.

But I got through it. I kept playing; or, rather, the instrument kept playing, using my mouth and my gooey fingers, leaving my mind free. And the only way I can think to describe it is that I focused my thoughts as if they were external and sent them out through the instrument. There's no better way to put it than that, and if you've done something like it you know what I mean, and if you haven't, well, try it. I knew the *what* of what I wanted to do; the instrument turned it into *how* and my power-soaked brain supplied the energy. You're doing it, and watching yourself do it, and then it's like you let your mind wander, only you direct where you want it to wander to. I guess it isn't wandering but it feels like it's flowing out of the instrument, floating, and watchingguidingwaiting and the notes of the music turn purple and the spell is going into each finger and out like it's all in your hands and—

It's a lot easier to do than it is to talk about. The magic part, the technique, was being handled for me; all I had to do was focus my thoughts, and, at the same time, keep my mind open and alert for contact. That's all. Yeah.

I made sure my breathing was slow and even—in through the nose, out through the mouth, not how you play an instrument, but like when practicing witchcraft. After all, witchcraft is nothing more than a means of controlling psychic energy the way sorcery is means of controlling amorphia. But then, sometimes you blend them, and strange things happen. I've seen that happen before—if you hang around people like Morrolan, you see that sort of thing.

That was the principle underlying the whole thing, really— sometimes if you're expecting someone to use one skill or another, and he comes back with a combination . . .

But let's not get ahead of ourselves.

At the time, I stood in front of three Jhereg mucky-mucks and three sorcerers, controlling powerful psychic and sorcerous forces, and tried to keep my mind open and relaxed. And I managed, and, except for being a bit shaky at the beginning, I even made it look easy. Pretty impressive, don't you think?

Just don't ask me about that middle part, because I'm still not sure what happened.

I lost sight of what those in the room were doing; the amulet was off, Loiosh was outside, and I wasn't even paying attention to what was going on around me. Kragar's words about being over-trusting clapped at the door, and I told them firmly that I wasn't home. Which was pretty much true.

Loiosh tried to tell me something, then, but I had no concentration to spare for him.

And I felt it—a hint, like a whispering. I willed it to become clearer, like when you can almost hear something and you strain to hear it better and it doesn't work; only this did. That's what I like about magic—things like straining to hear better actually work. And somewhere in the distance, the euphonium changed its tune; began to play something soft and soothing. What had it been playing before? I have no idea, I'd had no attention to spare. Didn't now, either, really—but I'm giving it to you as I recall it, which I'm sure bears at least some relationship to what happened.

Don't demand too much, all right?

Look, let's make this short: It worked. As I stood there, I felt the stirring in my brain as of someone reaching me, only, well, it wasn't someone reaching me. It was just there. Like a voice without a voice, if you will. Somewhere, I became aware that there was an odd silence, and realized I'd stopped playing.

I put the instrument down and looked at the Demon. "The orchard on the west side of your home, my lord, has room for three more trees, if they're placed carefully."

His face devoid of emotion, he nodded.

I took a deep breath. I only had so long until the effects of the egg wore off. "Who's next?" I said.

"Do you need to know?" asked Illitra.

I nodded. "I have to focus on someone; I'm not receiving every piece of psychic communication in the Empire. That would be a bit tiring, I think."

"When you're—"

"This isn't going to last long," I said. "I mean, using the egg is a cheat, because I'm neither a psychic expert nor a sorcery expert, so I need to get this done in a hurry. Let me finish, then I'll answer your questions. Who's next?"

"I'm ready," said the one called Diyann.

"Good then," I said. "Remember the ten-count, please."

Diyann concentrated a bit, then nodded. I set mouth and fingers to the euphonium and started playing a tune. At least, I suppose it was a tune. I wasn't exactly listening, and I certainly wasn't controlling it. I knew Diyann even less than I knew the Demon, which made it a better test, but, you know, a bit harder. I had to keep my eyes open, to watch him, to stare at him, to imagine myself inside his head.

I didn't know him; I didn't have to know him. For that matter, I didn't want to know him. I just had to focus on him. The music knew him—the spell wove through the air, my lungs, through the instrument, out to him, wrapping itself around him, testing, touching; he wouldn't know, he wouldn't feel it; and he wouldn't like it, later, when he learned what I was doing, how close I came to seeing his thoughts. I'd told the truth, but still, it's a near-run thing, and no one likes to have his mind read by a stranger.

I'd once almost put a knife into Daymar's eye for doing

that to one of my people, back when I had people. Back when killing was easier.

Never mind, never mind. If this worked, I'd be glad I left him breathing.

Focus. Concentrate. Music, music, almost seeing it, wrapping around his head, getting into his skin drawing invisible lines me to him to somewhere else to me; open. Must be open, don't *make* it happen; *let* it happen.

And, yes, there it was.

Again, I stopped. One thing I hadn't expected was how quickly it would become tiring. I took a couple of breaths and said, "The new exhibit of psiprints by Rusco is disappointing, but it's good to see that he's still taking chances, even so."

The Jhereg grunted, nodded, and even smiled a little. "I always enjoying seeing someone push himself," he said. "Very good."

The sorceress named Radfall glanced at him and they exchanged a nod. Then she went back to glaring at Illitra. I realized later how comical it was; at the time I was too busy concentrating on other things.

"All right, then," I said, looking at Poletra. "If you're ready—"

"No," he said. "It isn't necessary. I'm convinced."

"In that case," I said, "I can—"

That's as far as I got before the door burst open. Then things, as they say, happened fast.

16

MAKING TESTS
OR
MAKING ENEMIES

I reached for Lady Teldra, but Illitra made the smallest gesture at me, and my head lolled forward as I pretended I'd suddenly fallen asleep. All part of the plan, you see; something in the back of my mind went, "Ha! Called it!"

Not that hard; there were, after all, only four possibilities: a quick Morganti strike, for which I'd been watching; chains; paralysis; or a sleep spell. They'd gone for the sleep spell. I was fine with that.

But I guess Illitra was of the type who used both a clasp and a pin, because he wasn't done.

I couldn't move my arms. Or my legs. The euphonium fell to the floor with a kind of chirrupy ringing sound that, just for a crazy instant, made me wish my friend Aibynn were there to hear it. I really hoped I hadn't put a dent in Sara's instrument. I'd feel awful about that. But I could have been paralyzed holding it, which wouldn't have been any fun either.

My heart could move—it was pounding so loud I could hear it in my ears. I remember that. Sleep, yes; the obvious spell. But a paralysis spell too—they were taking no chance.

They wanted me Morganti, and if the only way to ensure that was to nail me while I was sleeping and paralyzed, well, that's just what they'd do.

I could talk, too—I suspect deliberately. "And here I trusted you," I said. Pretending to be asleep, at this point, didn't gain me much. And besides, I'd been so startled by the paralysis, my eyes had opened on their own.

The Demon glanced at me, but he didn't reply. He sat back and watched. I concluded he was probably the one who decided on both spells. He knew me too well, that one. I should really put something sharp into some vital portion of his anatomy. Assuming I had the chance.

I remained motionless, because I had no choice in the matter, and my mind raced. I know something of sorcery. I know it isn't easy to keep someone paralyzed. It takes concentration, and you have to maintain it or the guy'll slip out.

That's the thing about sorcery, you see: With witchcraft, it's all about gathering the energy to execute the spell. With sorcery, there's all the power you could ever want for anything. The question is, how do you handle it? How do you make it work for you, doing what you want, instead of just dissipating into nothing—or, worse, blowing up in your face, maybe taking a few people you like along with your face?

The word "spell" is misleading, or at least ambiguous.

When someone speaks of a witchcraft "spell," that's sort of just a fast way of saying a series of actions that will permit you to gather the power you want for a particular use, and simultaneously attuning it to that use. When someone speaks of a sorcery "spell," that means a series of actions, or words, or even drawn diagrams, that help you concentrate in the right way to produce a certain effect.

Got all that? I hope so. The lecturer will be asking questions about it tomorrow. Heh. And please don't ask me about wizardry, because, like they say, if you ask five wizards what the word means you'll get six answers.

Point is, I knew he was going to have to drop the spell, sooner or later. I once saw Morrolan maintain a paralysis spell for half an hour, while drinking wine and discussing the latest discoveries in natural history, but there aren't all that many Morrolans lying around. This guy was going to have to drop the spell.

And that gave him a problem, you see.

If he dropped it, there was nothing preventing me from sticking a dagger into his eye. Admittedly, I couldn't draw Lady Teldra, but I still had plenty of hardware. The object with something like this is to get the guy dead, not have a fight. Which meant that the paralysis spell should only have to last long enough to—

Yeah.

One of the bodyguards pulled a knife, and I knew at once that it was Morganti. I noticed, in a sort of distant way, that it was my favorite kind for shining: a long, slim stiletto. I wondered if he intended to stick it into my left eye, as a sort of ironic salute. They'd studied me well enough to know how I like to work, after all. If it had been me, that's what I'd have done.

But no, he'd been going for the more standard approach, up under the chin. He struck.

But, you see, I had all of this psychic energy flooding my brain, and there was no point in letting it go to waste. Sometimes you get fancy, sometimes you just do the only thing you can, and if it's a bit inelegant, well, that's how it goes.

The blade stopped about five inches from my skin.

"Problems?" I said.

The button-man looked at Poletra, which let me know who he worked for. Not that it mattered. Poletra said to the Demon, "You were right."

"He may have someone coming," said the Demon.

"Block is in place," said Farthia. "No teleports in or out."

"Necromantic gates?" said the Demon. "He knows at least two people who can pull that off."

"Covered," said Radfall. "If someone starts trying to break through, I'll let you know. It won't be quick."

"Goodness me," I observed. "A lot of magic flying around. I hope no one gets hurt."

They all ignored me. Of course, it's what I would have done. I was the target. My job was to die. Nothing I had to say could make any difference.

Now me, I had a whole different take on matters. But even if I couldn't participate in the discussion, I found it interesting.

"All right," said Poletra. "Let's kill his beasts, first."

"They're gone," said someone behind me. "Flew away as we were moving in."

"I see," said the Demon. He gave me a speculative look. I could see he had questions; he knew he wouldn't get answers if he asked them. Then he looked at someone over my right shoulder and said, "How long is his shielding spell going to last?"

"Can't say," said the sorcerer called Farthia, who had apparently moved to somewhere behind me. "He's using pure psychic energy, probably from the hawk's egg. It's pretty solid. Might be hours."

"I can't hold for hours," said Illitra.

The Demon frowned. "Did anyone," he said, "think to bring chains?"

"I have some rope," said Poletra.

"No good," said the Demon. "He's carrying too much edged hardware. We need chains, fetters, manacles, locks."

"I can have a set here in two minutes, if you'll drop the teleport block."

"No," said the Demon.

"How far out does the block extend?"

"Not far. A couple of hundred yards," said Farthia.

"Ten minutes then."

"I can hold him for that long," said Illitra.

Ten minutes. What could I do in ten minutes? Not much, in fact, what with not being able to move and all.

In the past, I've pulled off some capers that depended on exact timing. I was always proud of that. This time, I had been pleased that I didn't need to know exact timing—that I had like half an hour of slack built into the schedule.

But, you see, I had just squished that egg. My head was filled with psychic energy like it had never been before. And, while I didn't actually know how to manipulate psychic energy, I am something of an accomplished amateur witch, and psychic energy is what we use.

Which is why I was still alive—I was, quite literally, holding the knife back with my mind. Nice trick, huh? Wouldn't be able to do it for long, but they didn't know that. Now, if they hadn't been so determined to make it Morganti, they could have used that same paralysis spell to stop my heart. I think I could have used that same energy to keep my heart pumping— maybe. If they'd done that and come at me with the knife at the same time, I think I would have had problems. And, certainly, if the first attack had been to kill me instead of to make me fall asleep, they'd have had me before I was aware of it.

But they wanted it Morganti, and I could keep the knife away for a while longer. I was not, in other words, quite as helpless as they thought I was.

"Don't go thinking he's helpless," said the Demon. "I don't know what he had planned, but I know he planned for this. He always does. Be careful."

Bastard.

Meanwhile, the enforcer turned suddenly and tried to nail me with the stiletto again, but my grandfather didn't raise idiots; I'd kept the barrier up.

I hadn't made any progress beyond just staying alive by the time one of Poletra's enforcers came in with chains, padlocks, and no expression on his face. So I sat there, unable to move, while they stood me up, as I couldn't do it myself, and I was oddly pleased that when they did my back straightened; having me sitting there hunched over would have made me feel absurd.

They attached the manacles to the fetters in front of me, and several padlocks went click, click. Then the sorcerer released me, and, at the same time, passed his hands over each one of the locks; without my amulet on, I was able to detect a simple, basic enchantment—because enchanting an object to remain in a certain position is an entirely different matter from keeping a person that way. Like I said before: It's one thing to cast a spell on an object, another matter entirely to cast it on a person. I mean, without killing him. And by the way, almost everyone I know agrees it's bad form to kill someone by accident; and if you want to do it on purpose, there are better ways than by deliberately messing up a spell that's intended to do something else.

"I think we should get him out of here," said the Demon. "Whatever he had planned must have been set up for this place."

The older guy, Diyann, who hadn't said a word this entire time, now said, "Why?"

"I didn't realize it, but when he set the conditions for the meet, he wanted this exact room, this exact building. I should have caught on before. He might even have done something to my head so I picked this place. If he has something set up, it's for here. So let's get him out."

Look, I never claimed the Demon was an idiot.

They started dragging me toward the door, and that made it time for me to move. There was still all that power running around in my head, but I could feel it diminish. To the left, however, the guy wasn't trying to stab me anymore. I've always preferred those times when no one is trying to stab me.

The two guys hauling me took their job seriously—their grip on my arms was brutal. I was going to need to get clear of them before anything else. I was considering this when Poletra suddenly said, "Wait."

They stopped just as they were about to start dragging at me.

"Taltos," he said. "What's your game?"

I couldn't think of anything to say that would be to my advantage, so I didn't say anything. Rare for me, but it happens from time to time.

We all stood there, motionless, while he tried to see inside my skull; which was kind of funny, considering what we'd just been through. He didn't manage, however.

"What are you playing at, Taltos?"

I remained mute.

"Your little friends haven't done anything. Why? You always . . ." His voice trailed off as he stared at me. "The Demon is right. You have something planned."

I said, "You can just let me go. We'll say this never happened."

"Do you even have any idea why we're doing this, you fucking Easterner bug?"

Well, yeah I do. I even expected it.

"Feel free to tell me," I said.

"You know what you did. Everyone knows what you did. And you never learned your place, Easterner. And I hate the hair on your face, and the smirk on your lips. And some of the people you stepped on on the way up were friends of mine. Money? You think money will make up for everything you've done? Do you?"

"Uh, sorry. Did you ask me something? I drifted off there for a bit."

The Demon shrugged. "He's speaking for himself. Me, I've always liked you, Taltos. But business is business."

Yes, it is. To a Jhereg or an Orca. They were thinking like Orca, which happens a lot. If this worked, it meant they were also seeing things like a Hawk.

Because that's the thing about Hawks. They can spot a norska from miles away, but the guy holding the snare never enters into their calculation. With a Hawk, it's never about what they see, it's about what they don't see.

Meanwhile, I think if Poletra had clenched his jaw any harder, it would have broken. "We can find out what you're planning. We can hurt you. We can hurt you in ways you haven't had nightmares about."

"I don't know. I have some awfully vivid nightmares. When we're done, I'll tell you how you did."

"Bring him," he said.

I'd like to tell you that it was cold calculation to get him to do what I needed him to do, but that'd be crap. I didn't need him to do anything. If he'd walked away, I'd have been fine with that, and Loiosh and I would have had many delightful conversations about whether it was all the preparation that produced the result of not needing it, or it was all a big waste. No, I'd just been needling him because he'd pissed me off.

But he'd have done it anyway. So, as old Napper used to say, don't matter.

Yeah, old Napper. A good guy. Until they stuck a Morganti blade into him.

Verra.

No more time for doubt, no more room for screw-ups, no more attention for self-pity. And I know that somewhere, deep down, I was loving this. Loving it, and hating it, and, above all, doing it. As they tightened their grip on me, I relaxed my legs, so they were carrying all my weight. I couldn't reach Lady Teldra, and I couldn't drive my elbows into into their guts.

But I didn't have to.

They had me gripped so I couldn't get away, their thumbs carefully placed on the back of my arms, fingers in the direction they didn't want me to go. I straightened my legs and drove toward them, pushing against their thumbs with my arms, and for just a second I was free of them.

I threw myself between them and into the window behind me.

It came loose like it wasn't even attached—which it wasn't—and I went through it. I landed on my right shoulder, which I didn't like, and I had the wind knocked out of me. My momentum from the jump carried me over the cliff.

It was a long way down. I felt like I had a lot of time. I'm sure I didn't, really, but it seemed like I did. As I went down I was turning head over heels, but I can't tell you anything about what I saw. All I recall are flashes of color—gray for the rocks, green for the water, orange-red for the sky. Or maybe my imagination is filling in for what my memory won't tell me. I don't know. I fell. I do remember thinking that if I hadn't had the chains on, I would have been able to use the cleverly designed cloak to slow myself down and, with luck, made sure I landed in a good position.

"Boss?"

"So far, so good."

Then I hit.

Water is much harder than you think it ought to be. I mean, I'm sure it wasn't as bad as landing on solid rock, but I've landed on solid rock after a long fall, and I sure couldn't *feel* any difference. I didn't lose consciousness; but I wasn't quite all there as I submerged, either. And, what with the chains and all the other hardware I was carrying, I went down fast.

Breathing was an issue. I didn't have the amulet on, and spells for breathing underwater are pretty easy. The trouble is, using sorcery then and there felt like calling more attention to myself than I wanted to. It was going to take them a little while to find me, and I needed all of that time. But, in my befuddled state, what is more significant is that it was impossible to get my mind clear and focused enough for sorcery. To blow myself up right then trying to do a water-breathing spell would have made me feel ridiculous.

Besides, that isn't what I'd planned for, and now was very much *not* the time to start second-guessing myself. I went ahead with the plan.

I'd like to tell you that it took me five seconds to get out of the chains, but I'm just not that good. Even with Kiera's lock-pick, which I'd been carrying under my collar, it took me the better part of a minute. I had to hunch over to reach them.

And that water was cold, by the way. Very cold. I know that just a little east of that spot is a place where Easterners like to swim on hot days. All I can say is, they're made of sterner stuff than I am. In any case, the chains were gone, my lungs were bursting, and something in me said, "Wasn't I just in this position?" But this time, at least, I didn't have to cut my own throat. I pulled off my rapier sheath, removed the rapier, stuck one of the sheath ends in my mouth, and blew into it as I raised the other end over the surface. I just happened to know how deep the water was in this spot, having recently questioned a kid who had gotten an anchor for me.

You should know that that first good lungful of air is just as good when you haven't just cut your throat. I mean, in case you're ever in that position.

Problem solved.

Well, that problem solved. There was still the matter of being a few feet underwater with some killers after me.

"*Boss?*"

"*How are things up there?*"

"*Warm and dry, Boss. There?*"

I should have expected that. "*Loiosh, what's the sit—*"

"They're standing looking over the cliff talking about what sort of locate spell to do."

"All right. Taking their time, are they?"

"They've put a teleport block around the area."

"Yeah, I know."

"No, a new one. Tighter."

"All right. You stay out of the way. They have something planned for killing you and Rocza, and that's a worry I don't need right now."

"Got it, Boss. Is it time?"

"Almost."

"All right. I'm ready."

I replaced the lockpick under my collar, letting the torsion wrench fall because who cares.

I was at the bottom of the ocean-sea, breathing through a specially designed sword sheath. I'd been carrying it around for years, wondering if it would ever be useful, and here it was. So I was under water, knowing they'd find me soon, with a teleport block in place, and no way to effectively avoid a locating spell.

No problem.

I still had that psychic force buzzing around my skull—diminishing, but not gone. And I had at least a little time before they fished me out of the water, so I might as well do something useful. I couldn't break the spell on the cord holding Lady Teldra to her sheath, and I couldn't untie the knot (ever tried untying a wet knot under very cold water?). But I could manage to send my thoughts *through* the knot, tracing each turn; and once I'd done that, it was a simple matter to loosen it, loosen it more, and then let it fall off.

She came into my hand and I stood up and stepped toward shore, water dripping from my hair.

"*Okay, Loiosh. Now.*"

"*On it, Boss.*"

I tossed the rapier sheath aside and climbed out of the water. Lady Teldra was in the form I'd first seen her—an exceptionally long knife, narrow, straight blade, and only the smallest crossguard. And, of course, the tiny gold links that made up her hilt. I re-sheathed her for the moment. I took off my cloak and tossed it aside, because it was wet and very heavy. The harness around my shoulders was now revealed, with various pieces of cutlery hanging from it. Under the circumstances, that was all to the good.

How to get up the cliff? Well, as it happened, there was, just thirty or thirty-five feet away, a set of steps just recently hammered into the stone of the cliff. By recently, I mean yesterday. Steps and handholds, like a ladder built into the rock. Isn't that a lucky break?

It took me maybe a minute to climb it.

Why, you ask, didn't they see me?

Well, it's the oddest thing: just as I got out of the water, there came a thick, heavy fog—a fog that a simple breeze didn't seem to dissipate. Sure got lucky there, didn't I?

I could feel the counterspells working on the fog, and I figured I didn't have long before they managed to get rid of it. Well, fine, then. I opened the little box, withdrew the amulet, and slipped it around my neck. I could no longer sense the magic. Right around then, the fog dissipated, and there were the Jhereg. Three bosses, three sorcerers, and ten hired thugs.

And there was me, more or less in the middle of them,

holding Lady Teldra, who had changed shape, and now resembled a rapier, light and useful in my hand. I felt bad for the hired thugs. I used to be one myself.

Loiosh and Rocza came and landed on my shoulders, looking at those surrounding me, and hissing. In direct violation of my orders. Shows you how useful orders are, doesn't it?

But, all right.

Now, I just needed to survive.

I made tiny circles with Lady Teldra, while I also turned, so everyone knew exactly what he was facing.

"Well," I said. "All right, then. Who wants to start the party?"

"You aren't getting out of here alive," said Poletra.

"No? Well, who wants to go first, then?"

"Nicely done," said the Demon. "But even if you escape us now, this only puts you back where you were."

"Are you making me another offer, my lord?"

"Yes," he said. "Let us end this. We won't use the Morganti blade. We'll—"

"No!" said Poletra. "I want to see this—"

"It's business, not personal," said the Demon, with something of snap in his voice.

I said, "Hey, if the two of you want to have this out, I can come back later. Should I make an app—"

Then came a new voice into the mix. "Count Szurke?" and my knees almost turned to water; not from fear, from relief. It came over me in waves and torrents and it took more than just a little effort to keep my voice even when I replied.

"Yes," I managed. "That's me."

17

MAKING ENEMIES
OR
MAKING A STAND

"Boss. The weapon."

"Oh, right." I quickly sheathed Lady Teldra—no point in rubbing his nose in it, after all.

"I am Khaavren, Captain of the Imperial Guard, and I must ask you all to surrender your weapons."

Diyann, the silent one, took a step toward him. Khaavren seemed to have about thirty guardsmen with him, and they were spreading out in a nice circle. Diyann said, "I have no weapons. May I ask what this concerns?"

I cleared my throat. "I can answer that," I said.

I had everyone's attention again.

The Demon said, "Taltos. Well. What?"

I recited from memory, "'Whosoever shall, for monetary gain, or the equivalent in station, merchandise, or other considerations, put at risk Imperial security through the use of such arts or techniques as described in parts two or three above, shall be subject to any or all of the punishments described in section nine below.' Let me skip to paragraph six of section nine below, because being stripped of your House ti-tles doesn't matter much, and what's a few lashes? Here's the good part. 'The forfeiture of all monies, properties, wealth, and other interests. This to be extended to family and other associates as deemed appropriate by the Imperial Justicers.'"

I smiled. "That should cover it," I said. "As you can guess, 'part three above' is rather complex, but what you were just trying to do—eavesdrop on psychic communication—"

"It had nothing to do with Imperial security!" said Pole-tra.

I shrugged. "If you can convince the Justicers of that, why, I'm sure there will be no problem."

Poletra said, "But you—"

"I?"

"You taught it to us!"

"Oh? Did I receive gold for this service? Or anything else? In fact, it would seem that I got no benefit at all, however you want to calculate it."

"No, you received—" He broke off, his face—none too pretty at the best of times—twisting up. Even if he were will-ing to say, in front the Imperial Guard, that they'd been plan-ning to kill me, it wouldn't have helped him. Because I had received nothing. No consideration, no benefit. Because they had betrayed me.

The Demon looked like he was trying to fight off a smile. "All right," he said. "I can see half your play. Any and all wealth and property, and the right to keep digging until they've found everything, and then they take more. So, there's the rind. What's the fruit?"

I nodded to him. He really did know me. I turned to Khaavren and held out my signet ring. "My lord Captain," I said. "I present to you my identification as Imperial Count of Szurke. I hereby invoke my right to defer justice. I would, therefore, request and require that this arrest be temporarily suspended."

"You have that right, my lord," agreed Khaavren, keeping his face straight. "Suspended for how long?"

"Until my death or extended disappearance," I said.

"As you wish, my lord," said Khaavren. "But I must secure the identities of all of these—persons—so that, in the event of your death, we'll know where to look."

"Of course," I said. "Take your time."

Poletra glared and ground his teeth and vowed under his breath to do things to me that he knew very well he couldn't do. The Demon almost laughed aloud, and said, "Well played, Taltos." Diyann simply nodded. That guy was really scary. I think if I'd first gone to him instead of the Demon, this wouldn't have worked out so well for me.

But no point in dwelling on that.

"Will there be anything else, Count Szurke?"

I shook my head. "No, thank you, Captain."

The other Jhereg—the sorcerers and the thugs—were just sort of milling about, not sure of what they should be doing. I walked out past them, keeping my eyes forward, because if I'd caught anyone's eyes I'd have been gloating, and I don't like to do that.

I started back toward the road, which, once more, took me past the cliff. I went back into the room and picked up Sara's euphonium. I looked it over, and shook my head at the little ding in the side and the egg on the valves. I'd have to apologize to her. With luck, when she heard the whole story she wouldn't be too upset. I also grabbed Daymar's wand.

I looked around the room, feeling, I admit it, a little smug.

"*Boss, you did it!*"

"*Seems like.*"

I put the euphonium in its case, slung the case over my shoulder, and walked back outside. It was just starting to get dark, but I could still see the path that took me next to the cliff. I stepped onto it, once more overlooking the cliff. The Jhereg and the guards were gone.

So that's when they hit me.

This time, it wasn't Loiosh who let me know; I felt it myself. It was elegant, subtle, precise, deadly, and useless. From what I could figure, the attacker was a powerful sorcerer who knew I'd taken off my amulet, but didn't know I had put it back on again. I know that I felt the attack as a sharp point aimed at my head. The field produced by the amulet is so effective that when I'm any distance from the Orb, even that doesn't penetrate; so an attack so strong I knew it was happening meant I was up against someone who was very, very good.

I shouldn't complain—the first total idiot they send after me will probably be the one to get the job done.

"*Boss? Was that—*"

"*Yeah. Can you tell where it came from?*"

"*Sorry, it was too brief.*"

Well, okay. It had to be someone nearby. That meant one of the three sorcerers who'd been at the meeting. If I could find out who, I could maybe do something.

At which point I realized how ironic it was. If I could find the sorcerer, I could use the recently proven technique to listen in on the sorcerer reporting back, and learn who was behind it. Only I no longer had the hawk's egg, and if I removed the amulet, I'd be very quickly dead.

In the meantime, my only movement was ten or so steps away from the cliff. The sorcerer had to know the attack had failed, so what would the next step be? I didn't know, but I wasn't going to make it easy to build up a wind strong enough to sweep me over the cliff. Just because I'd survived a fall into the water didn't mean I cared to repeat the experience.

I shivered. I'd been too busy until now to realize that I was soaking wet, and cold. I hoped I wouldn't pick up the lung-squeeze, because it seemed I wouldn't be able to remove the amulet to have it cured, and that would be an awfully stupid way to die.

I kept thinking of stupid ways to die, as if, short of old age, there are any smart ways.

What would come next? I was also wondering where I'd miscalculated; why I was being attacked right when I figured I was all done with that. But I didn't have a lot of attention to spare to working that out, and the implications of it being a sorcerous attack, or anything else. What would come next?

"*Loiosh, see if you or Rocza can spot someone nearby who might be doing this.*"

He didn't reply, but they left my shoulders.

I drew Lady Teldra.

Lady, I don't know what sort of sorcerous skill you have, but if you can manage to find out where that attack came from, it would be pretty damned helpful right now.

Nothing.

Wait. Was my attention being drawn in a direction, or was I imagining it?

"*Loiosh, check off to the right, in the direction of those trees.*"

Yes, I became convinced of it. The communication was strange, and not in language, but there *was* communication, and if I'd had time, I would have been pleased about that; maybe I'd even have smiled.

I started walking toward the spell. I tried to get a feel for how far it away it was, but I couldn't get that. I kept walking, and I became aware that I was really, really angry. Angry enough to be stupid. Maybe angry at myself for whatever miscalculation I'd made so that after all of this, I was still a target. I don't know. But I was angry, and if there was any way to do it, someone was going to be very sad.

"*This way, Boss!*"

I walked a little faster.

I came over a rise and there she was about fifty feet away from me and backing up. Radfall. She looked at Lady Teldra, and me, and abruptly vanished. Try to kill someone, and then disappear before facing the consequences? I mean, really, is that honorable?

She hadn't teleported, though. I know what a teleport looks like, and it wasn't that.

"*Loiosh?*"

"*Yes, Boss. I have the scent. Should I—?*"

"*Not yet. Is she moving?*"

"*She just moved a few feet, and stopped. If you don't want me to attack, I could always shit on her head.*"

"*Tempting, but let's not call your presence to her attention just yet.*"

"*You never let me have any fun.*"

What would she do? I looked around. There weren't any heavy objects she could drop on my head, and there were no signs of a gathering storm that might produce a lightning strike that would miraculously hit me, and I was no longer standing next to the cliff. Boulders she could roll down on me?

No, nothing nearby. What would her play be, now that she knew I had the amulet back on?

"*She could surrender to us.*"

"*You're not helping. I need to know where she is well enough to have Lady Teldra break the invisibility.*"

"*Can she do that? I mean, from a distance?*"

"*We're about to find out.*"

I wondered if the teleport block was still up. Probably. This would be a good time to have Morrolan come charging to the rescue, but even he can't break through a good block without a lot of work, and I had no way to reach him.

Maybe the block, in fact, was why the sorceress was still there? Maybe she didn't want to do anything to me, but had no way to leave? Or maybe she had a plan. Or maybe she was trying to come up with one, and I needed to do something now before she managed.

Maybe, maybe, maybe. You can die of maybe.

You're way ahead of me, aren't you? You're sitting there, drinking your—whatever that is—trying not to smirk, and thinking, *That poor idiot Vlad. How could he not see what was coming?* Well let me tell you, smart guy, it's a lot harder when you're in the middle of it than it is just hearing about it, all right?

So, yeah, there I was, concentrating on the invisible sorceress, when the invisible assassin was coming up behind me. He was good; I didn't see him, I didn't hear him. Neither did Loiosh. Normally, something as simple as an invisibility spell wouldn't have accomplished anything, you know? But remember how I said you have to take time to set something up to do it right? I still believe that, only, well, they made a fine job of it with what can't have been more than twenty minutes of preparation.

Here's how it worked: Radfall cast a spell at me, figuring it would probably have no effect, but would alert me. Then she did a simple invisibility spell and wandered around a bit, because that way I'd have Loiosh and Rocza looking for her, and that got them out of the way. But then there was Lady Teldra, right? Out, in my hand, and if there's ever a time when you don't want to fuck with me, it's when I'm holding her, and I'm alert and ready.

And, yeah, while Loiosh, Lady Teldra, and I were all concentrating on finding the sorceress—concentrating enough that Lady Teldra was oblivious to an invisibility spell a lot closer—we missed what was, like, six feet away, in front of me to the left. Because that's how far the guy was when I felt the Morganti weapon, and he suddenly appeared.

I reacted, and—

How do you conceal the presence of a Morganti weapon? Here's one I never thought of: You have another one, even more powerful, in the area. I don't mean Lady Teldra—she's part of me, and I don't get the reaction I do from others. No, I mean that the one that suddenly appeared in front of me masked the one from behind.

It was a beautiful set-up.

I didn't suspect someone was behind me until much, much too late. In fact, my first clue was a grunt practically in my ear.

I turned, and saw the weapon, recognized what it was as the guy holding it stumbled onto his knees, wincing. He dropped the weapon. He remained still, on all fours, and I understood why he hadn't managed to finish me: there was a knife sticking out of his back.

I turned back to the other one, but he was quite sensibly backing away.

And about thirty feet away was someone I didn't recognize. A guy in Jhereg colors, looking like he'd just thrown something. Like, say, the knife that was sticking out of the back of the guy who'd almost put a Morganti blade into *my* back.

What the—?

Loiosh and Rocza were flying toward me at full speed, of course, but then Loiosh said, "*The sorceress is gone, Boss. Teleported.*"

I didn't answer him. My eyes were going back and forth between the guy who'd just thrown the knife, and the guy two feet away from me, on all fours, a Morganti dagger next to his hand, and a knife sticking out of his back.

That must have hurt.

I managed to keep my sympathy under control, while I studied the complete stranger who'd just saved my life. Then I took a step forward, putting my boot on the Morganti knife, just to be safe, and Lady Teldra made a second hole in the assassin's back, and he was gone before he had time to scream. I told her to go ahead and feed, too, because I was just in that sort of mood.

I looked at my savior and said, "Let me guess. Kragar sent you?"

He shook his head.

"Kiera?"

He shook his head again.

"Well then, who—"

"That'd be me," said the Demon, coming up behind him, flanked by a pair of bodyguards. "Looking out for my financial interests."

"Good shot," I told the guy.

"Thanks," he said. "I practice."

The Demon walked past him, and all three of them fell into a loose formation around him. They were all watching Lady Teldra. I wondered if they were going to ask me to sheath my weapon, or if they realized it would be wasted breath.

"I suppose," said the Demon, "we should talk."

"I guess so," I said.

"Want to go inside?" he asked

I shook my head. "I'm more comfortable in the open."

"All right."

He glanced at his bodyguards, and nodded a little, and they all moved out of earshot, though not without significant looks at the weapon I was holding. The Demon glanced down at the body, looked at me, and gave me a little smile.

"Isn't it nice that our interests line up again," he said.

"If they do."

I still wouldn't re-sheathe Lady Teldra. He pretended not to notice. "How could they not?"

"I don't know. Maybe I missed something. Maybe you just killed one of your own people to make it look good."

"You think I'd do that?"

"No. I don't think you would. But I don't know for sure."

"Nah," he said. "You didn't miss anything. You've set it up so it's in my—our—interest to keep you alive. Poletra hates it, but he isn't as stupid as he seems. He'll face facts."

"And the others? In particular, that Diyann guy?"

The Demon nodded. "You'll be all right, but don't make any mistakes. And don't think you can now push this as far as you want. I know Diyann. If you go too far, he'll get to the point where he'll cut his own throat just to cut yours."

"Yeah, that's how I read him. As long as he isn't there now."

"He isn't."

"Good. And the Jhereg has nothing to worry about from me. My plans are full of having nothing to do with the Organization again, ever."

"Good plan. We feel the same way about you."

"Evidently not," I said, and studied the dead guy.

He shook his head. "No," he said.

"You're sure it wasn't Poletra? So mad or scared he just barked out the order without thinking it through?"

"I'm sure," he said. "Trust me."

You gotta love a guy with a sense of humor. I said, "How can you be so sure? You say it wasn't you, but how can you know it wasn't someone else?"

"In the first place, because no one would be that suicidal, after the Council gave the order. And in the second place, because I know who it was."

"Oh? You going to tell me? Or is this information you plan to trade for something?"

He shrugged. "You'd get there anyway, sooner or later. It was the sorceresses."

"The Left Hand? What did I do to them?"

"Worst thing you could have done: you gave them an opportunity."

"I don't—"

"Radfall."

I shrugged. "So, she's Left Hand. I know. But she was hired by one—"

"No, that isn't it. She has, it seems, both an ear and a brain. She must have reported back fast." He chuckled. "Too bad we weren't using your new technique to listen in; would have saved some trouble."

I shook my head. "I don't get it. Reported what?"

"For a smart guy, Vlad, you're pretty stupid sometimes."

"If I'm stupid, how—"

"Don't go there."

"All right, then explain."

"This process. It's just their kind of thing, isn't it."

"I suppose."

"And it's huge. That's why we got greedy with it, and tried to get both it and you."

"Which I was counting on."

"Yeah, which you were counting on. Aren't you smart. And Terion was just killed, which sort of threw us off. Someone more suspicious than me might wonder if you had anything to do with that."

"Of course I didn't."

"Of course you didn't."

I said, "So that all worked. But, you were saying, the Left Hand?"

He nodded. "But the only thing better for them than having that process, is having that process without competition."

"Who—? Oh."

"Yeah."

"Let's see if I have this right. They kill me, the Empire strips half the Council of everything. The Jhereg—the Right Hand—is crippled, and the Left Hand gets the technique and to keep all the profits."

"Yep."

"I should have seen that coming."

"Yep."

"For a smart guy, I can be pretty stupid."

"Yeah," he said.

I said, "But, won't the Organization come down on them like, I don't know, like something that comes down on things?"

"Maybe. Maybe not. If it's clear they have all the power, then no. If it looks like we might able to make them pay, then yes."

"And so the ugliness continues."

"Yeah."

"And I'm just as deep in the middle of it as I ever was."

"Yeah."

"Think I can make a deal with them?"

"Is it true that you killed Crithnak's sister?"

"You know it's true."

"Morganti?"

"That part was sort of an accident."

"I don't think you can make a deal with them."

"All right."

I considered whether I should kill the Demon anyway, just on general principles. With me holding Lady Teldra, there was a pretty good chance his bodyguards couldn't protect him. But then I'd have the Jhereg after me again, because you don't put a shine on a Council member without permission from the rest of the Council, and far be it from me to break one of the unwritten Jhereg laws.

Again.

I finally sheathed Lady Teldra. To his credit, the Demon didn't show any special reaction. He said, "I have to say, even so, you came up with a good plan, and you made it work."

"Actually," I said, "there's one part of my plan that isn't complete yet."

"Oh?"

I dug into my pouch and pulled out a flask. I pulled the

orange out, and the knife with the hollow blade. I punctured the orange, and, calling on all of my skill and finesse, dribbled some of the liqueur into the orange.

The Demon watched with a sort of mild, detached interest.

I put the knife away and held the orange for about ten seconds, then sucked some of the liqueur back out through the hole I'd just cut.

Gods of the Paths, it was good!

I offered the orange to the Demon. He raised his eyebrows, shrugged, took it, drank.

"That's quite good," he said.

I nodded. "It's an old traditional drink from the East. Usually reserved for celebrating a triumph."

He handed the orange back. I had some more. "I'm not sure how much you have to celebrate," he said. "What with one thing and another."

I shrugged and had another sip.

"I guess we'll see," I said.

"That we will. Thanks for the drink."

"Thanks for the rescue."

"Take care, Taltos. We'll probably meet again."

"Maybe," I said.

He turned and walked away. I stood watching him until he and his bodyguards were well out of sight. Then I walked back to the edge of the cliff and stared out some more.

I had another drink. It was supposed to be a celebration of the end of a job, of my new freedom. Well, I guess it was a freedom of a different kind.

And, instead of the end of a job, it was the beginning of another.

I finished the orange and threw it over the cliff, onto Kieron's Rocks, where some bird would no doubt enjoy what was left of it. Darkness was falling; the wind shifted.

I stood on the cliff staring out over the ocean-sea. Below me were Kieron's Rocks. If I were into sacrificing everything for melodramatic gestures, I'd leap off the cliff. I'm perfectly willing to make a melodramatic gesture when it's called for, but I won't sacrifice everything for it.

"Boss?"

"Yeah."

"So, it isn't over. It's just that now it's the Left Hand instead?"

"Yeah."

"So this is just going to go on and on?"

"No."

"No?"

"No."

"Why?"

"Because I'm tired of it."

"Because—"

"And because there were Jhereg outside Cawti's house, and I'm tired of not being able to see my kid."

I walked a little ways up the coast, staying on the cliff edge. Years and years, I'd spent running. I'd counted on this to either end it, or end me. So, okay. Why change plans now?

The wind was in my face, and my cloak would have been billowing nicely if I hadn't tossed it away and it weren't soaking wet. Take that as a metaphor, if you will. Also I wouldn't have been as chilly, but that isn't as important as pulling off the whole billowing-cloak-hair-in-the-wind-on-the-cliff thing. Adrilankha was far behind me. I could keep going, of course. I could just keep going this way, and run, and run.

I could have done that a week ago.

"Boss?"

I tapped Lady Teldra's hilt with my finger, stopped, and faced the waves breaking beneath me.

"Yeah?"

"What are you going to do?"

I took off the amulet and weighed it in my hand. Then I took hold of the chain and swung it over my head.

"Boss!"

I let it go, and watched it arc over the cliff, over the beach, and fall into the ocean-sea.

"Come on," I said. "Let's get back to town, I really want my cloak."